Slaves of Isis

Slaves of Isis

MADAME DE MORVILLE

Stiletto Books

Published by Stiletto Books in 2000

First published in Great Britain in 2000 by Stiletto Books
An imprint of Dilston Press Limited, Hilmarton, Calne, SN11 8RZ, England

Dilston Press Limited Reg. No. 3411422

A CIP catalogue record for this book is available from the British Library

ISBN 0 9525463 6 1

Book designed and typeset by Andrew Burrell

Printed and bound in Great Britain by
MPG Books, Bodmin, Cornwall

Internet website: www.stilettobooks.com

I dedicate Slaves of Isis *to those of my readers who so religiously polish and in this way give earthly life to the shadows of the dark recesses of their minds. May you be led forward by the black shine of these illumined silhouettes, and by the sound of their booted tread be soon guided into the presence and service of the Divine.*

Madame de Morville

Contents

CONTENTS

Foreword

Many of you will already know me as Madame X, the agony aunt of Heel! magazine. Some of you will even recognize your own submissions to that publication which have been included in this book. May I congratulate you ahead of time for your contribution to the cause espoused in these pages, in case you are overly surprised when confronted by the verbatim reproduction of your innermost thoughts. It is not the job of an agony aunt to judge, but merely to prescribe the solution to the problem that her experience reminds her is most fitting. The editing of this text, therefore, has been restricted to my selection of submissions, and no altering of words or phrasing has been considered necessary, or undertaken. Let the servant speak with his own tongue, and freely, when offered the opportunity. With the polishing and the licking of his mistress' boot, that freedom is curtailed and rightly, and the conformity to appropriate behaviour then expected. In addition to these accounts of servitude, proposed and realised, by the male readers of Heel!, I have decided to include several of my own replies to specific inquiries of an everyday nature, relating to the equestrian and the domestic environments, in the hope that this advice might be taken and its more general application meet with public acceptance and approval. I am often accused by our female readership of having an excessive regard for compassion in matters where discipline, whether by the lady's boot or whip, is traditionally preferred, and in anticipation of this criticism of my supposed overindulgence and kindness towards the kneeling servant and his submission, who is, according to this line of thought, permitted too free a rein by my reluctance to erase thought and trample upon wayward misconception, I would make the following points in my own defence.

Either by natural inclination or by the enforcement of behaviour patterns deemed by his mistress suitable for the exploitation of potential in the normal man, the servant is led and sets out on an uncertain and difficult path. Though his uncertainty is not of course shared by the mistress who is cast in the role of patient counsellor and guide in his gradual or hurried progression to that goal of achievement which he will in time share fully with his dominating companion, the servant, or to speak frankly, the slave-to-be, finds himself in the process of becoming something utterly new. What, he knows not, and this goal or purpose, as yet ill-defined in his now dwindling mind, involving the reconstructing of his very being, becomes the source of an almost bestial frustration in the developing slave. There is created in him a growing and apparently irresistible need to forget the memory of what lies in the past, and to complete what was begun in perhaps the lightest and most theatrical of spirits, his conversion to that which is intended for his future by the mistress.

Within his reeling psyche, as if to confirm the rightness of his selection, of that original choice made by the mistress on his behalf, the instinctual and primal urge of the slave to reach his destination, wriggling there in beaten leather or rubber against imagined and opposing currents, in turn becomes a source of pleasurable enjoyment for the mistress, who delays the moment of her triumph, perversely denying herself for a while longer, observing the painful leaping and thrashing of the captivated slave splashing about in search of the polished shine of his mistress' half-submerged boots. By analogy, my indulgence towards the well-hooked servant is neither kind nor excessive, but carefully judged to prolong that intermediate period of his yearning, and the lengthy retention of the receding identity.

MADAME DE MORVILLE

Slaves of Isis

ONE

The Chameleon Tongue

Whether it would be possible to locate some distant point in the night sky and then to attach a hook there by which, with the further use of the imagination, that blackness could be pulled down into the human realm, causing a lingering atmosphere of doom and despair; then this would describe how I felt on my arrival at that ancient castle. Surely this dark setting belonged to the filmmaker's imagination, a black and white world of pain ruled over by some witch or bitch goddess with the captive servants who live in dread of her whip and those high-heeled boots. Certainly this was not a twentieth century type of environment, but a most unearthly place to which through carelessness of thought, the casual dreamer of fantasy might be drawn in his sleep, into an existence of perpetual drudgery and servitude. At that moment I became aware that I was dreaming, that I had become separated from my physical body which was asleep, and to which I would no doubt return after yet another other-worldly dream adventure. This however, as I later realised, was a miscalculation on my part of future events; for, by the severing of the connecting silver cord between the dream and physical bodies, or by means of the psychic pulling of the slave's physical body after his dream body into her cruel world, the dark goddess whom I was about to meet, regularly recruited lost dreamers, transforming them into her new slaves. I had been staring out into space while pretending the existence of this hook, with my consciousness not yet fully focused in that world, when I realised I was not alone there. Certainly, I had seen many uniformed women in the everyday of my world, but always retained the comforting notion that they would during their leisure, revert to more familiar behaviour. However, it did not require any surge of intuition or even careful deduction, but merely a recognition of the starkly obvious, to understand that for this uniformed woman, her clothing was quite as personal to her as her own skin. She was looking upwards as if to observe whatever it was that I had just seen. Leaning backwards with her arms folded above her tightly belted waist, her posture exaggerated by the black stiletto boots, she spoke as if addressing some spy whom she had caught in the act of espionage. 'There are no planes . . . No planes for you, Mister Journalist'. When she had finished her theatrical delivery of these words, perhaps intending that their full meaning should first sink into my mind, this goddess in uniform remained silently observing the black sky above, which seemed to possess no planets or stars, but instead was being criss-crossed by a network of searchlight beams, that when they rotated through a strip of ground showed some close or far off agricultural scene with male labourers exerting themselves in back-breaking toil beneath the gaze of other uniformed women. The apparently random motion of these light beams was, I soon realised, responsible for the construction out of their condensing light of the very landscapes in which the entrapped dreamers were forced to work so unendurably hard. And when the beams of light withdrew their shine, making dull the leather of the boots, belts, gloves and whips of the guards, the bodies of the dreamworkers seemed then to freeze in mid-activity, spellbound; the whole scene coming to life again as soon as another shaft of light cut across the sky towards these silent dreamworkers who therefore experienced no interval to their suffering at the hands and booted feet of the female inhabitants of this strange world. I half-expected that my imagined hook would soon be shown up by one of these rays which by the quality of their energy, seemed to determine the servile nature of the dreamworkers. Again, my wavering consciousness had surfaced amongst the shine of boots and the discipline of whips employed by these uniformed women, who were I now believed, the personification, the human forms taken by this alien light in its continuous control over the dreamworkers who were labouring there without any memory of the previous pleasures of their earthly existence, blindly accepting the orders and punishments given by such perfect beings, whose sublime leader remained with arms folded in silent contemplation of these scenes of suffering and devotion, from time to time flexing a riding-crop between her leather gloves.

'No planes for you, Mister Journalist . . . ' With some horror I noticed that by the force of their repetition, her words were being projected as individual letters that appeared and disappeared across the translucent and naked skin of my dream body, bizarrely mixing with and then erasing the appearance of the wording of my own thoughts, being superimposed and then highlighted in their place. As a consequence I was being forced into a state of mental blackout, being required to think the thoughts of one of her slaves. The word 'SLAVE' was being imprinted on the flesh of my chest by this transmission of her intent that now required my adoption of the slave's kneeling position and worship of her boots.

'I am the Death Goddess . . . you are my slave and messenger'. I felt and then read the projection of her thoughts across my skin. A series of hieroglyphic symbols appeared over each portion of my body, her spike-heeled boots being repeated in painful lines, pinning me like a cushion; this followed by the vertical repetition of her riding-crop alliterating my skin with pain, and evoking memories of the temple practices in Egypt when as priests we had attempted to map our journeys into the dream world.

Suddenly, the random motion of the light beams became coordinated, lighting up a straight path to the castle. Each overlapping circle of light seemed to project in turn the appearance of the departing goddess; only the occasional tapping of her boot with her riding-crop blurred sufficiently to suggest the unreality of her disappearing image . . .

I awoke in my room, it was three in the morning, I was in bed. I had been asleep. I turned on my bedside lamp to confirm my surroundings. Everything was as it should be, except that the curtains were wide open to the black night beyond. I got up and walked over to close them. A ray of light from some distant, flickering point, at first barely perceivable, was growing in intensity, travelling through the heavenly spheres at blinding speed like the tongue of some cosmic chameleon flicked out towards planet Earth, to retrieve my body, pulling me back into the core of its being.

Several times in some sort of rehearsal, I was re-projected out in a variety of leathery forms, products of the goddess' mind. And when the light condensed into her human form, I then experienced myself being incorporated within the shine of the leather instep of her boot, and sealed beneath the layer of polish that I had so recently kissed.

TWO

The Riding Habit

I had arrived there, at last. The timing of my arrival seemed, however, to be most inconvenient to those ladies to whom I had agreed to report. It was not for a while clear to me, in the fading afternoon light, what was the nature of the activities performed at the stables that had demanded my urgent participation. Certainly, as I stood by the office door beneath the arch that was, I was sure, the only entrance and exit to this perfectly square courtyard, with its high walls, I began to wonder whether I had indeed acted wisely and correctly in presenting myself there.

I knocked again at the door, but seeing through the glass panels of its upper section that the room remained dark as it had been during the twenty or thirty minutes since I first knocked, I ventured with pretended confidence out into the square.The stones that had gradually chilled my feet during my wait continued beyond the archway, and it was their unevenness, through decay, I realised, that accounted for their sparking and flashing, here and there, as in preparation for the night, horses and carriages were being moved and ro-ordered about me. Indeed, standing now in approximately the centre of the courtyard with the natural light almost gone, and with no alternative source of artificial light, I became at length disoriented, seeing no longer the outline of the tall women in riding attire that I had glimpsed with difficulty from beneath the arch, but rather the random and frenetic firing of spurs against the uneven cobble stones, which for an instant would shine the surface of some anonymous boot, before switching again to darkness followed by perhaps a pattern or formation of some six or eight boots, but never in pairs, which would have aided my attempt to locate and track their movement.

There was however some internal light at a door that, on one side, led into the interior of the stable building itself. And it was therefore possible to detect fully a pair of gleaming riding boots which had appeared over a distance across the cobble stones to have only an intermittent existence, once they stepped out into the light of this side door. Another observation that I mention here, was that individual booted movements by these equestrian women were hardly to be connected with the consequent echoing about the courtyard, such was the ricocheting sound that began to work upon my mind during that period of fruitless concentration.

Certainly what I had felt initially to have been an unwelcoming place, seemed in a strange fashion familiar to me, even to the extent that what had been my physical self-consciousness, standing alone there, amidst the unseen, routine movements of stable life, had turned into a feeling of being absorbed into the patterns of light and sound so continuously generated by the feet of these silent women, in their riding attire, with their horses. If it were feasible to be both at the point of panic, and to deeply resonate with your surroundings, such would be my description of my state of awareness at that time.

A certain jolting from this state followed my perception that the door through which more than twenty, even thirty women had passed, was being shut behind them, with the sound of repeated bolting. Then, looking around me and up to the stars of the night sky which had just previously seemed so dim and unimportant, I was in my confusion reacting to my next observation that the two huge curved doors were being shut by invisible hands beneath the archway. Physically, in the new stillness, I was again conscious of the coldness in my legs that had permeated through me. And though I cannot claim to have immediately retrieved my sense of purpose, I began to consider my position and predicament.

I had been to visit her regularly since we had been introduced . . . No, we had simply met about six months previously, she out riding, I walking along the edge, or as she determined, within the boundary of her land, which composed a huge estate, in places thickly forested to obscure the ancient house to which I was then summoned to receive retribution. Nothing too dramatic had occurred there; though she had often congratulated me on my change of attitude, which I believed had remained reasonably constant throughout that period, up until her sudden request that I come to the stables and not the main house, on my next visit, which should also be at a later time; dusk.

Indeed, from memory, during my time visiting the main house, the only requirement, and this after a period of some weeks of normal and pleasant conversation, was this: that whereas she had delighted in my learned reflex responses to her presence – for example, my kneeling before her, she wished to extend this encouraged, gradual turn of behaviour, by developing in me an instinctual response to her persona, which would she had said, require a deeper effort on my part. To guide me in this, and to ensure my attentiveness to her purpose, she took my lowered head between her gloved hands, slowly rotating my vision from her riding boots, up through the length of her riding habit, to her veiled face. I should add that my experience, my training so far, had required at all times that I refrain from addressing her face to face. This was, besides, given the kneeling position adopted once in her presence, a less and less natural inclination for me, perhaps confirmed by the fact of the variety of her shoes. Though she would on occasion continue indoors to wear the black riding habit in which she rode, she would on her return change into new shoes or boots.

My eyes had by then met hers, my head forcibly lifted up and then held in position by those leather gloves. Her unremitting downward gaze seemed to search for some sign or other, while establishing in me an increased compliance to her will, that accompanied my feeling of being in some way emptied. Minutes had passed when satisfied, she placed a hand on my head, pressing me down gradually until my lips touched the leather of the instep of her boot. She started to move my head methodically about each boot in turn until the moment when I was moving voluntarily across the leather, exploring the details of the heel, its shape and then its sharpness, beneath the darkness of the skirt that now enveloped me. I remained there, my body flattened across the polished floor, as if receiving some essential nourishment from this exercise. It had been, after that day, my duty and instinct to see to it that Madame's boots were fully polished. Often I had felt the frustration of attending her, yet without permission to remove whatever dirt or dust might have adhered in the time since my previous service to her boots. However, I had returned home between these episodes as normally as I had ventured out to visit her. Certainly I could vouch that no sort of unpleasant behaviour had been instilled in me. Rather to the contrary, I had felt fulfilled by my natural respect and admiration for her authority, her controlling of my sometimes wayward, undisciplined self.

I had, by then, closed my mind from my apparently hopeless position in the courtyard of her stables. At first, I thought her words were mine; she must have been standing there beside me all the time, in silence.

'A starry night, how propitious, don't you think, for your first night ride with me?'

I did not answer, but at the moment of recognition, I knelt down at her feet. She continued.

'Here you must learn new tricks, a new understanding . . . Together we will achieve for you the animal status that you have come to crave. It is through the bit, the bridle, spur and whip that you must strive to please me now. You have a choice to make right here, this very instant. I believe you were watching my riding staff pass through that door. I have been observing you carefully. Either go to these women who wait for you, to prepare you for me, who will keep you here within their midst, to train you as an animal, to make you finally forget your humanity . . . in a way, I suppose, to simplify your mind for our purposes. In your favour, I should remind you of your great progress to date. Look at you now on your knees, so attentive to my boots, this new pair with spurs that are sometimes cruel . . . Or, just in time, rediscover your humanity and leave this place. It is the time of decision. If you choose to leave, you shall not return to me or my house. You will perhaps, if I have exaggerated your discipline, be unfit to live your old life . . . Consider, slave, and decide'.

'I wish to serve you always, Madame . . . I have remembered these stables from some other time and gladly offer myself for final training'.

'Then go slave, to be trained, and returned to me . . . Here is your bridle which has remained here. Accept its control and now . . . take the bit inside your mouth. It shall not be removed . . . you shall not free yourself this time . . . nor shall you speak again . . . go to the women for your preparation, do not resist as you are strapped and bound to my pretty carriage . . . go now and they will bring you back to me . . . changed'.

THREE

Daydreams of Leather

Swinging through the air, on an upward arc to a point high above me, I watched her descend, her well-defined figure of polished leather accelerating against the backdrop of slowly moving clouds into which she had just risen. So wide was the arc she was travelling, and therefore so nearly invisible were the ropes that guided her swing, that each time it seemed implausible that she should again swoop all the way down, eventually being just a flashing gleam against the dark foliage of the yew trees that bordered one side of the lawn on which I was sitting. So close was the swing to the ground at its lowest point that she raised her booted feet and stiffened her legs in front, as she tore through the cooling air, leaving behind her a sound made by the rapid adjustment and extension of her legs.This split-second manoeuvre was no doubt facilitated by the design of her clothing. So perfect a covering did its smooth leather surface provide, that with this eccentricity of dress it was not evident whether her shoes grew out of, or were of a piece with the encasing outer garment. Whether she could have been described as booted or merely wearing black shoes with their curved stilleto heels, is surely for the fetishist to decide. At that age when these events happened, I was more surprised and curious, than developed in my comprehension of these esoteric matters. My questioning was otherwise, how had I arrived at this place of which I had no easy memory, and which seemed so deathly quiet other than the sound of the increasing number of women identically dressed who were to be seen swinging through the air above me, as if encouraged by the date of this summer's evening to suddenly appear like exotic insects at a river's bank, to mate and die, or to mate and kill? Certain trails of light remained hanging in the ether so that the resulting pattern emerged before my eyes, to be replaced in turn by another, each more fantastic as the numbers grew. What deficiency of daylight remained was being augmented by the moon and stars which through reflection of the leather shine now pinpointed the rhythmic movements of these women as they criss-crossed the lawn without collision at accelerating velocity, each figure arcing away into the night, to be replaced by another leather-clad figure, this time travelling at a different angle low across the grass, her boots extended, hissing by me.

When passing over the lake, and then into the moonlight, these numerous fleeting forms combined with greater clarity before my eyes. Yet I did, in my efforts to understand their presence and mine, look away from this enticement, mentally noting whatever other information was perceivable. A tall church spire rose from behind the yew hedge so that I could deduce that this hedge was both the border of the lawn and that of the churchyard. A number of trees, evergreens with flat, horizontal branches, filled much of the expanse of the skyline, perhaps providing secure points of anchorage for the many swings, which seemed during their arc to have an elasticity that caused on occasion their more sudden and unpredicted arrival above the lawn. Like antennae of some unidentifiable, exoskeletal insects, the booted feet seemed to be investigating my presence, inviting contact, seeking me out in ever greater numbers before retreating far out of my view.

Following this insect analogy, the comparison would be with the co-ordinated activity of fireflies communicating their joint intentions across the dark spaces of night-time. Though I do not know whether fireflies would have skimmed so close to the still surface of the lake, down to which the otherwise flat lawn sloped and up which, as I watched, one of these leathered forms swung to a halt, slowed by her gashing path through the water, and suddenly standing upright by the downward thrusting movement of heels into turf. Two more followed, whether by misjudgement or driven by instinct, and when balance was assured, they embraced with frenzied gesticulation, their whetted forms briefly merged in gleaming unison, before, as if timed by nature, separation and return to flight. A stiffness in my right arm reminded me that I was sitting back on a sheet of white linen that was stretched over grass, its contents the remains of a summer's tea-party held in the vicarage garden. Some jam was smeared in a streak across one corner, its source a cake compressed into the ground. Several cups and their saucers, again disturbed as if by some ungodly and violent visitation, were strewn over the white fabric. A cake tin, its lid pierced as if by the applied force of a shoe had rolled away onto the grass; a subsequent kick would have taken it all the way down the slope and into the water.

Two new leathered forms had arrived, their progress through the air halted as before by the motion of their heels, their downward thrust. The cake tin, their immediate target, was by mutual effort prised apart, as if their purpose was to feed, and quickly. In my study of this activity, and at the moment of my realisation that these two were the same women as previously, the approach of the third woman, skimming silently over the lake directly towards me went unnoticed. Without this time lowering her booted feet, as if resigned that all food had by now been consumed, she drove her heels straight at my stomach, producing a sudden heightening of sensation within me, an explosion of discomfort in my body, and my awakening. The shapely boot I found myself holding against my side belonged, I immediately realised, to one of the invited daughters of our new neighbours, whose arrival had been taken as another opportunity to cure me of my 'mental aberrations', primarily my daydreaming, that accompanied me on such social occasions. Such a cure seemed imminent when I detected the persistence of leather beneath her polite, long dress. The inappropriateness of the riding-crop which she had brought to show me, and which had been the subject of light-hearted comment by those other guests, had, I fear, taken hold of my mind, leading inevitably to reverie, and now to her punishment and correction of my behaviour.

There being no spectators, the garden being by then rid of the afternoon gathering, and without the necessity for more tedious exchanges between us, she had raised her gloved forefinger to her lips so as to preserve my silence, and ensure my contrite endurance of the first pain inflicted upon me by the whip in her other hand. Her purpose was to improve my understanding of her nature and that of her companions in leather, before my introduction to them. The whipping having induced in me a permanent acceptance of her control over me, a lead and neck collar was then taken from that exquisite handbag of black leather that matched so well her leather-clad figure which now emerged from the discarded summer dress. She led me down to the lake, stopping me with a sharp pull at the water's edge. Kneeling there, my head naturally inclined in observation of her booted feet, which drew out from me my subservience to her, I was mumbling words of adoration. She raised her whip-hand as if to slap across my face, then relented with a brief smile, before kicking me backwards into the water, and by the pressure of her boot upon the lead against my neck holding me there beneath her. Almost at once as if being baptised into some new world, my panic changed into expectation as I again perceived the many identically dressed women in polished leather swinging above me . . .

FOUR

The Rubber Poultice

Yes, he would forget this woman at the first opportunity, a fact that he had repeated to himself many times whilst driving through the night away from her house. Neither the heavy rain beating down on his car, nor the near invisibility of the road ahead had lessened that resolve in him. He would forget her and all her fetishistic displays, even before his journey's end. He drove on, his foot flat down on the accelerator, his eyes trained on the motion of those windscreen wipers, which were, he believed, his closest allies in his fight to be rid of her vile perversity. He would put the greatest distance between this evil woman and whatever destination awaited him when he had finally forgotten her nocturnal presence and her controlling ways. He would put her unspeakable behaviour behind him.

Being further and further distant from the strut and stamp of her boots, and therefore surely on the verge of becoming a free man again, tentatively at first, he voiced out loud his long overdue defiance of her revolting obsessions. Addressing whatever tree or night spirits inhabited that stretch of the highway, he dismissed as nonsense her constant belief in the irreversibility of a slave's training, and as for her repetition that a partially trained slave always returns to his mistress . . . What nonsense that had proved to be! Whatever small inclination to servitude had been incorporated within him by discipline would surely vanish by daybreak, thoroughly cleansed by the night rain. With his shoulders hunched in concentration over the steering-wheel, in a position reminiscent of that required in her presence, and that contradicted his optimistic mood, he drove into the night as if his life depended on it; his lone progress lit up by the downward streaking of lightning. Travelling at breakneck speed and without as yet having the nerve to slow his engine, even to look back over his shoulder, he passed yet another town lost in the darkness, though now he noticed the first lights being switched on in the homes of waking commuters, who would, no doubt, hurry to join him in his flight from that woman whose body seemed always to be encased in gleaming black rubber. Soon the first cars of the morning had driven onto the highway, perhaps to lead the way towards a new life. But puzzled looks and glances in his direction produced in him, for the first time since he had left her, a certain defensiveness of mind, and self-doubt.

Why had he been driving through the night with the roof of his car down? And why could he not bring himself to behave like them, and drive protected from the storm and the spray of water? The answers came to him as he again swerved out of his lane to overtake . . . Because for the first time in his life he had felt himself to be free, to be at one with Nature. Besides, he reasoned, it was too late for him, since he was already soaked through to the skin in a car that contained such buckets of water.

Yet, with this new attitude towards his exterior environment, he was beginning to fear the absence of water that would come with the inevitable cessation of this unseasonable weather. He was even dreading the opening of his car door, and the resulting outflow of accumulated rain-water. He felt uneasy. He was being observed by those without his understanding for the pleasures of water who drove alongside him when the traffic jammed. What did they know of Nature?

He would not become like them, he resolved, his tongue keeping up that continuous flicking at the drops of water on his upper lip. No, he had a higher purpose, a new life starting that morning. As if to reassure himself of these facts, he surveyed with indifference to their curiosity, the landscape ahead that now beckoned him to a future full of hope and promise. Soon he was travelling at speed away from their town, following the curve of the road that stretched out in front, still with the eagerness of a modern pilgrim.

It was almost daylight, sufficient for the headlights to be switched off, but not the windscreen wipers, for there appeared to be no prospect of the storm clearing. Not that this bothered, but rather encouraged him to maintain speed, to cover mile after mile in the service of his quest. How contemptible, he reflected, with the growing perspective of hindsight, had been her abuse of his hospitality then offered to welcome her and her bizarre entourage to their quiet and god-fearing neighbourhood. Had he not warned the others that her arrival heralded nothing but trouble and upset?

Overtaking a car, and accelerating away in his joy at having left his previous existence far behind, he punched the air above with his right fist. It was however, when he again rested his forearm against the car door, that he realised one possible cause of his new attitude towards the presence of water. He noticed something like a pad or square of black material hidden beneath the soaked and therefore transparent sleeve of his shirt. Full daylight aided this recognition of what felt by its gentle constriction of his arm and its smooth action, like some sort of healing poultice.

Because of his sensed need to hurry with his journey, he was forced in his study of this secreted material, to take quick sideways glances at his arm while watching the road in front for traffic. The level of concern soon required the unbuttoning of his sleeve and closer inspection. His response could not have been more horrified had he in fact discovered a family of leeches; for there, without his conscious memory of its origin, was a wide and closely-fitting strip of black rubber which he felt unable to touch with his free hand, let alone peel back, such was his phobic reaction to its surface.

This impasse of mind caused in him a desire to drive yet faster towards that planned destiny of which he had been so proud until this discovery. Believing the acceleration would in turn clarify his own thinking, he sped on past the next town, which he hardly recognised, due to his absorption with the condition of his arm, to be just one exit from his hometown where he worked as a salesman. The black material had, if he had but realised it, been acting upon him since the very time of its fitting the evening before.

And so, confused by the circularity of the route that had returned him fully captive to his mistress, he licked his upper lip as if to taste the air before taking the next turning off the highway, being guided forwards both by instinct and by fate. Any surge of resistance had failed to rescue his mind from the state of dazed passivity in which he was to arrive back at the gates leading to her house some fifteen hours later. However, the presumption and certainty of his return meant that adequate arrangements were in place for the remainder of his training in his chosen field as a salesman of equipment for cleaning swimmimg-pools.

It was by then midday. Two women stood together on the lawn polishing each other's skirts after the storm, oblivious in their concentration, to the screeching of his breaks. At their booted feet, with elbows and stomachs resting on the steaming ground, a group of five women continued to dispute amongst themselves. Each of their sudden emotions was punctuated by the scorpion-like thrusting of their heels into the air. They, too, were dressed in polished rubber and in their involvement, were oblivious to the salesman's return.

On the pediment high above the roof-line, where statues might have been expected to stand in vigil, instead the thigh boots of three reclining goddesses hung down over the stone as examples of what can be achieved by the disciplined application of polish. This sight stirred in the salesman his first vague memory of those events that had so traumatised his mind into a state of complete amnesia. He was now re-experiencing in flashback the slave's after-glow on executing to his mistress' satisfaction a domestic task, in this case the enforced cleaning over an extended period, of high-heeled boots.

This triggered memory in the mind of the salesman, still seated at his wheel and demonstrating a reluctance to leave the car, now bled backwards and forwards through mental association, into other aspects of his programme of training at the feet of his mistress. He was, he remembered, being prepared for the position of swimming-pool cleaner. This required another period of psychological adjustment, not least to the continual wearing of rubber clothing and his living full-time within the pool to ensure the water quality. Therefore, in order to secure his acceptance of this new life, and as a first step in his training, a band of rubber had been fitted to his arm. This had, to the dismay of his mistress, induced the reaction of panic. As always, the slave that has been partially trained, returns.

As if receiving through the heels of their boots some vital transmission, or being prompted by a prearranged sign, the women's attitude of indifference was shed at once, with a sudden spasm of their polished bodies, as though their sublime display was merely a pretence, a greeting planned in advance to influence the salesman's mind; being the next stage in the process of his distraction. Converging from all corners of the extensive garden, they now wriggled their way towards his high revving but out-of-gear car, with their whips uncoiled and freed for use. To the onlooker, who was innocent of their attraction, they might have appeared to have recently emerged through the pliable soil from the underworld, perhaps probing the surface in search of slave-workers for their queen.

Alerted, at last, to their deadly intent, and therefore returning his attention from his side-view across the lawn to the interior of the car, having some idea of escape in his near paralysed head, he believed for a moment that three and not two windscreen wipers were being dragged squeaking across the dry glass. Fumbling with the gear-stick, while at the same time looking at the road ahead through the windscreen, he recognised his new mistress standing there, astride, in front of the car, barring his way forward. She was holding a riding-crop in her right hand, which she tapped repeatedly against the open palm of her gloved left hand; each short rotation marking time with the motion of the wipers. Staring at him until her dark eyes had penetrated and transfixed his will, she then turned about, leading the way down the black tarmac track in the direction of the swimming-pool, to the scene of his previous panic. The salesman followed, his shoulders again hunched over the wheel, keeping an even distance of a few paces from her immaculate and shining form, despite the bumping and jostling of the accompanying women.

She had stopped at the side of the pool, turning to stare once more deep into his mesmerised eyes, which remained gazing upon her as the car door was pulled open by the frenzied women, and he was carried by the weight of released water over the edge and down into the pool, where his frantic efforts to climb back out were then discouraged by the use of whips and by the boots that lined the pool's four sides, that pressed down upon the grip of his failing fingers, until the point of exhaustion had been reached, and the boundaries of his new existence accepted.

After midnight, when the rest of her entourage had retired indoors, the mistress, dressed to gleaming perfection and in the highest of heels, stood beside the pool, to listen for sounds of cleaning in progress. Her new slave had indeed found the cleaner's rubber suit left floating there, and responded well. She lowered her boot into the water to test his abilities. After a brief interval, she sensed her slave blindly at work on its surfaces, before moving on to clean an adjacent area of the pool. He would, of course, require regular emptying to ensure proper suction and a long life. How much more convenient, she mused, than those appliances so rudely offered her by the salesman.

FIVE

Reflections of a Servant

You ask me for details. A strict account of events in chronological order will provide you with the clearest picture. And let me preface my observations with mention of the facts that most excuse my susceptibility to these remarkable ladies. I was fresh out of school, my academic career finished with a fluorish; exams passed and experiencing that widening of horizons typical in a boy who had just celebrated his nineteenth birthday with promises of sexual encounters from a number of pretty girls, but who would be, by a chance reply to an advertisement that promised sufficient rewards as to impress them, soon led down a different path, finally to lead to a quite different life, a life of servitude.

At the risk of confusing my reader, let me begin at the critical meeting with the lady who placed the innocent-looking advertisement in the local gazette which read: 'Boy wanted for the summer in a disciplined environment. Opportunity for self-improvement. Conditions of employment non-negotiable. Replies to Box 72''. The reply was written and sent off in a hurry, before an afternoon of entertainment planned as usual on the spur of the moment, involving the usual group of friends from around the village of Cordley, in Wales. Nothing was heard from the advertiser, and in the next issue of the gazette her advertisement was not repeated.

Concluding that the post was filled, I was thankful that the possible intrusion into my summer was now removed. I was at the same time regretting the lost opportunity for income when I received a telephone message that I should report for an interview for the advertised position, the other applicants having proven less than satisfactory, having, I quote, 'failed us and themselves, being unwilling to make the suitable adjustments of behaviour required of them'. I was to hurry there as 'there was little time to prepare me for the return of the owner of the property' on whose behalf the advertisement had been placed by her colleague, Ms Alice Court, who would be conducting my interview that afternoon.

Setting out half-heartedly, and following the instructions given by Ms Court, I had arrived at the mansion address within the allotted time to meet a lady whose kind nature seemed immediately to contrast most favourably with her brusque telephone manner. Indeed, I half-expected the sudden appearance during the interview of her more severe twin, perhaps equally clothed in a long black Victorian dress.

Preliminaries over, and responding to Ms Court's easy charm and concern for my well-being, I had signed the piece of paper that she jovially placed before me. Her mood changed abruptly: 'Now let's see what it is exactly that you have agreed to'. She had retrieved with a quick motion of her elegantly gloved hand the signed contract of employment, and began to read it back to me.

'There's obviously some mistake', I protested to Ms Court, hoping at once to return the conversation to its previous friendliness.

'Why do you think that?' she replied, continuing to look down at the legal detail contained in the document.

'Well, it's obviously a contract of employment for a woman . . . '

'Yes, how perceptive of you, and perhaps you have signed because of the very generous terms offered ?'

She pointed to a paragraph which stated what was surely an absurdly high rate of pay, but Ms Court assured me there was no error whatsoever in the terms of the contract, which she reminded me I was now committed to fulfil.

In my confusion at her insistence that I obey her terms to the letter, I had ignored the arrival of a second lady, also in a Victorian dress, who after picking up and reading the contract, declared in an impartial manner that it was clear that I was indeed to be a female employee until the expiry of my term of service.

Disconcerted by her matter-of-fact summary of my position, I intended, at that moment, to get up and to leave this antiquated house with its two outdated occupants.

'Have you been dressed as a girl before?' enquired the second lady with seeming concern. I did not reply, but her persistence then drew from me a quick denial which was noted down by Ms Court, while the second lady stood behind me, her leather gloves pressing down on my shoulders, ensuring by their increased pressure that each of their questions was answered in turn, correctly.

These questions became as time passed, more detailed, and with my resistance faltering, Ms Court was soon helping me in the selection of a daily routine most suited to my ability. The logic of the interview and the phrasing of my obligations under contract, required that over a 'reasonable period', I become completely 'feminised' and employed with the duties of a maid, whose appearance would be determined by one of or both my employers jointly, and which at any time may be changed as circumstances require. At last, as if the three of us had together put behind us some tedious but necessary activity, I was invited to see my room and to confirm that its character corresponded to the terms of the agreement.

The second lady was then formally introduced to me as Ms Spence, whose name I had just read in connection with my training as a maid. Seeing my comprehension, she smiled towards me, her black gloves clasping a riding-crop in front of her.

'Maids do not shake the hands of their superiors. They curtsey before them'.

I looked incredulously back at her. She gestured towards me, a new severity in her voice.

'Maids curtsey . . . a maid looks down at the feet and not the face of her superior'. I felt a certain paralysis. I did not wish to offend, but to curtsey seemed beyond what was then possible.

'Perhaps our maid will find it more easy to curtsey tomorrow, when she is dressed for work', suggested Ms Court. 'It has indeed been the case with previous employees and I anticipate no deviation here . . . she will make an adequate and good servant'.

'Do you have any questions, maid?' enquired Ms Spence.

'Yes', I muttered, no longer looking directly at her. 'The period of contract . . . How long? You see I have some important dates, invitations I have accepted, parties I must attend . . . '

'Stop right there, maid! The contract contains no expiry date, but can only be terminated by the joint agreement of Ms Court and myself'.

'I was thinking that perhaps if I conformed to these requests, I might soon be released'.

'Legal requirements . . . not requests. We are very pleased that after consideration you chose to spend your remaining life with us here . . . we both feel flattered. After all, the excitements here are few, and this old house where you will work is, as you see, quite shut away from the modern world.'

'What if I'm not good at my work. You will probably want to get rid of me?'

'Ms Spence will ensure that you perform well and that you will wish to stay here for a long time . . . your previous life will become, under her training, a forgotten memory'.

It all seemed so inevitable. I looked about me as if for the first time, to take in the environment where I would live my future as a trained maid in service to Ms Court and Ms Spence. The furnishing was medieval, the room vast, its floor pitted as if by the endless procession of ladies' heels. Reading my mind, Ms Court raised her long skirt, showing me her high-heeled shoes.

'Now maid, do you understand why you are here?' she asked.

'Yes, Madame'. I sank down on my knees before her, staring down to the ground.

'Continue maid. Speak your thoughts to us who own you as our servant'.

'How many others before me?'

'You are not the first', replied Ms Spence.

'What is my name?'

'Sara . . . It is the name on your uniform'.

'Am I to wear a uniform always?'

'Yes, of course. What else would a maid wear?'

I was feeling during these exchanges a growing weariness at the prospect ahead. The effort required to formulate replies was draining my reserves of energy. Ms Spence was observing my condition carefully, while Ms Court continued with her questioning about my new identity. Finally, at the point of collapse, swaying about on my knees in front of them, I repeated after Ms Court: 'My name is maid Sara . . . maid Sara . . . '

I had passed out at their feet and been taken to my room which when I was again conscious, was dark. I was seated and yet felt in some way separated from my body. I could not then move my arms and legs. I remained there sitting still in the darkness, trying to organise my mind, to understand my predicament. After a while, I felt something tugging at my left wrist, pulling it from side to side, lifting my arm into the air. It was as if another being had entered my passive body during my state of drowsiness, and was attempting to operate my limbs. My forearm, as if lowered by puppet strings was replaced on the arm of the chair. For some minutes I observed the darkness around me. Then the tugging resumed, this time my right arm was suspended. There was a clicking sound which released my arm which flopped back onto the armrest. The same clicking sound was repeated behind my neck.

I could smell tobacco smoke and then observed the lighted tip of a cigarette next to my upturned wrist. Then a downward pressure which did not burn me but rather produced the odour of burning plastic, easily distinguishable from tobacco smoke. The cigarette was moved up and down each wrist in turn, and was then applied with the same up-down motion to the back of my neck. I heard a door close, then silence.

Perhaps twenty minutes later I had the sensation of re-entering my body. I could clench my fingers. My legs felt re-animated. I rose from my seated position, shuffling forwards in the dark with my arms extended in front of me, until I touched the smooth surface of what seemed to be glass set into the wall. I was experiencing some constriction of my movements caused by my clothing which seemed different. My shoes also forced a compensation in my movement. I had found the light switch which I now pressed. The resulting light at first blinded me, and only slowly did I become accustomed to its brightness. What I eventually saw in front of me reflected in the mirror, and dazzled by the lightbulbs fixed around its edges, was a young girl, made up prettily, eager and keen to fulfill her promise as a maid. I raised my hand in disbelief, observing a corresponding movement in my reflection. My intention was to remove, to smear away the lipstick that now emphasised the feminine shape of my mouth. Instead, I watched my varnished fingertips move past my lips and upward to check a wayward hair and return it to the new feminine cut that supported a maid's mob-cap. Again, of their own volition, my hands returned to smooth the white apron now tied behind my maid's dress. For the first time, I looked at my feminised body directly, already becoming used to the sights of my transformation. Beneath the white cuffs of my uniform where the lighted cigarette had pressed I traced with manicured forefinger the plastic zips now fused together, and useless. The zip behind the collar of my uniform was also useless. I stood looking at myself in the mirror. I realised that if I held my hands tidily against my uniform, then the blemishes to my uniform were no longer apparent. I realised that at the end of my present employment, I would need to seek similar work as my uniform was quite irremovable. I curtseyed several times, knowing my employers' requirements, before kneeling down to a position with my head inclined to their imagined shoes.

I saw there the three discarded zip-sliders and the pliers used to remove them. I stood up, again smoothing my uniform about me so that no evidence of my sedentary hours would remain, causing a suspicion of laziness in my service. I then left my room closing the door behind me. I was surprised, though a maid has no right to be, to find both ladies waiting in the attic corridor for my reappearance

'Good evening, Sara'.

I curtseyed to Ms Spence.

'Sara, what took you so long?'

'I was changing, Madame'.

'You should have done that earlier, Sara'.

'Yes, Madame'.

'Whatever shall we do with you, Sara?'

I saw that the riding-crop that Ms Spence had with her during my afternoon interview had been replaced by a whip neatly coiled around her gloved hand, also being made from black leather, which over the future months she would wear as if it was a fashion accessory to be used often in my encouragement.

'Punish me, Madame'.

'Yes, Sara . . . you do understand?'

'Yes, Madame'.

The sudden brush of her hand across my cheek to remove a

tear-drop produced in me the strong desire to return hurriedly to my room. Ms Court steadied me by placing her arm about my shoulders.

'You have seen my shoes, maid. Now observe those of Ms Spence . . . '

Ms Spence raised her skirt to below her knees revealing to my intense admiration the high-heeled ladies' boots whose shape I had most revered.

'Punish me, Madame'.

'Yes, Sara'.

SIX

Aristotle's Praxis

I refer to the letter received by your magazine regarding the 'Training Dilemma' being experienced by one of your readers at her riding-school, and to the advice offered subsequently by equestriennes through your pages; the majority of which, perhaps predictably, advised that the most logical solution is to have such regular recourse to the whip, whether or not the behaviour of the animal justifies this harsh treatment, that no chance be given for him to fall back into his old ways. Let us not deny that preventative measures that take the form of severe punishments, will always have their place in the stable environment, and their application by the firm leather-gloved hand of woman has ensured good order for many, many years. I make no apology for the submission that we have required of our animals in the name of preserving the natural order. Nor should his acceptance of his new condition, and a show of improvement that becomes over time permanent, release us from our role as punishers both of transgressions past and those that will otherwise lie in the future. Like your reader from Taunton, I too sleep in my boots, polished and with whip in hand.

No; it is in the method and degree of punishment that I beg to differ from those opinions so far expressed. Does not the continued wearing of the bridle produce inevitably in his thought processes, however slowed by his reflex responsiveness to commands whether issued by voice or spur, that constant reminder of his servile nature? And is it not the case that on the occasion of its removal for remedial treatment to his lips that there is no revived effort to communicate directly with his owner, but again, that simple acceptance of fate with an animal's dignity that can appear most becoming to the disciplinarian? I would therefore make almost a religious distinction between the value to his rider of a horse that is brutally subdued in his first moments in the presence of his new owner, in substitution for that more traditional greeting of his kissing of her boots in turn, from the kneeling position, and her measured response that employs, dare I say it, the loving and compassionate use of the whip to which he is at the same time introduced, with the certain result of his association of riding-mistress with pleasure, and of pleasure with pain.

Following this conventional procedure, there will be a state of equilibrium immediately achieved, or to use a less modern term, established, by this involuntary response to boot and whip, between these apparent extremes of suffering and pleasure which in reality represents no such mid-point between opposing forces that are now identified in his animalistic mind as the same experiences to be found in the diverse circumstances that the mistress provides by the variety of her dress, the cut of her riding-habit, the spur on her boot and the pull of the bit on his new mouth applied through the tensing of reins.

Before I am accused of being soft or overly sentimental, or worse, of leaving the job of training my horse half-finished, which would indeed be the greater cruelty, let me return once more to the psychology of the situation. We have that rare and unusual thing within the grasp of our power, held beneath us by forces that worry and perplex his still thinking mind; a being who feels himself to be trapped by what he perceives to be the limited nature of his present servitude, with a lively memory of the time before his initiation into stable life, to which he feels some level of nostalgia, but also a rejection of what lies in the past and has become alien to him.

A choice, agonizing in its making and irreversible in its consequences, is nevertheless accepted by him. This agreement seemingly made with himself in the seclusion of the horse-box in which he has been shut away and tethered for the duration of the night hours, is in reality the product of the intelligent and moderate treatment of his flesh that has led him to the recognition of the destiny of his natural self, which is simply to be a means of transport, of practical use to his mistress, with therefore no continuing independence of will reserved for himself. His life's purpose has now been decided for him.

The night, even the hour of his acceptance of the logic of the situation, will be predicted by the riding-mistress whose abilities will include that second inner sight which allows for the deposit of leathery imagery within the animal's mind, and also the clear view at any time of his body's response to the heavy chain that hangs down from the white-washed ceiling above, to which his bridle is attached at the end of each day's exertion, and which determines his kneeling posture on the bed of straw.

A desire for complete subjugation has been created by her careful mode of training, and for a while the horse has suffered at this cross-roads, so to speak, unable either to turn back or follow through to the fulfilment that his nature demands.

Even with the bridle removed so that he may more easily eat his morning meal placed for the first time on the instep of his mistress' boot, he is for the reasons already given, quite unable to communicate this turn of psychological events, and by her equal reserve is unaware of the deep understanding she possesses of his dilemma and the timing of its resolution. An increased severity however is detected in her attitude towards him, to which he responds with outstretched tongue that of its own accord returns the reflective shine to her boot, but is dissuaded from this further worship of the second boot, by a flicking of her whip across each polish-stained cheek, and by their re-enclosure within the bridle which together with its bit, is buckled tight against his skin.

A yearning to progress rapidly through to the last stages of his equine training has overcome his machismo mind, which has of itself initiated the process of its own death to which the riding-mistress now feels, from that same compassion that I mentioned earlier, compelled to acquiesce. How much different this form of horse-training from its brutal counterpart in the riding-ring, when the horse is broken by lungeing-rein and whip, and sold on to the highest bid from the assembled ladies even before he has recovered his breathing? Surely it is fitting that the technique of enslavement that brought the father of science, Aristotle, to his knees, so that he might be tamely ridden by a woman, be used again after the rejection and death of that science which denied the Goddess.

Finally, if there is lingering doubt as to the advantages of my proposed method of training and the pleasures gained from what at first appears an unnecessarily protracted affair, let me recall for the amusement of your readers the day when I rode home from the nearby stables into whose care I had entrusted my as yet untrained horse for a period of one month, during which the most careful preparation of my stableyard was undertaken. In our light carriage, repainted for the day of his return, on one of those perfect summer afternoons that remains unforgettable, we drove together along the winding country lanes towards the gateway that opened to the stone facade of our marital home.

No words were exchanged on that day between us. No words were needed to confirm the triumph of Nature over man. Indeed, no communication whatsoever was then possible for him. He seemed for a moment to hesitate as if confused by the lessons of his training so recently received at the hands of the local equestriennes, and his memory of our previous coexistence. Detecting that condition of yearning of which I have written at perhaps too great a length, I raised my whip as if about to punish him for this unnecessary delay to the fruition of my plans. Reacting at once to the lashing then delivered, and with a final glance sideways at the familiar entrance to the house, he trotted ahead towards the horse-box that I had furnished with fresh straw ready for his home-coming. It had been a marvellous summer's day . . . marvellous for all the right

Footnote: To avoid confusion in the reader's mind, the publishers wish it to be known that the above letter was written by Madame X prior to her appointment as the agony aunt of Heel! magazine.

reasons. I should add that this slow method of training horses has proved as effective in the training of dogs; an activity that I know is dear to the hearts of your readers who write with their problems with dog-walking and eating disorders.

MADAME X

SEVEN

The Bridge of Sighs

True; her letter sent to my London address had contained a briefly worded warning for sufferers of asthmatic attacks not to visit her chateau. It had hardly caught my eye, then; yet here I was in the ice-house being repeatedly treated with body powder which provided a far from ideal atmosphere, even though I had not been a previous sufferer of such an attack. The powder's effect was quite obvious to see on each occasion when the large wooden door above me at the level of the outside expanse of lawn was abruptly opened delivering a shaft of powder-filled light across my rubber-encased exterior.

My hostess, the chatelaine, in whose grounds I was to have enjoyed a short break from the stresses of city life, was progressing with my enclosure in rubber in such rapid and mechanical fashion that I was doubting her awareness of my continued existence within. The poor light and low temperature would have contributed to her attitude, but I guessed a childhood fascination with the miniature world of insect predator bondage to be a factor too.

Adding further to my apprehension, as if to confirm that this rubberisation of my body was to last more than an afternoon, I was then to be sprayed with a coating of silicone. To ensure the evenness of this coating, my body was being spun round, under her guidance, at the end of a rope that hung down from the overhead rafter. A polishing cloth was now applied vigorously, which induced in me the beginnings of an acceptance of what was being planned for my future. My arms were not separately polished, however, due to their earlier withdrawal and binding behind my back within the rubber casing.

The slowing of my body's rotation, and its regular reversal of direction, permitted my hostess the closest scrutiny of my changed appearance; a process made more thorough by the gradual lowering of my body by the rope into a pit-like depression, which was filled with water and floating pieces of ice. The downward spiralling of my body into this pit made possible my simultaneous observation of the polished black rubber worn by my hostess. Though the rest of me was concealed by rubber, and now by water, my face, still naked, was greeted at the lowest point of my descent by the sight of her high heels, in which she seemed to be ascending in front of me. In response to a final request, as yet unspoken, before my submersion by the downward pressure of her shoe on my head, I was first required to kiss both shoes in turn. It is often the case that pleasure precedes pain.

Outside in the open air above, I had been walking through the garden near the ice-house, and from a distance, though my view was obscured by the scale of topiary formally laid out over the lawn in front of the chateau, I then observed a number of blocks of ice, each appearing to contain some frozen life-form, being sent skidding from the ice-house over the steaming lawn down the slope, slamming up against blocks of equal size already being gathered by the bridge which links the chateau itself with the woodlands beyond the river. As I watched from the edge of the lawn, with the growing concern that I might soon be noticed and identified, even included in this bizarre exercise from which I now recoiled, a number of blocks had collided together with force, breaking open to reveal their human contents. This consequence of the blocks smashing against each other was surely intended by the group of supervising women who were clad also in rubber, more in sympathy, I believed, with these rubberised men, than out of any environmental necessity.

The women took immediate control. Dislodged tubing was quickly reconnected and then checked. Each one of the 'crash survivors' was laid out on the grass for a period of revival; no opportunity being given, however, for the renewal of initiative. Besides, it was evident to even the most partial observer of these events that such creatures would not be suited for any return to human habitat.

I understood from their helpless condition that there was a kindness, even a logic, first in their encasement in rubber, then in their secondary protection from sunlight within the blocks of ice, and later, when secured by a length of rope to hooks embedded in the masonry of the bridge, in their release into the river.

The chatelaine was engaged similarly with my preparation, in the near-darkness of the ice-house. In a detached manner, as befitted someone who had returned time and time again to some routine task, each time advancing towards its completion, she now covered my face and neck with body powder, this time remaining with me after its application, ready to proceed with the final moulding of my face to the shape of the mask which, being attached to my neck, was floating in front of me. Taking a fist full of my hair in her rubber glove, she slapped my cheeks with the front and back of her free hand until my face was covered with a mixture of powder and tears. On each occasion that she slapped, the fixed position of her fist above my head caused the return of my cheeks into the path of her hand. Only then was she ready to proceed with the stretching of the rubber mask over my face, and its sealing behind my head.With the left and right nasal tubes pressed back inside my skull, and their subsequent, rythmic constriction between her thumb and forefinger, which produced a sudden tensing followed by relaxation of my body, the involuntary functions of my internal organs were, as this progressed, becoming fully under her control. As if to test the true functioning of the new mask, she unscrewed the disk over my mouth.

'Forgive me, Monsieur.You do understand?'

'Yes, Madame'.

'Goodbye, Monsieur'.

The disk was re-inserted into the mask. I felt the silicone spray directed at my head, then the final polishing and my body being lowered onto ice. A succession of images flashed across my mind in long sequences, until, with the cooling of my body, they flickered to a standstill, leaving me with that most recent image of Madame, before she had blinded me with her mask. Blackness had gained an uninterrupted hold. Months, perhaps years, elapsed, during which I remained there suspended, body and mind, in the ice-house, before it was my turn to be sawn into a block of ice, and after being attached by a length of rope to a hook, to be introduced into the river beneath the bridge, where I remain.

To describe our existence. For there are many of us here who hang, side by side, in the river's current at the end of our extended ropes that swing together over the water's surface, like the triple rows of a trireme's oars. You are right in supposing that we are denied by our condition the fulfilment of those basic instincts that are so cherished by your kind. We have developed a heightened sensitivity to that increase and then decrease of water currents. We feel the changing temperature of running water.

And what of our relationship with Madame? We feel the vibration of her tread upon the bridge above. It preserves the memory of our previous lives. It is her gift to us; our constant reminder, when we respond too much to this new type of existence, of those well-heeled boots in which at first she greeted each one of us, her guests.

EIGHT

The Icequeen's Shadow

Being aware of another man's ability or liability is not always sufficient for the purpose of aping that talent or lack of it. An immediate contact with the individual together with the hoped for explanation, perhaps coupled with a physical demonstration, may in the simpler cases be more than enough. However, neither of these options was at that time open to me.

Presumably, the nomadic peoples of the African desert can with ease distinguish between a mirage and the true landscape. And I had heard of no equivalent apparitions occurring in the eastern climes of Europe, certainly not in a ski resort, one that was overlooked by the most towering, snow-capped mountains upon which little fodder, if any, would ever be uncovered in the most unlikely circumstance that the grazing animals of the African plane be led along some circuitous route by their keepers, taking them all the way from the heat and haze of their natural habitats through Turkey and up to the freezing resorts of eastern Europe.

The travel brochures like to regale us with the most complimentary descriptions of those value-for-money ski resorts constructed on the spur of the moment with the subsidy of governments in need of foreign currency, and on land provided from the estate of some reluctant aristocrat whose preference for the solitude of her medieval retreat had to be weighed with an unwilling acceptance of the financial requirements of modernity.

The balance in such an arrangement in favour of the government committee typically ensures that the resulting resort has most of the appearance and facilities, including the nightlife, of its western European counterpart, though much of the ancient character of these well-hidden locations is of course destroyed in the process.

However, on this occasion, under the insistence of the owner of the land, those rights of way across the snowscape, called bridleways, which had become fixed by custom and usage through the centuries, and which in other instances might have ceased in the present to serve any further purpose, would, the committee officials agreed, be preserved. More controversial, but eventually accepted, was the landowner's request that the ancient curfew imposed on the village by her predecessors during the night hours should be maintained, as well as her time-honoured right to punish transgressors according to tradition. Lost in the detail of the small print of the agreement, and only finalised at the eleventh hour as the bulldozers were arriving, this late concession by the committee, all of whom had grown frustrated by her refusal to appear in person at their public hearings, was left unscrutinised, without any regard to the possible medieval nature of feudal tradition.

So it was that each night for the first week of our stay there, the chalet girls repeated verbatim the small print of the travel brochure which we too had failed to scrutinise, warning us of the threat of unknown retribution should we venture from our candlelit cabin out into the dark, until boyish bravado got the better of our initial fear of the 'Icequeen' as she had by then been named. Surely, if she did indeed exist which we now doubted, having seen no evidence of hoofprints in the snow or marks left by her sleigh, she would not venture out into this blizzard. She seemed to us to be a fiction thought up by the authorities perhaps to cover up inadequate staffing levels or fuel for the ski lifts. With this logic to support us, and with the certainty that the driving snow would conceal our nocturnal adventure, we pushed back the door and disappered in the blizzard, leaving behind a panic-stricken chalet girl who had been about to tell us of the disappearance of those other skiers.

Soon losing sight of the village and one by one, my companions, my thoughts turned from irritation with the anachronism of a curfew imposed on holidaymakers, to the realisation that I had become quite lost in the mountains, and that my only chance of being rescued from these sub-zero temperatures, since the local people would never break the curfew, was the Icequeen herself. If only she had been real after all, whether she was dressed in furs or leather, it did not matter; I prayed for the punishment that would surely accompany my rescue.

Out of breath from skating and gliding on my skis, a long way from the chalet, with no recognizable landmarks in sight, in my desire to live through the night I began to dream up the most absurd fantasies which I would soon experience at the feet of my rescuer whose sleigh-bells I pretended to hear, whose whip I pretended to fear. Somewhere in these mountains, its turrets dripping with icicles, its drawbridge now lowered to the ground and leading into a torch-lit hall of flagstones and blazing fire, was perched the enchanted castle of the Icequeen. I saw her in leather, in front of the flames, her dark silhouette framed by the drawbridge gates, pacing up and down in boots impatient for the bell-tower to strike the curfew hour. Only then would her immense shadow freeze against the stone wall, patiently waiting, whip in hand, for the Icequeen's return and punishment of the new servant.

The storm had passed into the next valley, and I was standing in the stillness that followed, looking out upon a vast expanse of blanketing snow, which glistened under the moonlight. So alien was this scene that surrounded me, and so filled was I with silent wonder, that if the Icequeen had then appeared in a sleigh pulled by swans or some chosen bird of prey, or by a team of winged elves, I would have accepted that their claim to reality far exceeded my own.

I was losing my grip on their world; any moment I would be woken from this spectacle by the mundane brush of a stiletto boot dangling from the descending chair-lift. I looked up. Sure enough, it had all been a dream; for there as usual was the chair-lift slowly climbing above the ski slopes, filled as usual to capacity, each chair carrying two skiers dressed in leather with stiletto heels and whips that hung down beside them, occasionally flicking at the heads below. Guests of the Icequeen at her mountain retreat? It would have taken a nomad to ski in Bulgaria.

NINE

The Prodigal Slave

Lying back on the smooth deck, I dreamt of an undiscovered temple and of how I would awaken a Goddess from an ancient sleep. For this had been the purpose given me by the dream which had sent me from that world in a boat without compass or crew. Equipped only with a map of the island as it once had been in Vulcan's past, and with the light heart of youth, I had climbed above the fields of cultivated fruits tended by the women dressed in black, that stretched in an upward curve from the shore to the steep slopes of the mountain strewn with the boulders of past eruptions. No longer was its peak capped with the white marble of her temple.

Recalling then the contours of the Himalayas, whose snow-bound heights are but the visible supports of more ethereal structures, I began to imagine the temple as it had been in ancient times in the sky above the centre of the volcano's crater, and attempted to calculate the expected trajectories of flying stone. But no sign was there of evidence of the remnants of a lost temple.

Scaling the last few breathless steps to the rim of the volcano, I peered through fading light into its forbidding interior before starting my descent down the northern side of the crater, down to the red molten core of the mountain's heart. Traversing for hours across sheer rock, employing the full grip of my fingers and toes, hurrying when the moon shone, then clinging tight until its return from behind the cover of clouds, all the time driven on by the impetus of the instructions received from the leatherclad woman of my dream . . . I encountered a sizable impediment to my downward progress: an outcrop of smooth black lava that had in the distant past sealed over what appeared in the half-light to be the protruding shape of a temple. A flight of steps preserved beneath layers of volcanic ash jutted out from the rock face, leading up to the temple doors. I had found the temple to the Goddess, complete and intact, sunk beneath its former lofty, sun-splashed splendour and embedded within the cooling lava stone.

Pulling myself up onto the steps with a final burst of effort, I had collapsed with my face resting down on the soft black ash which seemed then to bind with the perspiration of my skin into a kind of protective coating. Perhaps it was appropriate that my naked flesh took on this dark aspect of a shape-shifting demon that might belong in such an infernal place. For what further transformations could be expected within a temple untouched for two thousand years to which I had been led by the most persuasive of whips . . . should I now hammer at its doors with loose stone to break open Vulcan's seal?

I started to chip against the temple's blackened entrance, disturbing shard after shard of stone until the blows delivered seemed almost to be anticipated by the crumbling veneer, and echoes from within near deafened my head. I turned to see the last of the dislodged rubble hurtling down into the abyss below. Whatever

Goddess still lived behind the exposed doors had by now been woken from the deepest of sleep. Surely, I reasoned, my task had already been accomplished and I should return to the waiting boat lest it leave without me; lest it leave me in the thrall of a Goddess whose priestesses in their temple clothing of rubber still awaited her return with ready sacrifices, and ungrateful of my service might arrest me on my daylight journey back through their fields. Or so I imagined.

I pressed lightly at first against each of the two doors that had remained locked together since antiquity, but there was no movement in their hinges. I tried again with the full commitment of my musculature, at the same time fearing that I was about to be confronted by some whip-wielding Goddess unacquainted with the more moderate behaviour of our times. My feeling of frustration was therefore tempered with relief as I sat exhausted on the topmost step, slumped against the doors, about to plan my escape from the crater when I fell back onto the cool marble floor of a silent temple. I did not move from my kneeling position while my eyes were adjusting to the vast scale of the temple's inner space.

A white linen sheet was draped over the reclining statue of a woman, which lay upon a slab of stone, the lid of a sarcophagus which rose out of a pool of dark water that surrounded its rectangular base. It seemed impossible that any lifeform could have survived that period of suspended animation; yet trapped within the folds of linen at the noblewoman's feet, two fluttering birds had revived sufficiently to attempt discourse and escape. Like glove-puppets that had been vitalised by the shafts of incoming moonlight, what messages drawn from the woman's deep consciousness were being silently exchanged in this dialogue which grew increasingly more animated until both birds flew sideways off the lid, taking with them the sheet that now floated in the water.

From behind this cover there appeared a figure sheathed in black, almost invisible to me after the period of my concentration on the white of the linen. Her sculpted upper body lay back on the sarcophagus' lid, asleep. The polished legs had been dragged by their whirling ankle-wings over the edge of the stone slab, where they hung down beside the sarcophagus, their surfaces being reflected in the dark pool below. Again the ankle-wings unfurled themselves into the moonlit air, seemingly panicked by their closeness to water or proximity to the stiletto heels. Lacking as yet any true coordination, they caused the Goddess to kick out, to writhe about and then to waken.

Slipping down into the pool she crossed its width before stepping out onto the marble floor, where she stood dripping water onto the ground about her feet. Her unblinking eyes stared at the dark liquid as if to reclaim their focus by observing its slow trickling over the marble to where I was kneeling. Would this Goddess whose divine proportions I now faced in awe, remember the reason for my presence in her temple; how dressed in leather she had ordered me from the dreamworld to serve her earthly form? She tilted her head to one side, seeing me from the corner of her eye, then raised and lowered her right arm, mechanically, with difficulty, repeating this movement until flexibility had returned, and I was no longer able to distinguish the finish of one practised whiplash from the next. She reached for the coil of leather at her waist, pulling it away from her to unleash its full length, and spoke her first word for two thousand years.

'Sssll . . . ave!!!'

With the spontaneity of a relationship renewed, I threw myself forward towards her feet, the better to receive her extended greeting, which was not limited to a polite whipping, given the independent volition of her recently revived right arm that prevented a more regular show of affection. Uncertain of her limbs which retained within their fibres the memories of suffering inflicted, she walked with an uneven tread over my body, dragging the whip through my spreading blood which flowed over the marble into the dark pool whose water had turned the porous stone of the sarcophagus red. She stopped at the open doors; her black silhouette now poised to leave the temple of her entombment. I watched the ankle-wings whirl beside the polish of her legs, lifting her clear of the steps into the shafts of returning moonlight.

TEN

The Schizophrenic Boot

'Letter to the editress, on the "Wearing of Boots", the lady's name and address having been withheld at her own request. We may reveal to the readers of Heel! magazine, in the same confidence, that the correspondent has been a past contributor of authoritative and widely acclaimed articles on the subject of the naming of Ladies' Boots. Her insightful comment and progressive recommendations in this matter, tirelessly proposed in the crusading spirit, have at last and thankfully prevailed over the error of the "anonymous approach" to the labelling of boots, which has been the regrettable cause of so much unnecessary distress and confusion, most particularly with the uninformed debate and palaver at the recent elections over the multiple voting of booted ladies:

> DEAR BOOT-LOVERS,
> I am regularly asked to give a date, a time-span, even the season, on or within which a boot and its pair, if they are to be named together, at once, should be so christened; in short, I feel sometimes that I am expected to provide a measure of exactitude, of scientific precision, to an aspect of a lady's behaviour which must be considered to be entirely sublime and in every case beyond the determination of mere reason.

Certain guidelines but not instruction, which is of course reserved to the polishing servant, may be usefully provided, and no more.

My reply to my questioning and sincere colleague is itself made in the form of an innocent enquiry. For example, does the reader believe herself to be in receipt of an intolerable and personal insult when her footwear, if here supposed to be animate in its own right, might at the same time feel badly treated, or slighted by some act of disrespect? Is the moment savoured when again, if indeed the boot is at first removed, the leather which has been prepared for inspection and touch by the boot-slave, is slid over and becomes fused, at least imaginatively, with the mistress' expectant flesh? If the answer to these two questions is "Yes", both times, then it would be correct, advisable and timely, to delve further into the unique and blossoming relationship of boot and mistress. The reader may in the meditative privacy and midst of her self-questioning and doubt, choose her own phrasing, with the sensitive variation of my words, which are, nevertheless, and this should be borne in mind, based on the experience of countless exchanges with the lady who has arrived at this point of open and complete self-discovery.

And does one boot differ from the other such that the mistress inclined by nature to kick out and strike with her right side, discovers that it is with her left boot and heel that she has dispatched so summarily the subject of her repulsed and dispassionate gaze – that kneeling, servile object of her sudden disapproval; and all this contrary to what might have been guessed before the deadly delivery to the head and body of the clumsy slave? And is the other boot, though more reticent, and preferring to play on like the proverbial cat with the cornered mouse, more expressive by the arching instep or lengthened and raised boot-tip, of the contempt with which the misdemeaning man is held in the eyes of the impatient mistress, perhaps made late for a meeting, prearranged and of great importance? For in the character of its conduct lies inevitably the clue to the identity and sexual recognition of the female boot, and the resolution to this dilemma of the new wife and mistress, much reported within these pages, of which name to choose for boot and slave. Yes, certainly, the polishing and soon to be feminized slave will bear the name of the boot that kicks, and be baptized the very same.

What is the complex and true nature of the indwelling life within the polished and shaped leather of reshaped bull, and the sharpened heel now turned against the sex of its previous incarnation, and carrying within, instead, the new memories of the female host? Was not the heeled boot of the suffragette tethered also beneath the long dress, to the patriarchal gates, and with this troubled past of darkened imagery still unavenged, seeks out the opportunity to punish and then to punish, without appeasement? It is the deliberate and feminine naming of that schizophrenic boot which has so far remained at odds with and appears unconvinced of its new role and purpose, that, as precocious readers will have already surmised, forces through the still glimmering and bullish consciousness an acceptance of its new female identity and loyalty. And after the mutual baptism of boot and polishing slave, it is common for the mistress to say in her own defence, when exaggeration has entered into and played a decisive part in her relationship, and if the word "common" may be applied to a mode of living which is as yet in modern times, quite exceptional . . . it is common to hear of her complaint that the "boot struck first, and I but followed in its wake" as appalled as any bystander by the irreversibility and magnitude of the crime. Let the reader remind herself, and often, that in the training of the servant, as in the breaking-in of new boots, strict timing and restraint are the boot-lover's key to that elusive and frequently discussed state of marital bliss.

MADAME X

A second extract from this fascinating account of the making of a good boot-slave will be published by the kind permission of Madame X in our july issue, available from the shops on June 16th, or directly by subscription. Readers' comments welcomed!'

ELEVEN

The Rubber Arachnid

The giant leaves of amazonian lilies were floating above a scaffold of tangled vegetation that became visible only when I withdrew my paddle from the water, and shafts of sunlight then lit the subterranean world below. I was not there as some voyeur of the remnants of a lost civilisation, who with the advantages of hindsight had come to gloat over one of history's catastrophes. I was hunting for food, for the mutant lifeforms released from the nearby gene factory that had been submerged somewhere beneath me, a victim of the recent floods that had cleansed the planet's surface of most of the transgenic creatures. The result had been the same as before, when in the time of Atlantis, the divine Goddess had drowned those man-made species materialized by the magicians' parrot-like reciting of mantras.

How ironic it was, that those culprit scientists responsible for the present deluge had avoided its depths by being impaled at the end of poles, high above the water. Like clowns who had brought only one stilt each to the circus and then been set upon by the disappointed crowd, these shaven-headed men had been made up with happy smiling faces, giving them the appearance of products from their Frankenstein past.

The sentence of impalement had been taken from the pages of a book in the town library, when news of rising water levels had reached its population. For it had been the librarian's interest in Vlad, the ruler of Transylvania and impaler of thousands, whose life had so contrasted with her own humdrum existence, and her purchase for the library of several biographies, that had suggested this medieval punishment to the elders meeting as the streets had begun to fill with water.The impaling of the scientists had in most details followed the medieval accounts contained in the biographies. For example, the smoothing of the end of the pole before insertion prevented excessive rupture of internal organs and ensured a period of lofty reflection prior to death. Also, the greasing of the poles.

Switching the paddle from one side of the boat to the other, I was weaving my way through the growing density of these vertical poles that rose ten to twenty feet out of the water. My suspicion that the smiling scientists would have been impaled near to their workplace, convinced me that I was close to my quarry and a rare meal of transgenic flesh, if I could stomach it.

The white coats that hung down over the tops of the poles provided a most surreal setting in which to hunt. I was being reminded of that Turkish king, who had fled Transylvania without engaging Vlad in battle, so repelled was he by the sight of a ravine filled with impaled citizens. I then noticed that long strands of a black material had been wound round a number of the corpses as if some effort had been made to preserve the flesh. In many instances, so complete was the body's capture within a compact bundle of the black fibre that even the smiling faces were concealed. Each of these black cocoons was linked by a rubbery thread that ran down the length of the pole and disappeared into the water. Once more, the sun shone through this forest of branchless trees with their shiny black fruit. I could see fleeting movements of equally black creatures thirty feet underwater. Fearing that the progress of my wooden boat would have been watched, and certain now of a connection between the fabrication of the cocoons and the spidery forms below, I transferred my weight onto one of the huge lily leaves whose existence was perhaps also the product of the scientist's skill.

No sooner had I removed the paddle, placing it beside me against the upturned edge of the leaf, than the entire wooden structure was enveloped in a black cocoon, spun by the giant legs of a spider that had rapidly climbed up through the thick stalks and positioned itself immediately under the boat, presumably intending to trap me inside this rubbery sarcophagus.

Sitting crosslegged, as still and inconspicuously as possible, I watched the darkness of night descend, until the wriggling of the cocoons was no longer visible. In my determination not to fall asleep and overbalance into the water, I began to consider the probable nature of the creatures below. A female spider, eight foot across, would be outrageous even in the islands of the Galapagos. So some human contribution to its appearance had been made. Had they been created to produce a new type of biodegradable rubber? Were they now treating the laboratory of their birth as their natural habitat? And what sort of beings would eventually emerge from those cocoons, whose wriggling indicated metamorphosis perhaps resulting from their injection with spider genes?

I could hear the sound of a cocoon being pulled down a pole by its rubbery thread into the water, no doubt to satisfy the appetite of one of these transgenic arachnids. This was to be repeated at intervals throughout the night, and by morning a flotilla of discarded cocoons, whose occupants had been sucked out after injection with digestive juices, was floating around me. It was then that I seized my chance to escape by concealing my body within one of the cocoons that had been emptied of all nutrients. Pulling open the hole previously made by the spider's mouthparts, I squeezed inside . . .

Being carried by the surging floodwater through the gaps between the lily leaves out into the fast current, I had felt the rubber casing of the cocoon being pierced and my skin punctured, three or four times, but was experiencing no physical transformation that I could detect. It seemed that not only the spiders understood the directions of the current, for I was to be greeted by some amazonian women when eventually I had reached dry land, and my body was pulled clear of the water by a gaff plunged into the side of the cocoon.

In my relief at being rescued, it did not cross my mind that I would be mistaken for a transgenic lifeform. My arrival had nonetheless been expected by these long-limbed descendants of the Cloud People whose ancestors were survivors of the atlantean flood. If I had been able to see through the cocoon's surface, with my anthropologist's eye, I would have noted their rubber skins and spike-heeled boots which would have been used to finish prey that had been caught within the radius of their hunting whips.

Otherwise the women took with them a bow and quiver of

arrows. It had been the scientists' fear of being attacked as intruders in this ancient rain-forest, that had led to the bribing of this community of amazons with pairs of boots made from spider rubber, which were delivered to them regularly by the predictable current.

My body started to wriggle involuntarily inside the cocoon, whilst I was being rolled across the forest floor by the force of the women's boots. From within, I could hear the sounds of the distant beating of drums, coming ever closer as my mutating form was pushed and kicked up the steep incline towards a temple, which rose above the forest canopy, but was covered to the point of concealment by the weight of thousand year old vines. Only the twin domes with their cladding of rubber could be seen, shining like beacons in the night sky. In the dark interior beneath, spiders worked at their unceasing production of rubber fibre. Legs were constantly being broken by the priestess' whip or singed by the encircling ring of fire, or when fast production and not dexterity was required; bound together.

A pair of boots, their heels as high as a man, stood polished on either side of the temple gates. Created by the industry of countless spiders, and fused into being by the light of the full moon, their surfaces still perspired from recent use by the Goddess. Was it intended that I should now join the temple spiders in their manufacture of rubber for the Goddess' wardrobe? My attempts at mouthing words of protest served only to produce the first secretion of black liquid.

TWELVE

The Museum of Time

The brush of her coat turned me around. For a moment, I believed that she, too, was standing on tiptoes in the effort to more closely inspect the Goddesses of the Heavens who seemed equally intent on meeting us half way, in the mid-air below the museum ceiling of the Louvre, Paris. Perhaps they pressed down on their high heels, pushing away from the canopic stone above us, in the same polished boots that were worn by this woman standing beside me admiring the map of the celestial vault taken from the Temple of Denderah in Egypt, where thousands of years before the priestesses greeted their Goddesses, Hathor and Isis.

She did seem Egyptian in her appearance according to my sidereal glances, as my head continued to spin. Her coat made from black fur and the long leather gloves both attracted and repulsed my confused and buzzing mind. She was dressed as a fashionable Parisienne, no doubt about that; her boots were too perfect to have been crafted in Egyptian times, unless those Goddesses whose lofty sphere echoed their booted progress through the zodiac's constellations, had once brought to their temple some examples to share with their priestesses.

Again the strange sensation of being enclosed within a tube or tunnel that extended down from the domed roof of the temple, returned to me, and I was aware of the ring of tourists that were circling this invisible barrier, trying to penetrate its magnetic field, in which I stood held by the presence of this resurrected priestess of Isis. Her position directly beneath the dome's centre seemed to free this beautiful woman from the pressure of forces circulating within the sealed chamber that we occupied together, now that the people outside were no longer visible.

The central position adopted, I believed, by chance by the priestess was, I have since realised, being used to activate those forces that through their increase caused this tunnel effect to bulge outwards, centrifugally, soon establishing a spheroidal shape of which the temple roof appeared to be the lid that spun and expanded the internal volume. The museum floor that had seemed so secure was, in an instant, substituted with an open area of sand surrounded by a wooden fence of joined, waist-high panels, that produced in result an area some ten times larger by diameter than that section of ceiling under which I had been considering the advantages of taking a train rather than a plane, back to London after a long weekend of exploration; neither of which would have been practical to reach this destination from the past.

My companion whose body had lifted clear of the wooden floor of the museum just before this sudden change of scene, so that her boots seemed to push against my face in the urgency of their climb, landed just after me, at the central point of this arena, where like a parachutist failing to break his fall, I lay looking in a daze at the shining boots that had settled upon my reconstituted body. Standing over me, as if fully concerned about my states of body and mind, the priestess was repeating a name to me, my name, but from a slave past that was infinitely more real to me, than that of any parallel existence of mine in Paris.

I felt both her leather gloves smacking successively against my cheeks, reviving me with their sandy touch, leading me to tears by this forced repatriation of my soul in a past that I had sought to escape by a knowledge of alchemical formulae. What I saw next would leave any but the dead, struck dumb by the force of its beauty and by fear of its potential. In my first circuit around this sandy arena designated by Isis herself as the place of training for her horses, I saw such a number of superbly dressed Parisiennes who enjoyed this dual nationality by virtue of the section of the temple vortex transported from Egypt, and by their recollection of ritual through membership of secret societies whose history had begun at Denderah.

The tiered seats, again of polished wood, provided a 360 degree view of the shape-shifting transformations experienced by those returned slaves who had in ignorance wandered onto the plate of the vortex like the nonchalant house-mouse who steps onto the trap without time to regret the irreversibility of the events to follow. Pulling against the rapidly inserted and tightened bridle and bit, with what must have been seen as a maddened look in my eye, or even the first sign of transformation, I caught repeated glimpses of the women beneath their travelling coats of fur: clothing that suggested an Arctic destination and not the sweltering heat of the Sahara. To the last woman, they were wearing leather polished to match the gleam of their black, stiletto heeled boots cut beneath the knee, over which the hem of their dresses rested.

Only then did I notice in their eyes the constancy of their stare as if determined not to miss some new phase in my development within the horse-ring. There was no conversation between them. Indeed, I would say that I was the unwilling subject of their rapt attention, and that my deliverance to their Goddess apparently required their unremitting support.

The very heat of the ring, were the viewing stands themselves empty, would have soon slowed my pace at the end of the lungeing-rein. The first slack in its length became evident as I drifted from the perimeter fence, no longer fighting its pull, and relieved that this reluctance of mine was met with only a few reminders from the whip that had been wriggling after me throughout this period of training. With my legs buckling and turning to rubber beneath me, I fell to my knees, and then forward onto the sand that had worked its way into my burning feet.

A murmur went through this audience of several hundred women, as if to acknowledge the appearance of some celebrated equestrienne whose unheralded arrival had taken these fixated priestesses of both temple and fashion, by complete surprise. Yet in retrospect, I believe it was my final collapse there on the ground that elicited this response, because it was then that they left their seats in hurried silence, and took their positions immediately behind the wooden fence. Whether Isis had appeared in the sky at that precise time and been observed, is unknown to me.

With her fur-coat left like the cape of a bull-fighter in the middle of the ring, the only woman there, except perhaps Isis herself, to be wearing riding-clothes, now accepted as if in ritual from the youngest in the crowd, a pair of the highest heeled boots into which, to gasps of appreciation, she inserted her feet. Perhaps I was taking part in an event whose origin predates our version of history, being the precursor of the modern bullfight; for, like the banderillas applied cruelly to the flesh of the selected beast, I was, I feared, about to be so mistreated and then dispatched. Again, the women looked to the sky in patient expectation, as if for a sign from their Goddess whose heavenly tread, I believed I also could hear in the total silence that then ensued. But no sign was given as they waited, immaculate in their unmoving boots, until moonlight had replaced sunlight in the shining of their leather. Had I been spared like the god, Seth, by the will of Isis?

The equestrienne, slow to concede to the Goddess' verdict, and treating my body as if it had indeed been gored by her heels of death, then tied in quick well-practised knots, a coil of rope under my arm, wedging its fibre into the pit, and then round my neck, before mounting a horse to the approval of the crowd, and dragging me away back from the desert towards the temple complex. Once there, my body was taken to what Egyptologists refer to as being a mud-brick 'sanatorium' where I was quickly bathed to cure the cuts of the whip, in the waters sacred to the Goddess, before being deposited in a sealed cubicle of limited space, on my back to 'incubate' or to await the appearance of the Goddess within my dreaming.

How long I had been there I do not know, nor am I sure whether in that world time can be relied upon to go forward without going sometimes sideways or in reverse when the Goddess turns the temple's zodiac in the anti-clockwise direction. But the blizzard of snow, this time, not sand, was real enough, as was the reappearance of the Parisiennes pressing keenly in greater numbers against the wooden fence. The sensation of shaking that ushered in this recreation of the desert arena had faded, leaving me to survive or die in this black and white dream in the moonlight. As I ran once more at the end of the leash of the woman I had carelessly stood next to in the museum, my feet this time frozen by the powdery snow that was falling still, I was avoiding as often as I was able during my circuit of the perimeter, those ominous patches of blood red colour that remained upon the floor of the riding-school.

Exhaustion set in earlier, due to the previous exertion, and the whipping of my back ceased so that the women in furs might request of their Goddess their preferred reward. But the invisible Goddess shook her invisible head in denial, and the blizzard blew again, until the women had gone and I was alone with only bridle and bit, and endless snow. Like the ant that listens for the echo of human steps upon the floorboards overhead, my equine ears were pricked to the sound of Isis' booted tread descending from the roof within her zodiacal sphere, where by the shaking of the dice within her leather gloved hand, the cycles of life are decided. One shake and I would be returned to the museum's vortex, to be captured by this horse trainer and led to a third and then a fourth riding-school, until the Goddess' dice had fallen in her favour. Another shake and I would see the Goddess herself wrapped warm in the snow, out looking for her human steed lost in one of her empty worlds.

A blackening vortex of swirling particles greeted these thoughts of mine, turning this way and that, pinpointing my position in space and time, before becoming fixed like the photographer's image, into magnificent form in front of where I knelt in readiness to apply my training in the transport of the Goddess. In her glove, a riding-whip had replaced the set of dice, which lay with her discarded fur-coat upon the snow; circular spots of black about to be crushed like ice beneath her booted feet.

'I am Isis, the Goddess. I am worshipped in Paris. Return with the priestess who brought you to me. I give you to her . . . Die to be reborn!'

THIRTEEN

The Human Parrot

DEAR BOOT-LOVERS,

It seems no time at all since I last addressed you and your questions and concerns about the female boot which appears, by the volume and nature of correspondence, to be in very good health and in this wintry season to be multiplying spectacularly in numbers, so that on occasion on the street corner, dressed beneath an umbrella in my favourite rubber raincoat, I feel myself to be moved, even overwhelmed, by the promiscuous display of polished leather and heels that greets my disbelieving eye.

With a happy and restorative tap of riding-crop against new boot, and a confirming glance at my tight-waisted and stiletto-booted reflection, stretched out and rippling below the curb-stone in the neon light, I then proceed to cross over to the other side, untouched by the spray of the screeching car. I am met by so many haughty, disdaining faces that I believe I have been transported to the set of some musical, where the harmony of clicking heels has replaced the usual composition. I walk on through the dancing, rain-soaked crowd, through the rehearsal of strutting boot and swirling cape, past the shop-window of artificially splashed rain- and foot-wear, up the steps and into the offices of Heel! magazine, where I discover the letters, heart-felt and sometimes over-enthusiastic, left on my desk by you, the boot-lover and captive reader.

You may have guessed that the procreation of the boot and therefore of the boot-slave is the subject foremost in my mind at this time. Let me, therefore, metaphorically speaking, if not in fact, sweep under the carpet, under the twin heels of my own boots, those missives that have failed to register a polite and appropriate level of interest in the topic chosen by your agony aunt and upon which she wishes briefly to dwell.

Let us progress without further ado, to this matter of growing importance and relevance in the life of the modern woman, but with first a grateful acknowledgement to the mistress who has written with such concern to ask about the well-being of my caged bird that sings from beyond my ink-well with a parrot's capacity to mimic the human voice. He is indeed in excellent spirits and has, since her last asking, exceeded by his range even that of the much praised bird, by his convincing and everpresent portrayal also of the manners and kneeling appearance of the boot-slave, so that when the little door is open and I insert some generous portion of seed and nuts within my tight-fisted leather glove, no sign of winged flight or confused flapping is discernible, merely the preservation of that posture which resembles more the demeanour of the trained circus animal that leaps through rings.

For that reason, and to add novelty to the idea, I have attached a silver necklace above his shivering body that with its leash includes, with the door unlocked, the distance to the ink-well, which he fills when my attention is diverted with my replying to your letters, and to the leatherbound sheets of blotting-paper, from which, I believe, he silently and slowly tears manageable pieces with which to follow at a safe and undetected pace, my writing nib.

Was he long ago the gift of a satisfied reader, or did he provide his service freely, of his own accord and volition, if a slave can be said to possess the gift of his slavery, which in truth is recognized in him by the predatory female and wrested from him for her purpose? The leather drape sent in by this mistress with the offer of some privacy for the bird and intended by the detail of her letter to be placed over the cage at the time of my quitting the office for the torrential rains outside, has I am sure, though changes of expression are hard to distinguish in the inclined face and the stiffness of limbs beside his kneeling form . . . been a compassionate and pleasantly scented contribution to office life.

The ankle-cuffs, too, have proved after the prolonged and awkward time had by the manicured nails of my staff in their attachment, another success for which I, who have been required by fate to handle the advance of his training and discipline, remain indebted; only his singing has ceased and that at the acceptable price of his improved performance around the desk. How sad that the miniature key has, we are told, no duplicate; for the original here has quite disappeared.

Suffice it to say that as this mistress might have supposed, we have not just the single song-bird who refuses, it seems, to sing; but an entire aviary with which we must contend daily. It is not the binding of the beak, but the resignation to captivity that is in each case the cause of that cessation of complaint and chattering by the clipped bird, and their substitution by his unconvincing repetition from the now limited repertoire of the single word, 'Heel!'.

Only by the improvement of diction, the result of his confinement within our offices, does the prospect of his release become at length a serious and realistic possibility, and later the anticipated reality; not of course by the bird who has relinquished all such desire for his reintroduction into the wild, and will resist by attempted pecking the grasping, protected hand that finally enters his cage to return to him that once treasured and often championed freedom.

The human parrot, so transformed in our presence, will when challenged on the affairs of politics or some matter of etiquette, in a public place, respond decisively and repetitively with his practised restatement of the exclamation, 'Heel!'. Such advertising is their invaluable and continuing contribution to our magazine. We have merely provided this closed and feminine environment, and then a selection of rubber clothing, for their eventual and empty-headed mimicking of the predatory female.

I fear that I have been distracted from my intended subject

by the mistress' concern for the human parrot. I will no doubt be referring in a subsequent issue of Heel! to the procreation of the female boot and the necessary increase in the population of its counterpart, the boot-slave.

MADAME X

As many of our readers will already know from her personal replies to their letters, Madame X has kindly agreed to her appointment as the agony aunt of Heel! magazine. Do send your experiences and inquiries directly to her at our Paris address. The Editress.

FOURTEEN

The Mannequin's Dream

The following account was written down after a lucid dream during an otherwise sleepless night in the heat-wave of 1972. No attempt is made to improve on the quality of text which remains in its original, scribbled form; hopefully conveying by its haphazard construction the immediacy of events that may prove relevant and rewarding in the life of the reader:

> A sea-palace. A massive entrance. A girl's beneath it. She's dressed in leather. She's late. She struts straight at the camera. She'd like to smash it . . . Camera backs up into palace followed by girl. White marble of palace contrasts starkly with black of patent-leather. Repeated sparking of stiletto boots against flagstones. Sprays of sea-water exploding from their polished surface. The sound of boot heels ricocheting like bullets overhead. Pointed boot tips kicking into thin air. Pythonic wriggling of smooth hips and thighs filling the screen . . . Camera pulls to side and stops at double-doors opposite entrance. Close-up of leather girl in profile. She knows that doors will open for her. They do. I see that she's handcuffed. Wooden doors slam shut behind her. I wake fully within the dream, within her leather-encased frame. I see

through her eyes. I know this palace. I've been here before. I know this girl. I've been her before . . .

Row upon row of booted women dressed in polished leather. A vast indoor amphitheatre beneath a white marble dome. Boots hanging down from tiered seats. Boots entwined in serpentine clusters . . . I remember that I'm late to school. Impatient clicking of heels on marble. Need excuse fast to explain being late again for class. Why am I wearing these handcuffs? This is not the first time. Do I do it deliberately?

'She works nights as a mannequin in a specialist store.'

I recognize voice and face of beautiful reclining girl in fourth row. She's always there when I arrive late in dreams. The reason why I am late. I am her bondage slave. I'm sure of it . . . The Mistress points me to empty seat in fourth row. Her own dress code is strict enough, but practical for the teaching of domestic science. She uncoils whip.

'Hand up anyone who believes that she is immortal!'

For students of bondage, such gestures of defiance are no longer possible. Experience of bondage leads to realism in this respect . . . Girl in fourth row is forcing my elbows together and locks them in place above handcuffs. Is she protecting me from myself? Was thinking of volunteering for demonstration of domestic violence. Feelings of submission towards this sublime Mistress who teaches domestic science with a whip. Who is this divine being? A Goddess of what? The Bitch Goddess of Pain?

'Is there anyone here who believes that she is not mortal?'

To further protect me from base desire, my ankles are

being forced and locked together. My body is then polished to erase the signs of struggle. Am I taking part in some esoteric ritual of transformation? The class slaves are being secured by stages. Becoming immobilized. Marbleized. Prepared for the black marble sarcophagus upon which the Mistress sits cross-legged, whip in hand . . . I attempt to mouth words of protest.

'Please, Mistress, could I be exempt Domestic Science . . . ?'

Nothing escapes from gag being fastened in my mouth beneath rubber mask stretched taut over my face. I am gaining appearance of Egyptian dead. I remember this ritual from previous times. The whipping of the class slaves will soon begin. Then the immersion of bound and helpless bodies into the salt-water of the sarcophagus.

'Whom, then, do you believe is immortal?'

'Bitch Goddess of Pain . . . Bitch Goddess of Pain . . . Bitch Goddess of Pain . . . Bitch Goddess of Pain . . . '

Who could forget this mantra of the would-be bitch goddess? Her chosen path to immortality. Not self-discipline but the disciplining of others. Now demonstrated to its limits by the whip-hand of the Mistress. The Bitch Goddess of Pain. Followed by the slave's full immersion within the overflowing sarcophagus. Then his reawakening within the world of mortal men.

Footnote: The "Bitch Goddess of Pain", or "Pain", or "Bitch Goddess", as she is known to the man in the modern street, was in classical times the embodiment of the Hellenic spirit, the thirteenth Olympian and principal Goddess of Homer's religion. She is the sibling of Pan, daughter of Hermes and Dryope.

Her sanctuary is on the island of Thasos where the first of the black sarcophagi was discovered in 1883 by Sir William Pencader, to contain "such unseasonable and unfathomable quantities of dark water concealing in its depths the body of a sleeping drunk of undistinguishable appearance, left for dead by his oppressors, but preserved in life by the salt of his wounds and English attire worn against the unnatural elements of that place . . . For a man to venture out at night and to recklessly deposit himself at the mercy of this Goddess within the boundary of her shrine, as a dreamer with dreaming on his mind, is to be rewarded by an insensibility to pain enviable by gods and men alike, and an unsatisfiable appetite for that pain, received not in manly pursuits, but in the company of woman."

FIFTEEN

Son et Lumière

Staring into the darkness of the night through closed eyes, I watched in the silence as slowly the blackness drained from within the volume of my skull until a blazing light had filled my waking head, that turned to the left and right to hear the whispered words of 'Sound' and 'Light'. About to drown and feeling dead, my body soon severed from its earthly bed, I rose above the sunken skies, through the opening of my eye, then floated in the distant night upon a sea of coral light.

Moving like eels, together, writhing and wriggling their inky mass toward me, the death angels approached, engulfing me in their rubbery embrace, taking me to their polished bosom to nourish my dying heart. Held by suction to this shifting host, I was dragged along within its coordinated motion, as it reared above the placid sea like some gigantic Goddess of the deep, then dived below into the emerging seasons of an embryonic earth, encasing me within its gleaming shape.

Bouncing over the surface of the sea with my body held within this Goddess' womanly vice, my heart was beating to the rhythm of a new life. Moving through the cool water between her colossal thighs, it was like being carried within the rubber folds of an enveloping sail that skimmed above the smooth surface, moulding my body into some amphibian form, while the Goddess' dark milk worked inside me, in the rubberisation of my organs. The more firm the sea felt beneath, the more ardently my body constructed layers of rubber tissue to protect itself, until I was released from the Goddess' care and thrown up onto the pristine shore of an alien landscape.

Half-expecting to find myself incorporated in the flesh of a seal-like mammal, I was relieved by the observation that my body had retained its human character; except that it would require that I inhabit near to water to keep the newly formed skin moist and that I sleep in caves away from the sunlight that would perish its smooth surface. I was indeed in a privileged position; for it was from outside my hermit's dwelling of stone that I greeted the sight of the Goddess from whose womb I had so recently been reborn, when she emerged from the waves at nightfall and progressed inland, having first added to her tree-top height with high heels in which she towered over the uneven ground.

One night, long after my arrival there, when I lay separated from the dust of the cave floor by rubbery layers of discarded skin, in a light sleep, I woke to the sight of a gleaming hand, seemingly cut off at the wrist, writing on the cave wall beside me the three words: 'Son et Lumière'. As these words were being written onto stone, the Goddess whispered each syllable so that it echoed about in my head with such vibratory force that I was compelled to leave the safety of the cave and to follow the Goddess' bootprints inland to wherever her crushing stride might lead.

On an elevated plane where green grass grew over fertile soil to a uniform length to the edge of a lake that reflected moonlight, I stood panting under a tree unclear as to the route taken across the open ground ahead by the Goddess, whose bootprints seemed to point towards the water. Bent over in exhaustion after my rapid ascent through the undergrowth strewn with branches of trees kicked aside by the action of her boots, I knelt amongst the broken timber that had so harmed my skin that I feared the process of its renewal was about to begin, which for its duration would render me helpless.

My arms began to stiffen against me, quickly attaining that rigidity experienced prior to the sloughing off of the outer layer of rubbery skin. My head then tilted forward in jerky, involuntary movements until my chin began to lock against my throat. Defying the process as best I could by turning my head from side to side in what soon became slow motion, I was at the same time reacting to the sound of whispering in the night air, unable in my condition to block its access to my mind with peeling hands.

From out of the corners of my rotating eyeballs, as if responding to this new call of the death angels, I watched hundreds like me leaving the sanctuary of the forest that ringed the expanse of grass, walking like zombis out into the predatory moonlight, adding their own voices to the mantra of the Goddess :

Son et Lumière . . . Son et Lumière . . . Son et Lumière . . .

Evenly spaced apart around this tranquil lake, the advance of the rubberised men towards its icy water was brought to a sudden halt, their robotic movements stilled by the whispered command issuing from the blurred energy of the death angels into whose multiple identities the Goddess had again transformed herself, circling in a swarm above the silent men, whose repetitive mouthing of the mantra had finally ceased.

What fate was I being spared from by my body's preoccupation with re-skinning itself? A humming sound now accompanied this gathering of angels of death who swarmed together under the moon, swirling in the air with bursts of blinding speed, all the time circling above the numbed forms below. The humming became gradually more shrill, culminating in a high-pitched shriek when piercing rays of starlight projecting through the swarm caused the materialising of the first pair of stiletto boots on the grass beneath; this followed by repeated shrieking as with each shaft of light that pierced the swarm and then touched the ground, new shoes and boots appeared ready for the angels' tread, until their full numbers had landed at the lake beside the rubber slaves.

How to interpret what I saw with the conviction that Truth should carry? Had my rubbery life in this land of the Goddess been intended to preserve in me after my death those vital juices and substances given me at birth, to which I had added by my own living, so that in some subsequent ceremony by a sacred lake, that life-force might be taken back into the creatrix's being and my emptied skin be returned like that of a grape to nourish the ground on which the angels danced filled with the blackness sucked from the neck of the rubber slaves?

The dancing grew more exotic. The dancers, drunk on human experience, offered each other the touch of their smooth limbs, pressing tightly against their partners until all gaps between them had been closed, and in a rolling ball of glowing rubber they plunged into the lake. All was then quiet, and I was about to thank the stars that I had escaped this second death, when a gleaming shape reared up through its surface. The Goddess had been recreated beneath the dark waters of her sacred lake, and in her hand was coiled a whip; the product of the hearts and minds of well-digested men. Replenished by this human feast, she stood above the grassy plane in gleaming boots admired by slave and stars alike. I wondered as I knelt and watched, whether I had not been saved by Providence for the purpose of their future repair.

SIXTEEN

Nefertiti's Left Eye

DEAR BOOT-LOVERS,

In a previous issue of Heel!, in a reader's letter which I decided to title *The Museum of Time*, reference was made to the vortex within the museum of the Louvre in Paris where a section of the ancient temple at Denderah, Egypt, has been installed, and which has, quite unknown to those who imported the stone structure there, provided a most convenient place for capture and transfer of the unwitting citizen, in an instant and by activation of this mobile vortex, to the sands of the distant Nile.

Perhaps it is time to confirm a fact often suspected in the content of the letter of the earnest reader, that the staff at the Paris office of Heel! possess what may best be described, in the simplest manner for the purpose of explanation, a dual nationality, having allegiance therefore to both ancient Egypt and also modern France.

It is understood even by the stooping and note-taking archaeologist who in this matter may be compared to his more elegant counterpart beside the catwalks of Paris, that the Goddesses of Ancient Egypt continued to be clothed in the sheath dress and depicted in stone in this fashion when the populace below took to wearing the practical garment. Hence we are seen by those citizens who accompany us to the temple at Denderah, tightly garbed and always polished.

Possibly, as this is to be a short issue which limits the space reserved for comment by your agony aunt, I should take this opportunity before my own imminent departure to that distant place where all has been prepared and is ready once more for the celebration of the zodiacal cycle, to furnish the reader who may in trepidation be now anticipating his selection by Heel! for participation there, with one or two answers. And by the extrapolation of the half-truth painstakingly stumbled upon by the kneeling and confused egyptologist, let me here reveal another piece of the truth, armed with which you may pretend to defend yourself from the influence of our nocturnal contacts by which you will be notified of the requirement that you attend, regardless of those demands that routine living makes upon your unimportant time. For, as in the case of the aspiring dictator who appears on the balcony to deliver his speech, only to find that a second and then a third would-be dictator has each chosen the same hour to appear at opposite and adjacent balconies, none of your mundane activities is deemed indispensable or without substitute when weighed against the pleasure of our amusement.

We are not restricted at Heel! to the chance approach of the casual citizen to the museum of the Louvre where we may be imagined to loiter impatiently, maintaining a perfection of appearance should the slave-to-be happen along that morning or afternoon, whatever time of day we guess might be most productive for the purpose of his capture, then to lead him on by the clicking of our boot-heels through so many rooms of inferior exhibits to the Denderah vortex where his progress, rapid until now, is arrested by the sudden release of a leather glove onto that precise spot which will ensure his final bondage. If this were the case, we would hardly have the time to address your concerns and weaknesses through this monthly journal.

Most contacts are made as previously stated in these pages, while the male sleeps and dreams in a process of self-selection by which the Death Goddess is alerted to the changed nature of his dreaming as he is drawn toward his new compliant existence at her feet. There are, of course, more intrusive means to enslave the free man as he ponders his lowly status in comparison to that of the living Goddess when confronted by, for example, the sculpted bust of Nefertiti in the Egyptian museum in Berlin, or the many other objects scattered about the globe in places where the viewer is afforded the time and silence to briefly contemplate his life when set against some representation of the Divine Goddess whose booted, bronzed statue peers down at him from the half-light of eternity. It should be remembered that Heel! is merely the external organisation of a society of the greatest antiquity, with origins before time itself was born. What is not clearly understood by the archaeologist who attempts, when all his logic has failed him, to explain away the untimely disappearance of his academic colleague by resorting to what he perceives to be base superstition, is that each of these artifacts possessing the power to move a man to awed despair, exists and is created as one of an identical pair. The bust of Nefertiti at Berlin and its veiled double concealed in Egypt therefore operate as a unit in the removal of the stunned museum visitor to the chamber beneath the undisturbed sands of Denderah. The academic's conviction that the Berlin bust was unfinished and therefore no left eye was ever inserted in its socket is partially correct if we add that the omission was intentional and is duplicated in its Egyptian counterpart.

However, the second eye, unlike the third, would be clearly visible to the human eye were it not for its concealment within the gloved hand of the captress who may by the means of the second sight afforded by its touch, be seated amongst the chatter of the aviary at the Paris office of Heel!, or robed officially in the priestly chamber at Denderah. It is through the feminine energy and transmissive power of the third-eye vortex remaining within the duplicated object whether in the exhibition of the high-heeled boot that slowly rotates in the spotlit darkness above the silenced museum visitor or the long-necked bust of Nefertiti so admired by dictators as insane as the man Hitler, that the transfer of flesh from the crowded room where the tourists throng, to the dark place of ritual in Egypt, successfully is performed.

When, by the rubbing of leather against the smooth surface of the uninserted eye, the isolated man is then sucked into the spheroidal shape of the instep of the exhibited boot, or Nefertiti's bust, disappearing in a flash from those surroundings before re-emerging in miniature in Egypt, either within the duplicate boot or through the almond-shaped opening of the socket of the left eye, immediately he is caught in the web of the veil that is drawn across her painted face, or is imprisoned by the vertiginous wall of boot leather. There is, you understand, no need for the regular appearance of Heel! staff either at the museum of the Louvre, or in the chamber of transformation at Denderah.

So, with the periodic arrival of the officiating priestess the accumulation of dying and dead men are extracted from the webbing of Nefertiti's equestrienne's veil, and taken individually, like the precious butterfly with wings clipped, within the darkness of leather gloves, away to the ritual of the gifting of his flesh for the cyclical rebirth of Isis' boots. I will not limit the imagination that I am sure runs wild in the minds of those soon to be selected readers who will offer their bodies to the Goddess, by revealing beforehand the process of their assimilation into boot leather, or the fashions to be worn by the Paris staff at Heel! who are to observe your sacrifice, except that the Goddess Isis will be clothed in a sheath dress of leather above her waiting boots, and that Nefertiti herself whose body our retarded archaeologist still seeks to find, will be presiding as high priestess.

How wonderful to have this opportunity to relate to those of my readers who will remain in Paris, that the demi-goddess Nefertiti is to visit our offices, soon afterwards, bringing in her retinue through the Denderah vortex at the Louvre, we are led to believe, some of her Egyptian birds to keep company with our own variously garbed parrots that are secured to their perches here at Heel!. Feathers together with leather; what sounds of singing and calling may then be heard! In this way, the close and ancient ties between our two offices are preserved by your generous sacrifice. Outside, of course, where the cries of flesh ripped and torn away by piercing talons are figments of imagination, the streets of Paris will be silenced, save for the clicking of heels, as these catwalking figures of leather and rubber emerging from the Louvre, then register in the simple minds of mortal men.

MADAME X

SEVENTEEN

Infernal Proserpina

As luck would have it, I had missed the last boat to the temple of Philae, or rather to the islet of Agilkia, where the pylons, obelisks and hypostyle hall of Isis' temple had been resurrected, rescued from the dam-builders from its ancient site which is today submerged beneath the still water of an artificial lake that appeared to shine synthetically beneath the moon by whose light I lay reading alone on the sand bank. Nor was it clear to me whether I would find the Goddess above water on the dry land of Agilkia, or whether in her mood of fury she had dressed herself in the protective clothing of the dam-divers, piecing together the rubber taken from their bodies, which were, if my guide-book was to be trusted, found washed up naked on the sand like the 'sacrifices of old'.

Had she remained below the four metres of water that covered her sacred island of Philae, which was I now read, nothing less than the site of a vortex connecting this planet to her star, Syrius? And had the axis of her temple at Philae, like the temple I had seen days before at Denderah, been aligned to the heliacal rising of Sirius? I felt sure that it had, and with this conviction I shut the guide-book, my companion for the duration of this journey to the source of the African Nile, where I had dreamed of a meeting with the Goddess Isis and her priestesses.

Placing its hardback cover between the back of my head and the cooling sand, I reverted to that attitude of self-reliance with which I always travelled in those regions where psychic impressions reach back and forth through the millennia, confirming or denying in an instant the hard-won conclusions settled upon by the slow research of sand-dusting academics.

Gazing up at the night sky long enough to internalize its pattern of glittering stars that arced above my weary head, I closed the lids of my eyes to observe their continued motion within the dark space of my imagination that then seemed to expand sideways and downwards into the desert sand into whose warmth my body had sunk, until I had lost distinction between flesh and sand, and between sand and the starlight, which flashed back into form in front of my blinded vision.

I had become the mind of Lucius Apuleius, magician priest, the author of Metamorphoses; and entered the scene of his meeting with the Goddess in the second century AD. As to what I heard and saw during this experience, let me quote directly from his text:

> About the first watch of the night when as I had slept my first sleep, I awoke with sudden fear and saw the moon shining bright as when it is at the full and seeming as though she had leaped out of the lake. Then I thought with myself that this was the most secret time, when that goddess had most puissance and force, considering that all human things be governed by her providence; and that not only all beasts private and tame, wild and savage, be made strong by the

governance of her light and godhead, but also things inanimate and without life; and I considered that all bodies in the heavens, the earth, and the seas be by her increasing motions increased, and by her diminishing motions diminished: then as weary of all my cruel fortune and calamity, I found good hope and sovereign remedy, though it were very late, to be delivered from my misery, by invocation and prayer to the excellent beauty of this powerful goddess. Wherefore, shaking off my drowsy sleep I arose with a joyful face, and moved by a great affection to purify myself, I plunged my head seven times into the water of the lake; which number seven is convenable and agreeable to holy and divine things, as the worthy sage and philosopher Pythagoras has declared. Then very lively and joyfully, though with a weeping countenance, I made a lengthy oration to the puissant goddess.

There appeared to me from the midst of the lake a divine and venerable face, worshipped even by the gods themselves. Then, little by little, I seemed to see the whole figure of her body, bright and mounting out of the lake and standing before me: wherefore I purpose to describe her divine semblance, if the poverty of my human speech will suffer me, or the divine power give me a power of eloquence rich enough to express it.

First, she had a great abundance of hair, flowing and curling, dispersed and scattered about her divine neck; on the crown of her head she bore many garlands interlaced with flowers, and in the middle of her forehead was a plain circlet in fashion of a mirror, or rather resembling the moon by the light it gave forth; and this was borne on either side by serpents that seemed to rise from the furrows of the earth, and above it were blades of corn set out.

Her vestment was of the finest linen yielding diverse colours, somewhere white and shining, somewhere yellow like the crocus flower, somewhere rosy red, somewhere flaming; and [which troubled my sight and spirit sore] her cloak was utterly dark and obscure covered with shining black, and being wrapped round her from under her left arm to her right shoulder in manner of a shield, part of it fell down, pleated in most subtle fashion, to the skirts of her garment so that the welts appeared comely.

Here and there upon the edge thereof and throughout its surface the stars glimpsed, and in the middle of them was placed the moon in mid-month, which shone like the flame of fire; and round about the whole length of the border of that goodly robe was a crown or garland wreathing unbroken, made with all flowers and all fruits. Things quite diverse did she bear: for in her right hand she had a timbrel of brass, a flat piece of metal carved in manner of a girdle, wherein passed not many rods in the periphery of it; and when with her arm she moved these triple chords, they gave forth a shrill and clear sound. In her left hand she bore a cup of gold like unto a boat, upon the handle of whereof, in the upper part which is best seen, an asp lifted up his head with a wide-swelling throat. Her scented feet were covered with shoes interlaced and wrought with victorious palm. Thus, the divine shape, breathing out the pleasant spices of fertile Arabia, disdained not her holy voice to utter these words to me:

Behold, Lucius, I am come; your weeping and prayer have moved me to succour you. I am she that is the natural mother of all things, mistress and governess of all the elements, the initial progeny of worlds, chief of the powers divine, queen of all that are in Hell, the principal of them that dwell in Heaven, manifested alone and under one form of all the gods and goddesses. At my will the planets of the sky, the wholesome winds of the seas, and the lamentable silences of hell be disposed; my name, my divinity is adored throughout the world, in divers manners, in variable customs, and by many names. For the Phrygians that are the first of all men call me The Mother of the Gods at Pessinus; the Athenians, which are sprung from their own soil, Cecropian Minerva; the Cyprians, which are girt about by the sea, Paphian Venus; the Cretans which bear arrows, Dictynnian Diana; the Sicilians, which speak three tongues, Infernal Proserpina; the Eleusinians, their ancient goddess Ceres; some Juno, other Bellona, other Hecate, other Rhamnusia, and principally both sort of the Ethiopians which dwell in the Orient and are enlightened by the morning rays of the sun, and the Egyptians, which are excellent in all kind of ancient doctrine and by their proper ceremonies accustom to worship me, do call me by my true name, Queen Isis. Behold, I am come to take pity on your fortune and turbulation; behold I am present to favour and aid you; leave off your weeping and lamentation, put away all your sorrow, for behold the healthful day which is ordained by my providence.

With all this said, Queen Isis, the Goddess, took the helmet at Lucius' side, raising it to his head, where it was to be locked in place causing a return to the condition of darkness that from experience often precedes the various degrees of enlightenment associated with this relic from temple initiations past. After a short interval, light flooded into view as if by the throwing of an invisible switch or by the sudden insertion into my brain of the scientist's microchip that forced upon our dual identity, Lucius' and mine, the promised gift of providence.

A network of golden lines appeared before me, extending outwards from my concealed face, reconstructing for my senses the artificiality of the lake whose luminous surface was lit this time, not by moonlight, but from below, by whatever source radiated from within the Goddess' temple. Shadows played beneath the water that I thought at first to be the projection of particles of sand locked within the space of the helmet, which were, I was sure, responsible for the reappearance of the constellations, and the prominence of the star of Isis.

Whether by innate faith, or by the confidence gained from the support of these interlocking lines that had formed a reinforcing grid which was spread out over the water, the first amphibian species now emerged with tentative, uncertain steps onto the smooth surface of this primeval lake that seemed prepared for some cosmic game of chance, to be played by giants with rules devised by gods.

As the centuries raced across the screen of my vision, and countless kinds of armoured dinosaur and bewildered beast rose from beneath the glowing lake; their fleeting shapes assembled upon a chosen square, before each in turn is substituted by some other newer breed . . . I was witnessing, fast forward, the catwalk of Life, a fashion-show staged for the Goddess.

Included were Neanderthals that screamed; then much later Neapolitans with their ice-creams; adults with their offspring; all criss-crossing the lighted stage in perfect order, until my century is reached and I sense that Lucius has seen ahead of me some outrage against the Goddess' Law to which he draws my attention . . .

Grotesque misshapen creatures, mutated by that self-appointed lawmaker, man, move in silence over this virtual grid; their path through evolution distorted by the evil will of scientific men. But Lucius has spotted something else, a dark shadow seen circling beneath the bubbling surface to where these jovial fellows in technicians' garb discuss their latest violation, ignorant still of the Goddess' fury. The light below that was their vital source of life is now eclipsed and down into the blackness the geneticists descend, removed from sight, and in their place the shadow grows above the lake until waist-deep she stands, the Goddess Isis dressed in rubber.

No coil of whip this time, but the snake-headed sceptre with its charge of destruction delivered as a lightning-bolt against the walls of Aswan Dam. I struggle to release the catches snapped across the screen and neck of Lucius' helmet, determined to be the first to see the full, black-booted figure of the Goddess; her shining form exposed by the retreating waters of a broken dam. But I am being returned to the mundane world of daylight and the chattering tourist, and Lucius to his other world . . .

EIGHTEEN

The Snow Leopard

Dear Boot-Lovers,

I had arrived back from Denderah to find what? To discover not that the Paris office of Heel! has been the victim of some random break-in or that any burglar has even been seen in this vicinity during the collective absence of the female staff, but rather, and almost too sad to relate, some sort of cooperative venture between the normally segregated groups or categories of office slave, with its object the disloyal and wholesale vacating of these premises of both its human and bird life, undeniably has been attempted without any responsible thought being, it seems, first given to the planned behaviour, or decent sentiment entertained before its fortunately and perhaps inevitably unsuccessful execution.

How did it happen and what was the trigger that initiated the thought process apparently experienced by such numbers of kneeling and otherwise duty-bound slaves? Was it noticed that a vessel of stagnant and stale water left behind beneath the leather drape of one of the locked cages that surround this desk was drunk more urgently by the thirsty bird than we could have judged or imagined, provoking some residue of unextinguished humanity to surface, even to rear up, in the form of concerned compassion in the usually numbed skull of one of these accomplices, who breaks free from his bonds intending then to fetch new water for the squawking fowl? . . . Exclude this as a likely possibility since the beaker of water lies just beyond the reach of the bird secured to his perch; a fact that soon after his introduction to life within the cage ceases to produce from his confused person any more revolt or calling of names, as his silence becomes the order of the day and night.

To digress and to provide useful information for the lady reader who is perhaps wishing to put to one side, albeit for the period of just a short break in the sun or under the moon, her selflessly performed domestic chores, and closing the bolted door behind her, enjoy some peace and quiet away from her caged bird, let me add, in order to hasten the acquiescent silence of the slave-to-be who, it may regrettably transpire, possesses a political bent of character, and is without therefore melody or harmony in his parrot-like song, that a leather mask modelled in its main details and rigidity of fabric on the shaped hood required to still the voice and breathing of the Egyptian falcon should first be crafted, then fitted snugly about the face and head of the bird which can be supposed by this measure and safely predicted to become immediately more accepting of his terminal existence.

What is the number of politicians still unknowing in their

gabbling and gibbering, their playing for time and offending of the Goddess, who remain ignorant to this day despite the availability everywhere of the answer-laden texts of the Egyptian deity Seth whose existence was once spared for this bookish purpose by the Goddess Isis? Which politician can talk a modicum of sense who has not yet consulted the text of Seth's book titled, *Dreams, 'Evolution', and Value Fulfillment*, which has been re-released to human consciousness by that American writer, Jane Roberts, and is in print still? . . . None, of course.

Suspicion fell upon that boot-polishing category of slave who during his circuit through the various rooms temporarily emptied of the office staff of Heel!, preserves through the mobility of his crouching limbs the near-convincing appearance of having retained in the midst of this concentration of divine women some limited physical freedom, and by inference mental autonomy, that might be developed into more furtive activity in our absence; for example the passionate rubbing and polishing of the phantom boot when none of those stilettoed pairs are anywhere to be encountered.

Let me patiently explain the situation here, which may at the same time be read as an apology to that visiting dominatrix whose address we do not have, who trusting her balance in the highest of boot heels to the convenient hand-rail which she held in her long-fingered and leather-gloved hand while she ascended, step by step, to the level of this office, suddenly was distracted by the passage in the opposite downward direction of a boot-polisher, who seemingly dismissive of her perilous condition, rudely dislodged her grip, passing by her at the most unreasonable speed. I can assure this lady that the slave has been punished and then punished for this affront to her dignity and the perfection of her figure.

I shall try to make clear by calling a spade a spade and a slave a slave, that in addition to the transvestite and caged birds which we have in our compassion taken in, or which the lady reader at the end of her tether has brought to us with fractured bones or broken spirit, and which we then endeavour to mend, remoulding the slave's body, which is reset in bondage, into some new evolutionary fashion, there is also a separately organised system of servitude operated here whereby the ogling boot-slave that has found his way to the revolving doors of our office and lingers there in hope, is with that same compassion permitted entry on the grounds that his life also is to be reshaped to the future benefit of Heel!. He is made to kneel, his legs fixed onto a low platform that runs smoothly over this marble office floor on a number of invisible ball-bearings.

About his neck securing the blinding rubber hood is a silver ring which is attached at the back by a metallic link, about a foot long and also of silver, to what was mistaken by the dominatrix to be the hand-rail, along which the boot-polishing slave with only his hands free passes at accelerating and decelerating speed; the motivating force that takes him smartly from A to B is the slap delivered percussively and dismissively across his rubber cheek by the member of staff whose boots are finally polished so that she might in relief return again to her work on Heel! magazine.

Obviously if a stiletto boot is cleaned on one level of the office building and the boot-polisher is required next on a higher level, perhaps around a corner and through a doorway where sits another staff member, impatiently, unable to continue with her work until her boots are also polished, a judgement is made by the gloved hand of the now satisfied wearer of boots as to the velocity of slap that will carry the slave accurately up the staircase and the precise distance to the waiting boot-tip. To your surprise, the staff at Heel! are naturally gifted without practice or rehearsal with this ability to send a slave the correct distance up and down stairs.

At night the boot-polishers are gathered together in a line, side by side, their wrists neatly tied behind them, silent and still in the darkness of the polishing-room where a long cable of twisted steel fibre is permanently tensed, wall to wall, opposite a row of twelve cushioned and comfortable seats, and where there is such slapping, to and fro, and fierce whipping theatrically performed that might naturally be considered by the outsider looking in, to be the ritualized and formal parting of mistress from slave at the end of another hard day's work at Heel!.

It is quite feasible, if we admit that the lock to the polishing-room was found on our return to be intact and sound, and each bird motionless on his perch as he had been left, that the blanket punishment of slaves designed to include in its ambit all of those unknown culprits, was premature and too harshly administered since we have just this minute discovered on the premises of Heel! on the back of that descending slave, the paw and claw marks of a Himalayan snow leopard that we believe had accompanied the visiting dominatrix. If this cat has remained here, perhaps on a bed of cooling snow up on the moonlit roof, then surely her feline movement and fiery temper was solely responsible for the triggering of the alarm that has caused the sprinkling of fine jets of water throughout our offices. Fortunately we are each well-equipped and prepared in our rubber raincoats for this very eventuality.

MADAME X

NINETEEN

Amazone in Bronze

'I write and write, my body strapped against an ancient roof, its tiles smooth and black. From the lawn below, this roof seems just a sheet of leather, it wriggles in the sun. It is of course the clouds and fountain spray that so distort, and the slow writhing of the slaves. The beat of Nature thrills their minds; her whip is flexed across the unseen canvas, releasing by its sting the seeds of other worlds before concealed by dry routine. The unreal appears real. Reason escapes its bondage, and like some dumb night creature stumbles blinded before the Goddess. I write and write, my body strapped . . . it is a writer's discipline.'

In the spring snow of white cherry blossom that swept across the neglected, overgrown orchard which had sprung up around the classical statuary of the seventeenth century mausoleum and burial-ground, where the bronze figures of Goddesses lazed back on rectangular slabs of stone, sealing by their weight the fates of the forgotten occupants beneath the lids of crumbling sarcophagi, I had stopped beside the blackened and booted form of the most dressed, albeit in leather, and seemingly living of these silent deities.

For a long while I had been kneeling there, at last fearing her arousal by my attention to her smoothed skin and the time of moonlit night, when, from out of the distant dark, being buffeted in the petal-filled air and finally trapped pressed tight against the curved and leathered shape, a piece of paper in certain hand-writing that was my own, then gripped her polished thigh above the fêting bank of blossom that rose beside the dated stone until the Goddess reclined horizontal and alone upon this soft bed of snow and pagan throne.

From what other night of Goddesses bathed beneath this penetrating light had I been writing from some exalted but constricted height and with what confidence of a final reader had I despatched this note of warning and of fact within the universal draught that blew with bated breath upon this restless and unearthly scene where waking from a timeless dream the statues, each unblinking, their sight still focussed on that distant place, then shuddered into life?

With metal whip still flexed above the glowing surface of her breasts between the fingers of her leather gloves, her thigh-boots, black, stilettoed and still uncovered by the blizzard and drift of white, still protruding below the knee above the disapproving pyre, their stark and pointed outline distracting from the lettered threat, continued then to gleam and shine and next to tremble beneath the caressing of my craving and expectant heart.

An explosion of white confetti was returned into the air, falling upon some mortal's effigy in its state of decay and disrepair, and exposing the coiling seated figure of a whipping Goddess whose forcing hand returned my lips to the worship of her boot, when of a sudden its instep domed and smooth became within my head the contours of an ancient cave whose occupant was myself and the others of the human dead.

In front of them, supported on an easel, a safe distance back from the cave's entrance through which foam was being spat from a battering sea reminiscent of the northern Mediterranean, but perhaps in the ancient time of this Goddess, the canvas of a painting titled 'The Amazone' was being examined by each in turn as if attempting to unravel from the detail on its surface, some insight into their condition and predicament; an alchemical key that would release them back to their previous lives of normal joys and sorrows. I joined these blank and staring faces in their study of the Amazone and the statuary of her garden and the roof of her white-stoned chateau.

There was the most complex maze planted with yew trees, which had trapped within its evergreen walls the night creatures referred to on the page of script. Beside this maze, along an avenue of equally spaced statues, some gaps were evident, which were to be connected by the eye with the scenes of flagellation nearby presided over by the animated statues of variously garbed Goddesses. In the bottom left corner of the painting, incongruously, was the cave in which I was standing.

Inside its craggy interior, on the ground beside the painting, was a pair of riding-boots, which seemed to belong to the Amazone who was about to enter the cave presumably to wear them. My eye then followed the line of statues towards a magnificent house with its mansart roof of black slates, against which the blackened writhing bodies already described, were strapped. Floating down from the roof were just visible a large number of individual book pages, several of which were being carried in the perhaps stiffening breeze over the tall maze where clutching hands reached above the yew trees to catch them. Beyond the maze, further from the house, in a wild and unpruned orchard, a kneeling gardener, his head held down over a stiletto boot, was being whipped by a woman dressed entirely, from the top of her head to boot-tip, in polished and tightly fitting leather or rubber.

On the other side of the avenue of statues was a black metallic pyramid that appeared to hover above the lawn. I was reminded at that moment of how the egyptian priesthood used to visualize the pyramidal shape at the back of their skulls in order to shift into other, adjacent worlds. Some force contained within the molecules of the painting now urged me to repeat this visualization while concentrating on the many scenes of suffering and of boot-worship depicted on the way to and on the flight of steps leading up to the chateau.

I was experiencing that fear of annihilation described often by the shaman's apprentice when he is for the first time about to switch into another existence. The painting's canvas began to flap about, blown by a wind otherwise absent from the cave but possibly the product of the storm clouds evident in the sky above the chateau; this motion increasing with the period of my enforced visualization of the pyramid.

Then I clearly perceived, with the inflow of new energy inside my head, that the figure of the Amazone portrayed in miniature entering the cave where her boots had been left, apparently in great haste, was being superimposed over the full length of the canvas which was being transformed into a larger than life portrait of this active Goddess, in those boots and with a riding-whip flexed between the fingers of her leather-gloved hands.

She stood staring outwards, her eyes fixed on mine, appearing all the time darker and more real. A sequence of images was being projected onto the screen of my mind: a scene of celebration of a boy's birthday or his coming of age, in which he is being tossed again, higher and higher, in a sheet of rubber, by booted women encased in the same polished material that identified them as belonging to this other world of the equestrian Goddess.

The timing of the release of the boy into the air and his subsequent capture was being synchronized with the expansion and contracting of the painting's surface, until I could no longer distinguish between rubber and canvas. A gust of wind blew into the cave from behind me, throwing me forwards into the blackness. I knew not to resist. Like the initiate thrown into the dark depths of the sacred pool, I had to keep swimming down until I had resurfaced within the space of the Amazone's portrait.

Suddenly, I was rolling and tumbling over the grass towards the chateau, my rubber-encased form propelled from the pyramid in the direction of the steps, where it came to an abrupt halt with my sealed-in face pressed up against the shine of the Amazone's boot. Immediate efforts that might for clarity of portrayal be compared to the smacking at birth of the newly-born child, with the difference that the riding-whip was here employed, failed to permit an easing and freeing up of the passage of my breathing which was both blocked and sealed over by a layer of newly-formed rubber. Only by the practice of the unenergetic occupation of the writer hoisted up by knotted rope to the altitude of the roof and fixed in place, could there be sufficient intake of oxygen through the restricted nasal access, which was belatedly provided by the downward pressure onto my face of a mercifully sharp heel.

TWENTY

The Renaissance Woman

The attributing of the title, 'Renaissance Woman', to those few equestriennes who have been noticed practising casting techniques and that coordination of hand and rod in the reeling in of the hooked fish, is not always fitting, given that the two occupations are not often seen to be enjoyed simultaneously over the same period, but rather successively, so that one pastime, fly fishing, is first dispensed with before the new activity, horse riding, is then embraced. The first pleasure becomes in this case merely the learning ground, that provides by its different elements a foretaste of the greater pleasure which lies ahead, in anticipation of which the young disciplinarian may rehearse in all weathers from the safety of the river-bank.

It is argued that the two pursuits of fishing and riding, one belonging to the present and the other to the future, coexist in the imaginative mind of the fisherwoman who is by her keen desire for the equestrian life, so transported forward in time as to feel herself bilocated, being both at the side of the river with rod and fishing-line, playing with some hapless fish, and at the same time employing the lungeing-rein and whip with her favourite horse that grows compliant by this exercise. The significant factor is therefore her perception of the act performed, and not that of the onlooker for whom a fish is a fish, and a horse is a horse. In her own eyes at least, she is indeed a modern version of the Renaissance woman set apart from others by the rivalry and equal contribution of her diverse talents.

Substance is added to this view by the evidence of her chosen attire, being inappropriate for the world of fishing, which is the riding-habit, hat, boots and leather gloves, which together with the veil, suggest an ambivalence of attitude, even the confusion that the fish might otherwise suspect the identity of his whip-wielding captress who reels him in, and as a result, attempt to flee from the prospect of a fate perhaps worse than death.

Then there is the question of whether someone so far removed by her elegant figure and the theatre of her mind from the typical waterside gathering of the weekending civil servant – from all that is mundane and dreary; whether such a divine individual, so perfect in posture and appearance, can be conceived as being truly involved with their dull and aesthetically destitute world of average happenings and average sensation.

Such dullness is not normally acquainted with the words of an ancient deity or the degree of relevance of those words to the subject at hand; nor with the tradition in pharaonic Egypt for the young priestess to read from the *Book of Seth* at the time of the rising of Sirius, a passage that concerns the nature of pleasure and its apparent opposite, pain. A translation of the text is contained in the modern edition, now re-titled *Dreams, 'Evolution', and Value Fulfillment*, a copy of which I found by chance on a river-bank left open on this page:

Some sects have believed that spiritual understanding came as the result of bodily agony, and their self-inflicted pain became their versions of pleasure. It is usually said that animals, and also man, avoid pain and seek pleasure – and so any courting of pain, except under certain conditions, is seen as unnatural behaviour. It is not unnatural. It is an eccentric behaviour pattern.

On a quite unconscious level you possess a biological self-image that is quite different from the self that you see in a mirror. It is a knowledge of bodily form from the inside out, so to speak, composed of cellular shapes and organizations, operating at the maximum. The simple cell has a curiosity about its environment, and on your much more advanced cellular level your own curiosity is unbounded. It is primarily felt as a curiosity about shapes: the urge to touch, to explore, to feel edges and smooth places.

The appearance of the man of masochistic and supersensual inclination who by the training rod or whip of his mistress is to be initiated into transformations of flesh and identity, signifies not the deplorable relinquishing of his humanity, but that person's evolution from the depths of ignorant despair, back to the distant shine of the Goddess' boots, whose existence is now a persistent and very persuasive reality that surfaces within his evolving mind.

Returning then to the equestrienne who is casting upon the water with riding-whip held firmly in her black leather glove, and with spurred boots submerged by way of bait; and by a study of the contents of her fishing-net, we may discover the confirming proof that she is without question the Renaissance woman of many disciplines. For there, concealed beneath a bed of reeds, behind the net's thick mesh, is the day's catch which by the amazement it causes, will require our closer scrutiny.

It is normal for the fish to be relieved and its mouth freed of the hook that wrested away its liberty so decisively, and this for reasons that oppose cruelty and continuous suffering. There would also be expected soon afterwards those signs of revival from the stagnated and dazed state. What opportunity here, when the catch is bound, front and back, to prevent striking at the net and the bidding for escape? What reason then for the discovery of a horse's bit inserted within the rubbery jaws of the human amphibian that had before our return been drawn so inevitably from the murky depths by the twofold invitation of riding-whip and boots?

To look on the bright side of all this, and to speak on behalf of this speechless creature of rubber. No blinkered man shall again his vision of the divine, foul. No sharp gaff can now puncture and deflate his aspiration to serve and to be trained. His Rubicon is crossed. Besides, her carriage is light to pull, and well-maintained, with the best in reins and straps. This Venus exceeds in her dress and manner that other Venus of the Renaissance whose unnatural birth is recorded in paint on Botticelli's windswept canvas, and immortal life reflected by Titian. The dark side of the companionship of the equestrienne should, however, remain undescribed.

TWENTY-ONE

Valley of the Queens

Dear Boot-Lovers,

To return repeatedly, in a magazine for the promotion of right relations between the sexes in modern society, to those matters both esoteric and occult that may appear at first disconnected from the correction of shallow science and unrelated to the subject-matter at hand, will stretch the reader's patience to breaking-point, but I would appeal to that elasticity of mind and body that was required by the Egyptian priestess of her bound slave. In dwelling once more upon the darker aspects of her vocation, it is my great hope that the reader will be led out into the bright and liberating light of the Goddess.

Various shining and stunted pieces of statuary had been discovered in Thebes, whose models must surely have complained when being sculpted into the cuboidal shape of the polished stone of these block statues with their smoothed away corners. To be preserved at death by the processes of mummification, must to these fast disappearing men have been the preferred method of defying its reality and facing eternity from within the privacy of the encasing tomb. Yet perhaps, just as the resting-place of pharaohs was indicative of their elevated status in life, it is also appropriate that the form of burial selected and the posture taken in death should be reflective of the slave's opposite status. Thus far and no further, given the impoverished imagination and profound aesthetic lack of politician and academic alike, has reason been advanced to explain the still lively expressions of the faces that seem to the uncritical observer to have pushed up through the topmost surface of the black cuboids in a last defiance of the priestess' will, before being frozen in mid-emotion, with neck half-exposed and soon also to be polished black, and finally moved into convenient position to receive the equally polished skirt of the priestess.

Egyptologists spend and waste long years on their careful investigation of the orderly covering of the mummified pharaoh, with layer upon layer of material, after the removal of the vital organs and their storage in canopic jars nearby in the burial chamber. There is a linearity to the accompanying thought processes which appeals to their rigidity of mind that nevertheless manages to completely miss the point of embalmment, which is to preserve a link to physical matter, and provide a way back at some future specified date, into full corporeal being. Inevitably, chambers of temporary death, awaiting the rematerialization of their contents, have been naively reopened releasing from their stony entombment those dark forces which history had shut away for good reason.

The preparation of the slave for his preservation and continuing service to the priestess is not so well documented. A full description, were that possible in so short a space, would include elements that are even today recognizably mundane, and those with which the deadened western mind can no longer cope. An example of the former would be the initial markings made upon the slave's stomach, which can be compared to a woman's treatment of the soles of a newly acquired pair of patent leather, stiletto heeled, thigh or calf length boots, to prevent slipping when first walking in them upon smooth surfaces, whether human or inanimate. In this case, rather than deep cuts being made to allow for intestinal removal, there is instead a fierce scratching with long, manicured nails of the first layers of skin. This is not of itself a painful act, though the slave will be gagged and writhing limited to jerking movements against the bondage ropes. Nor, if there is a degree of suffering, is that the intended purpose; rather it is the inscription of certain symbols borrowed from the reference books of the alchemist that begins the slave's transformation into whatever item of, for example, furniture, that is at the time agreed upon amongst the priestesses. The mixture and colour of rubber to be added, according to the nature of this proposed mutation, to the stoned form of the slave is now determined, and different symbols are written over the expanding rib cage, this time their imprint made necessarily by the light touch of a mason's chisel.

The slave's gulping for air is interrupted more regularly by the dribbling, then spewing of a rubbery saliva, until with his progress being closely watched by the surrounding group of booted women, in the torch-lit recesses of their temple, where cries for help are always met with the stony silence that follows such dreadful echoing of the repeated sound, there is a noticeable change to the slave's features. Some full spectrum of emotion has been crossed; the accusing looks are replaced by the look of acceptance that is writ across the statue's face, that is remodelled in an instant to the happy stare which still greets the museum visitor as she settles upon him dressed in the same polished skin as worn by the priestess many centuries before. This account of ancient practice excludes any attempt to unravel the magical science of vibration or to give out information as to the chakral energies exploited to accomplish this work; but is written in reply to letters received about the recent find in the Valley of the Queens of a great number of 'stacked drums in a darkened, subterranean chamber, in quantities too large to comprehend, over which, it appeared in the half-light of the flickering candle, numerous black serpents slithered upon their contradictory paths, as if left by history to be guardians of this hellish place, until at some appointed hour, the contents of this terrible stock-pile was released upon an unsuspecting world.' I am quoting from a journal published shortly after the event, which is representative of the language used at the time of the first press releases. We now know most of the facts, and I am not therefore revealing anything new when I make the following observations based on the updated reports that we all read and hear by the hour. We are not on this occasion dealing with some hidden supply of unused fuel, which by its huge scale might of itself alter the course of global conflict, making victors of the vanquished. Nor was there a single snake found within the whole subterranean expanse. Rather the discovery was that around the neck of each of the slave statues to which I have referred, a length of coiled whip had been tightened, in confirmation of the last detail of the slave's conversion from which I have so far spared the reader and to which I must now briefly return. At the time when accusation turns into resignation and then reverts once more to adoration, the eyes of the slave, any slave undergoing the above process of bodily concretion, and this is clearly shown by the light of the burning torch held up close to his face by the officiating priestess . . . the eyes of the slave become glazed over, fixed in a stony stare, yet still with life within, still seeking communion with this priestess. A layer of material now covers the lenses which resist depression by her thumb and forefinger. In a seemingly callous rejection of his final wish, but in reality out of sympathy for his evident suffering that is being prolonged needlessly, she takes from around her waist the bull-whip which is to be coiled carefully about his neck, and then by the sudden gripping of its length between her leather-gloved hands, is in one continuous movement pulled and tightened, in this way completing the last agonizing step of a transformation that was so routinely performed in an Egypt which was dominated by the ever-present fear of this abuse of priestly power. The block statue was then left for a period of three days before being for the first time sat upon.

It is my belief, based on my reputation for some expertise in the occult, that the retention of the whip, fully tightened about the slave's neck, is in the most strange fashion his only lifeline by which his rubberized body may at some future date be reanimated. If my translation of the hieroglyphs found stamped upon the statues by the press of the priestess' boot does indeed prove accurate, we may just have woken the dead from a very deep sleep that was intended by zodiacal motion to last beyond our time, and be about to witness the rebirth of a global order founded upon the Templar magic of leatherclad priestesses released from their state of suspended animation and preparing to lead mankind forward into the new millennium, serving again beneath the shining banner of their Goddesses, Hathor, Isis and Nephthys.

To test my theory, I suggest an experiment in which a small number of the block statues from which the vibrational life-line of the priestess' whip has already been removed, be cracked open and the fragments of shell be separated for inspection. In the position corresponding to the stomach of a kneeling figure, you will discover a left or right boot with stiletto heel whose polished surface will unfold in the sunlight like some dormant plant that is woken by the spring season. Within the adjacent statue you will find its pair, if I am correct. This army of the Goddess will march on the stomachs of its slaves.

Madame X

TWENTY-TWO

The Pygmalion Man

The Pharaoh Ramesses prayed a second time to the temple statue animated by the god Khonsu, Expeller of Demons, who, in response, left that temple in his stony form and travelled to the land of Bekhten to rid the daughter of a Syrian vassal of the demon that possessed her body. Centuries later, a Roman soldier inquired of the goddess Juno, after the conquest of the city of Veii, whether she would abandon her position on the city walls and return with his army to Rome. Her statue consents with a nod of the head, answering, 'Yes, I will'. Historian, Titus Livy, comments that during the lifting of the figure by the soldiers, it seemed immediately to lose its immense weight, and then to follow them.

In the nineteenth century, the French newspapers recorded accounts of the repeated disappearance in the summer and autumn of 1876 of the statue of the Madonna at Lourdes, which runs away to the woods behind her usual residence, the parish church, with the sexton following in desperate pursuit.

That the gods once danced with handmaidens in the foothills of Olympus is known to every informed mortal, but of their recent reappearance within the gardens of the chateau of Versailles where their statues are said to congregate after nightfall, almost nothing has been reported to date, to my knowledge. Certain signs of this activity of the garden statues have, however, been observed by the visiting public, particularly by those with psychic vision, in broad daylight.

Of the disappearance of the Tai Chi masters in 1964 perhaps too much has already been written, and it may be reasonably supposed that nothing of import could be gained by considering yet again the facts of that case to determine whether we can or cannot add it to the examples given above of the history of animated statuary. I do not therefore propose to take that route, but rather to relate an experience with which I am fully conversant as the sole participant, that through its parallel evidence lends gravity to the proof and acceptance of the unfortunate fate of the Tai Chi masters from Wu-Tang.

On the evening of my departure for Versailles, I practised in front of the looking-glass those postures and slow, continuous movements that I believed to have been performed by the masters beneath the statue to the Goddess immediately prior to their reported disappearance. After twenty minutes of observing this stranger in eastern garb mimicking my every move, I settled at my desk and reread for the umpteenth time the description of the moment of enlightenment provided in an ancient manuscript about the life of a Tai Chi master:

> A beam of light flashed before my eyes . . . suddenly I started to tremble and then felt immobilized. The ground beneath my feet began to shake, and I was bathed with rays of pure light streaming down from heaven. A golden mist engulfed my body . . .

I had shut the book knowing that I knew the rest by heart, and opened instead Book 4 of *The Early Sessions Of The Seth Material*, by J. Roberts and read from session 170 which had been dictated supposedly by the Egyptian god, Seth:

> I do not imagine that this information will save the world. It will take more than myself and twenty gods beside to handle that problem . . .

I had reason to believe, and my years of research justified this belief, that the pantheon of gods referred to here by Seth, had abandoned Mount Olympus at the invitation of King Louis of France and now lived unseen amongst the picnicking visitors to the great gardens of Versailles.

I checked that my travel arrangements made hastily that morning before the first of the day's appointments, were indeed in order. I would be taking the night train, in this way intending to avoid comment on my somewhat exotic clothing in which I would arrive at Versailles in the frame of mind of a Tai Chi master. The journey promised to be and was uneventful, allowing for the careful application of black hair-dye that would complete with conviction my disguise, and perhaps cause the Goddess to select a scientist for the experience of enlightenment.

From my window-seat, I was picturing myself not as some dull academic, but in the light of the intrepid explorers of old; yet I would be venturing, if I was indeed to be blessed by the Goddess, into the astral world, the playground of the gods. At the least, I would experience the time travel, the time-slips to the future and to the past, for which Versailles is rightly notorious. My research into the phenomenon had thrown up fifteen such instances, including that of the composer Sibelius, who witnessed the deathbed scene in the royal chamber. And had not King Louis himself told the cardinal behind closed doors of the numbers of goddesses who shared his gardens. But the Tai Chi masters of Wu-Tang had exceeded all of these tales of time travel and sightings of deities, by charming the Goddess with their slow dance.

I had already decided that on my arrival at Versailles I would first mingle with the other tourists in the gardens, appearing as a visitor from the east with a polite word for whoever should approach me; but that towards dusk, I would remove myself from their company and then hide behind some tree where I was to practise the slow dance that I had rehearsed countless times in anticipation of this one chance to turn the head of a Goddess.

All had gone according to plan and as the gardens emptied of the last of the tourists, I began to move amongst the statues that I had identified earlier. Remembering the sensations described by the Tai Chi master at the moment of his enlightenment, I would be using my body as a kind of detector so that on each occasion that I passed in front of the statue of a Goddess, the presence or absence of similar sensations would indicate whether or not that statue was in the state of suspended animation that would respond to my dance.

Towards midnight, with my face streaked with a mixture of sweat and hair-dye, and about to concede that I had made the greatest fool of myself, I found myself performing in front of a rectangular block of stone upon which, logic dictated, there should have been another of the long-limbed goddesses. Shaken by this sudden realisation, I stopped dancing, making no further movement in the darkness, as I considered the reality that each of the other statues was about to awaken, whether animated by the time of night or by my own continuous efforts.

A beam of light flashed in my eyes; a projection from the hand of the statue that reached towards me. Her sculpted figure, the perfection of its lines, drew from me the gasps of tongue-tied admiration that are normally reserved for the dominatrix, for whom I momentarily mistook this Goddess whose surface shone with the same polished gleam as that of a 'Lady of the Night'. I started to dance, as I had planned; yet, like the Tai Chi masters before me, I felt the confirming sensations of trembling and immobilization that brought me to my knees, my head inclined to those high-heeled boots, with my arms stiff beside me.

So this was to be the time of my enlightenment. The Goddess leant back away from me as if in preparation for some esoteric rite. My body was at once bathed with a heavenly light, and warm, golden mist covered my face. Then the rod of initiation beat down on my expectant skin with glorious repetition and I heard in the distance the words of the Goddess: 'Chien!..Chien!..Chien!' Three times and then silence; for I had lost consciousness from the severity of a whipping that in hindsight was the natural talent of this ill-chosen statue. The road to enlightenment, it seems, is long, and I have returned many times with my tribute to the Goddess and been rewarded with the golden shower of the Tai Chi master.

TWENTY-THREE

The Dark Goddess

Each time that I jumped, I had jumped late, and far from seizing the object of my desire and being carried by it through the thin air, I had landed back on the firm ground from which I had sprung, having grabbed at nothing in the anticipation of something, in this case a shoe or some proportion of a boot, crossing the dark sky above me from another world, through our own and into the next. It is always a question of faith, upon which the greatest reliance must be placed, for strategy and timing, so that what is unseen, and continues to be unseen, until the last moment, as inaudibly the boot crashes sideways through the overlapping space of other worlds, being coloured and then re-coloured by the spectrum of unearthly light, by the well-timed leap is at last apprehended and the shiny surface held tight through the impact, the shaman or slave-man being taken with it out of this world and into the next.

To leap upwards in an ill-chosen location, and thereby incur that other penalty, an explosion within the skull, however protected on the outside by soft bandaging across the face [to dampen the driving impact of the boot's impatient leather], is to court sudden death by the incorporation of cranial bone and facial tissue within the boot-tip, smooth instep, heel and sole of the newly emerged and about to disappear, fetish-wear. The coincidence of shared space must therefore be avoided at all costs, save by the suicide with his determined plan to persist after death in this form, being joined within its polished shape by countless others selected for this grim existence by the Dark Goddess.

No; the skill is to so familiarize yourself, through constant meditation upon, even worship of her oddly shaped shoes and boots, that a blind faith in the timing and certainty of their appearance is developed, whether this is known to the Goddess or not, which by the synchronization of the slave's mind with the consciousness of her boot [composed increasingly of the minds of decomposed men], makes practical this sudden leap of the imagination that is the shaman's method of encountering those parallel and usually inaccessible worlds.

Do not first begin to test the night air, casually, through a general disbelief in the proposition and process here outlined, and the warnings given; yet with the vague hope of immediate contact with a goddess, without the years of service required to attempt, safely, this traversing of universal boundaries. For without that affinity for the stiletto boot of the type worn by the Dark Goddess, you will without doubt fail to cling tightly enough, in sufficient proximity to the contours of its black leather, and be lost to the night between worlds; assuming that is, you do not first become one of those regrettable additions to the statistic of headless deaths that are today recorded in such numbers. With practice of this religious service to the boot which may be carried on within reason wherever an example may be found, even in an open public place, whenever receptivity to the nature of your advance is by the turn of a heel, indicated . . . with practice, what had seemed at first to be nothing more than a necessary preliminary, reluctantly performed, a means to the shamanic state of mind, becomes in time the obsessional pursuit of the slave-man who arrives at and, without noticing, surpasses his goal which is of course the development of faith, and a linking of his being to that of the Dark Goddess. It is then that fate intervenes, and his enlightened state, his slave's vibration, meets with a response from within the leather of booted feet, which may be transmitted up to the distracted consciousness of the earthly goddess under whose heel he is instantly trapped, collared and then led, and by her uncoiled whip, repeatedly bled in the effort to cleanse him finally of his machismo past and instil instead a masochism for the future. Up until this point in his self-initiation to boot-slave, he has had to rely on his own wits, and the wording of esoteric texts which may prove arduous and off-putting in their demands; but it is the chance meeting, perhaps during the night walk down a winding, moonlit bridle-path, that has finalized his condition and prepares him by the forced insertion of the equestrienne's boot within his by now, elastic jaws, for his abrupt transfer to the next world. A target is set up, and by the stiff extension of her gleaming boot away from the released stirrup, is held out in the still night air as an offering, or human sacrifice, to the rapidly approaching Goddess . . .

The slave's work is almost done. A period of waiting, even relaxation, follows as scudding clouds enter and leave the night sky above in quick, evenly-spaced succession, projecting and then reprojecting this idyllic, equestrian scene. The slave swallows hard in apprehension, taking the boot deeper into his expanding throat, mixing its fibres and molecules with his own, and by the resulting interpenetration, becoming with each gulping intake of breath, more nearly attuned to the collective mind of the unseen boot of the Dark Goddess.

Wide-eyed and increasingly serpentine, the slave's flesh is, moment by moment, being re-moulded in an envelope of skin about the contours of the riding-boot; here and there exhibiting through the surfacing black that characteristic shine and deadly intent of well-polished leather. A heel begins to form below his waist; the contraction of his now useless limbs is soon complete. The frontal lobe of his brain is beaten flat as if by its repeated impact against the taut leather of a woman's skirt.

With the impending collision of man and boot, and the transformation of the one into the other, a helter-skelter of dark thoughts and images crosses the restricted and changed mind of the slave who has lost his head over smooth leather and heels, and his parted lips to the circular leather rim of the black boot that fits so tightly beside the equestrienne's long elegant leg.

The slave's vision flashes back through the centuries to a scene of execution, of guillotined men and the women knitting and stitching in the crowd, who by their needles and strong thread now contribute to the finished shine of this modern leather riding-boot, fixing by their craft and dexterity the fast hardening skin that still pulses with sealed-in life, frozen in motion by the stroboscopic beat of earthly light. Their eyes meet, the slave's and the equestrienne's, the executioner with her prisoner strapped beneath her, beneath the guillotine's slicing blade that descends in a blinding, metallic flash, transporting him bodily from this world.

TWENTY-FOUR

Pandora's Boots

No; the discovery of fashionable leather clothing secreted in a crevice on Mount Olympus does not constitute a final proof of the birth there of the Goddess. If Pallas Athena was, as ancient myth has supposed, the couturière of Olympus who had created the curved heel and ill-humour of the stiletto boot in a polished pair of which Pandora, the first woman, was to seduce and control mankind, then why do we read in the classics that the Goddess Aphrodite gloried in her own nakedness, and refrained from appearing to her lovers Anchises and Adonis in leather and boots, which according to this argument, would have been available on each return to that overestimated and stunted mountain?

To be less far-fetched in our thinking, and less dismissive of sound logic, let us recall that Titian, a man born as humans are, first dressed the immodest Goddess after centuries of exaggerated nudity, in a gown of furs in his painting, 'Venus With A Mirror'. It is but one further step to take, to acknowledge that this outfit is the second product of the inventiveness of the human mind which, being superimposed upon fake flesh, has concealed that earlier figment of the human imagination, as the fig-leaf conceals the absent truth of the priapic statue. It was therefore on the basis of disbelief that I accepted this position as the outside arbiter of an apparent dispute between two Goddesses, Pallas Athena and Aphrodite; a dispute which I must not prejudge as unreal, or so it had been requested of me by the injured parties to the dispute, the townsmen of Ikaria, near Athens.

Let us be clear that over time, any statue made even of the hardest stone and representing even the most immortal of Goddesses will lose the smooth sheen characteristic of the freshly sculpted figure released from the studio into the glare of publicity that in ancient times greeted the first appearance in the street of a Goddess, whether she was dressed fashionably for the moment, or was divested of all clothing by the requirements of her reputation as is the case with the mundane lives of film stars and the like. Much later and equally regrettably, with the wear and tear of time, and the proximity to seismic disturbance, a limb, or two, will fall to the ground amongst the autumnal detritus. Nor is the bronze statue more or less favoured than the marble by Time, by the god Cronos, were he indeed to exist. The green encrustation, called patina, that covers the bronze Goddess of more recent antiquity evidences the very same ravages of time.

We must not therefore, by contrast, jump to quick conclusions when assessing the appearance of one Goddess in comparison to another, even when the short distance from one to the other, and the combative nature of the one and the disaffection of the other, might be suggestive of some dramatic exchange of force between them during the nocturnal hours, that would so easily solve the mystery of the sudden damage and deterioration apparent after so many centuries of relative stability in their physical expression. Less easily refuted, from the point of view of the objective and enquiring observer, is the argument of the unlikelihood of the predictable alternation of wounding from one statue to the other, which has seemed to proceed, back and forth, as if a slow engagement, too slow or too fast for mortal eyes, was in fact occurring before our very limited vision. One blow delivered to dislodge the snake's head from its coil on Pallas Athena's arm or to pierce with a fingernail the eye of the Gorgon on her breast, or which glances from her shield, is on each occasion returned by the thrusting and cut of her sword upon the naked form of Aphrodite, without leather and boots to blunt the attack.

Science can rightly be expected to supply solutions and to make explicable that which superstition has left unexplained. The investigative techniques employed at Ikaria are simple to communicate but required the greatest precision in execution if results were to be forthcoming, and the worthless misspending of time avoided. The human eye does not as yet accelerate and decelerate in its perception of the exterior world which it is forced to experience in evenly-spaced consecutive moments, quite apart from those variations in time that may more truly represent Nature's own variety of perception, and may be available to that list of deities who pretend to a freedom from the confines of human time.

The synchronization of cameras focussed over many months on the two opposing figures of Pallas Athena and Aphrodite, and the transfer of their images to the laboratory environment, where they are subjected to a process of transformation within different time scales, revealed to us, astonishingly, not just the apparent trembling of marble and change of expression of Aphrodite or grimacing of Pallas Athena, but within the background of stars and their galaxies, a rhythm of movement that corresponded to the Goddesses earthly encounter, such that a reverse suffered physically was felt at once in their greater struggle within the Heavens.

For this calculation, we drew on the common knowledge of ancient esotericism, that there is a darkness within the darkness known to man which appears as brilliant light to the perception of the Goddess. By allocating those seven most brilliant points of double-darkness, called 'chakras', to the physiques of both Goddesses in turn, in proportion to their size and contours, and then by correspondence detecting the similar outline of their heavenly forms, our computers began to predict, scarcely had we finished entering the complete data for final analysis, the actual outcome of this prolonged struggle, in favour of Pallas Athena.

A scientist, like any other person, should admit to the error of emotionality, its influence and effect on his work: we found significant evidence of animation within the material of each statue, such that it was considered reasonable behaviour to retrieve from the crevice at the summit of Mount Olympus, those items of clothing we believe the Goddess Pallas Athena withheld from her opponent for the purpose of her defeat, which included protective leather, a whip and stiletto boots. Whether by the coincidence of chance or in response to the gifts left at the feet of the perfected form of Aphrodite, it is here recorded, for the sake of completeness, the fact of the emergence on our skins on the night of our departure from Ikaria, of what we have termed archaically to be 'stigmas', being those tattoo-like marks made with a branding-iron on slaves of the Goddess, depicting the black stiletto boot, invention of the

Goddess Pallas Athena. Whether we are rewarded by one Goddess or condemned by the other, is not for the scientist to anticipate.

TWENTY-FIVE

Portrait of a Fantast

Dear Boot-Lovers,

Compliance and not complaint is what is required of the male reader of Heel!. So it is with such disappointment that when I have waded through the wet streets of Paris to be with you again as your agony aunt, I find, seated now at my desk beyond the hour when even with my deeply-felt devotion to you I can reasonably be expected to attend to your needs, that those of you who have so far been selected to be waterproofed in rubber as I in your service am at this moment, though admittedly not with the same permanence of enclosure, have ganged up on me your eternal friend and confidante in this matter, and written me letters with the foulest and most ungrateful content!

Was not the rubber chosen for the obscuration of your physical form of the highest quality in every case? Could more have been done by myself and the staff at Heel! to comfort you in the first days after your coating in rubber, when as each of you says, friends became scarce and opportunities for employment reduced? Were we not there for you even if only with the sound of our voices that advised you in your new-found place of darkness? Did we not take turns to visit and from the patience of our invisibility press down upon your healing body until your re-emergence from the safety of the cooling bath was judged in your best interest? Yet I read repeatedly that our heels were too sharp and that our weight was too carelessly distributed during, what was from our point of view, and consider this, the slow and most dull process as bonding of skin and black rubber so tediously completed itself.

Where some measure of gratitude might have been anticipated, we have received nothing but the most flagrant ingratitude, so that as I search through your letters, alone at night except for the kneeling slave who could not believe his eyes if sight of your vulgar correspondence were still permitted him . . . searching for that single reader on whom, as is my nature, I might liberally bestow a full measure of praise and practical advice at dealing with his transformed condition, I find only insult and regret. How fruitless to regret what is in the past and unchangeable! Perhaps if my delivery were as brusque and my letters as ill-formed as your own, then this would be my only advice to you this month.

However, as is my nature, and realising the difficulty inevitably posed for you in conveying to paper any objections to what has occurred to you, so that on occasion the letter that you have sent seems to be written by some demented typewriter with its own mind, except when briefly, for a phrase or two, your own thoughts and messages succeed in communicating themselves from behind the rubber mask, I will attempt as always to alleviate your concerns in any way that seems acceptable to your agony aunt. So wounding is the meaning of these unspoken words to the staff at Heel! and to this kneeling fellow who by your actions has suffered the pain of the whip, that if the silent majority who have not written on this subject were assumed by inference to concur with the views here expressed, my patient response could not at all be guaranteed, nor that of the membership of Heel! who have rescued you from unemployment and so resourcefully found alternative use for your useless limbs whose coordination can be relied upon to clean and polish the boot placed within their grasp, and no more.

Let us reconsider the facts, in the cool hour of the night, if that is possible for you who must return to the bath regularly to avoid the unhealthiest rise in temperature, and so dispense with nostalgia for a life lost, and the illogicality that may be read into the mind and portrait of the fantast . . . Contrary to the experience of that long-dead patriarch, King Canute, who failed so miserably to arouse the passion of the Goddess of the Deep when seated enthroned beside the sea and intending by his command the return of the foaming waters, his daughter – and this revelation of royal history has been religiously withheld from public scrutiny – later when she was herself seated on her father's abandoned throne succeeded by the offer of her polished boots that sought by their extension to engage with their smoothness the attention of the then molten, moonlit sea. Her differing nature, however, produced not the retreat of the Goddess of the Deep but her advance against the lunar motion of the tide, further up the sandy beach until the lapping waves had shown divine approval of the material of the shining boots. In this fashion, the rubber that has been applied to your skin causing forgetfulness of self and of the polite manners owed to me, your agony aunt, is tested still to this day against the verdict of the salt and spray of surging waves. To put the matter inside the proverbial shell, you are contained by the very best in rubber approved for the purpose of your enslavement by divine intervention. For that one might expect the expression of gratitude through your uninterrupted care of our boots!

By comparison, the lot of the male reader of Heel! who is under the control of our Egyptian office, will by my description of individual suffering as it is enforced on that continent, relieve the open-minded European reader of doubt as to the relative pleasantness of his situation and prevent the onset of that depressive state that is everywhere referred to in these letters. The parasitic spread of what has been termed the disease Onchocerciasis, or river blindness, which is delivered to the recipient of this agonizing condition by the bite of the blackfly produces in this evolutionary experiment the most intense itching which precedes the forming of leathery skin that will, if the experiment continues, produce a surface flexible enough for sweat pores and ease of movement. With this comforting news I will leave you to ponder your future and to return mentally to the fold of the rubber slave.

If there is to be a repeat of your rude behaviour, not only will I feel unable to address you in the familiar and affectionately as 'Boot-Lovers', but I may conclude that my own hand has been reluctantly forced to request a supply of this African blackfly, lest your work with our boots becomes by degree impaired.

MADAME X

TWENTY-SIX

The Stalagmite Men

What are we being led to believe in this case? That there exists a subterranean world into whose cavernous depths a team of eminent archaeologists suddenly descends, crashing through the thin ice of the ancient burial-ground that is being so meticulously disinterred. Then, recovering from the shock of their fall, they are amazed to find themselves within some vaulted chamber whose vast dimensions have most certainly been exaggerated, with its array of stalactites and stalagmites onto whose sharp points whole phalanxes of frozen men have been impaled so that even the necrophilic appetite of the archaeologist is more than sated without any further removal of ice and detritus.

Communication between the archaeologists proves difficult, and a number of these highly experienced men become separated and lost it seems at the very first opportunity, responding to the 'beguiling harmony of sounds' that echoes about the cave's volume, disorienting their minds and producing in them the behaviour patterns of the zombi, which are attributed in this published report to a combination of factors, including the paranormal explanations typically resorted to when good science has not been thoroughly pursued.

There is also a subterranean river that rushes by them and disappears again into the darkness of what seems to be, to their concussed minds, a very large worm-hole, thereby adding to the Alice-in-Wonderland imagery in which the detail of the entire report is couched. Surely it is time for the first intrusion of common sense into what fast develops into an account that is scandalously supportive of the reality of alien forces at work beneath the Earth's surface.

We understand that the moon, again in their inexcusably unscientific language, 'peered down' on them – various signs of the Zodiac being also mentioned – through the gap left by their fall through the chamber's roof. We do know from the written account that this light showed a 'wild blizzard' to be blowing outside above the cave's calm interior, producing no doubt, according to the changing direction of wind current, the sound of the 'swishing of invisible whips and the noise of their cracking that ricochets so menacingly amongst these stalactites' above the heads of the remaining group which had not succumbed to those earlier sounds that we can in hindsight attribute to the dripping of icicles in the raised temperature of their newly exposed environment, which have now begun to crack and fall to the ground.

Time goes by, and they are surviving adequately in appropriate clothing in conditions that would not have appeared too inhospitable to the three Icelandic guides who accompanied the team to the site, with rifles for their protection from inquisitive or hungry bears. With each hour that passes, however, the hole through which they, and mercifully their food rations, had tumbled is closing above them under the weight of fresh snow. Various estimates as to the food supply and survival times are made, and it is agreed that some alternative exit must be found. They synchronize watches, and agree to return to the vaulted chamber after two hours of exploration in the cave's tunnels.

Did the archaeologists find their way out of this labyrinthian trap that in addition to its human contents which, as described, were jabbed through and then suspended in mid-air, showed signs of being used in prehistoric times to catch the larger dinosaurs, whose skin and discarded bones were preserved in a heap on the white ice of the cave's floor? No they did not; and as with the last words of antarctic explorer, Captain Scott, we are left to piece together at our leisure the contradictory evidence contained in the journal left behind and identified as being that of the 'German professor', and the forensic detail included in the report. Their bodies, to give you the full picture, were never found, except for 'Exhibit A: Male cadaver, aged 26: Whipped but otherwise unbroken', which had joined its ancient companions that dangled on the ends of stalactites, kept fresh in this larder for a giant.

Respect is always deserved by the dead, but when pen and paper are provided to the man condemned to die, whether by hanging or by means of some other contraption, fanciful and bogus revelations often deny him this last opportunity for redemption in the eyes of his contemporaries and whatever god he may trust. The professor, through his version of events, would have us believe that several others of his party were pierced onto the stalactites 'like insects pressed onto the sharp point of a thorn and preserved in this way by the beak of the predator bird.' None were found. So are we to believe that cannibalism became a fact amongst this polite party of archaeologists, or as was written in his scribbled account, that a 'serpentine being of such tremendous girth as hardly to be accomodated within the tunnel where the half of it remained unseen, such was the length,' had access from below to the frozen corpses of the cave?

Cave paintings, pictograms whose codes are indescipherable even to our finest scientific minds, were concealed behind the walls of ice that were later excavated, demonstrating an abundant but decadent civilisation which would have preceded the timing of the Ice Ages so far revealed by the archaeologist. There was the usual illustration of shamanic transformation, with women emerging in stages from the glossy skin of seals. Evidence also of the clothing worn abounded in the hidden recesses of the cave which confirmed each cultural shift displayed simultaneously across the encircling wall. Best preserved for the clarity of its detail, and of interest to both the anthropologist and fetishist, is the ritual foot-bath that mixed hygiene with a reinforcement of the matriarchal order. The wall-painting shows a young man of around twenty years of age, with apparently healthy muscular definition, with his skull sealed within a close-fitting mask that blinds his eyes but is open at the mouth where the shape of a stiletto shoe is built into the encasement and is equally polished so that it appears to be of a piece with the layer of rubbery material that is stretched tight over the length of his body, which lies submissively on its back with knees up to take the weight of the seated woman. A metallic collar round his neck receives in its groove the curved heel of the shoe; its downward pressure ensures his motionless obedience through the period when his tongue's unseen but frenetic activity thoroughly cleans and services the skin of her foot. To the left of this image is another that represents the preparation of the slave who will undergo this ritual which may be repeated at the beginning and end of each day. We see four or five cubes of ice being forced inside his mouth which is held closed by the gloved hands of the woman who is about to enjoy a refreshing foot-bath.

Then there is the series of wall-paintings at the entrance to the tunnel through which the icy water of the river flows into the impenetrable darkness beyond. Dressed in black rubber or gleaming seal-skin to make this hazardous journey to the very depths of the underworld, we watch the women about to enter the tunnel in a spherically-shaped craft onto which bodies, live and dead, are being loaded by six stiletto-booted and uniformed guards with whips in their hands, which in one picture they are preparing to use and with which, in the next, after this moment of premeditation, they are lashing the reluctant men who are depicted both during and after their punishment.

It is easy for us to distinguish in this idealized representation, a German professor of archaeology and his worthy assistants standing and kneeling in equal numbers beneath the circular opening in the cave's roof, which appears almost to be blocked by the fullness of the moon that does indeed seem to peer down within. Whether these impatient women are descended from the matriarchal line and continue by some informal arrangement to supply the human diet of an infernal and over-sized serpent is pure and inexcusable conjecture on my part.

TWENTY-SEVEN

Ride to the Chateau

To fall asleep, and then to fall asleep again, within the dream, in a dream shared with one other, your lover, is to awaken fully within that dream, for ever, provided that both are identically entwined upon the dream bed as on the physical bed, which can, given the momentum usually involved, be hard to achieve at precisely the right time. Yet, it does happen, and often, and accounts for more disappearances of men and women than has been credited, and is the technique used on occasion by the shaman and the yogi, but with the more deliberate intention of moving between worlds and in this case from the posture of the celibate, who may, however, given his history of abstinence, suffer from that lapse of concentration, at the moment of departure, that delivers him into a world which is perhaps not of his natural choosing, into the world of the Dark Goddess. Indeed, the insertion of such sexual imaginings into his waking and dreaming minds, both heightened through the lack of past release to the point of reverence for the divine, is the skill of that group of unearthly beings, from whom the fantastic behaviour of the dominatrix is derived.

The lone figure therefore lies on the floor of his hermit's cave, ascetic to the last in all his habits, his desires all long since stilled in him by that continuous practice of self-discipline that has marked him out from other men. He revives in himself that half-remembered art of careless youth; but with the immediate influx of sexual imagery soon to be refined in his ritualistic mind by the urgings of these beings into worship of this Goddess, who settles upon him at the time of climax, binding him to her, while he fights against the exhaustion that will lead to his sleep within her dream, he now relinquishes the struggle, finally abandoning his soul for the fetishistic discipline that is the unending experience that lies ahead for such as he.

That there are volunteers for this kind of experience, who prepare themselves for an equal number of years with the same devotion to their purpose as the religious man, and with the same measure of discipline, though this time applied from the outside by the force of a supervising priestess or mistress, rather than through the enlightening words of a master of matters arcane, will no doubt perplex the mind of the reader who has yet to be selected by the dominatrix's unearthly counterpart for the lengthy process of initiation through the joint stimuli of whippings and boot-worship.

Much space is set aside in the secular media prompted by this wave of millennial fever, for astrological charts and prediction, and questions concerning the whereabouts of each individual's planet or star of origin, and in the more serious literature there is some discussion and debate about the disturbing matter of the control of this planet's evolution by secret societies, ancient in their origin, competitive in their attempts to manipulate humanity's progress. It is believed that these societies are in turn overseen by those star beings of whose invisibility next to nothing is known, save by the members of their earthly organisations who by means of the whip and the stiletto boot seek even before the new millennium is begun, to pervert the very course of history into the service of their Goddess.

The writer of religious history, unlike the fiction-writer, should not bring to his work those intrusive details of his own private life, which may be of dubious interest to the circle of family and friends, but are superfluous to the successful recounting of facts, which inevitably suffers as a consequence, serving but to confuse the reader whose time must remain the most important factor in this one-sided form of communication. Let me simply and without the burden of elaboration, state that my birth into this world was unorthodox, being also my escape from captivity in another to which I had been taken in the manner already described, from a past incarnation as a holy man whose followers had delighted in their belief that I had left them for a more spiritual existence. Imagine my distress when one after the other, imitating those techniques of advancement that had been given them at our mountain retreat, I was to witness their arrival at my side, all bound and gagged and accompanied in their torment by fabulous women in polished black.

Let me therefore strive to remedy the situation by making known the much-needed improvements to the esoteric techniques that we taught at the lamaserie, and which are unfortunately being transmitted by the wonders of modern technology to the occident where their uncorrected practice would prove a disaster, and where those thigh-booted agents of the Goddess are already dominant and everywhere available to conduct the neophyte away from the norms of proud civilisation, ready for his further transport to the distant realms of this unforgiving deity.

We were assigned by birth and training to be the keepers of the sacred places of which modern man has little remaining knowledge. The greater part of the period of my training was spent in solitude, in an underground cave where I became highly developed in my powers of visualization, and other psychic skills with which I will not bother the reader who has not the leisure available in the Himalayan mountain. I propose a technique based upon this inner sight which will according to a man's degree of enlightenment and the cycle of his incarnations, be a safe and practical method of moving between worlds.

As the sacred place carries embedded within its rock the hidden access to other worlds, which is felt at first as a pull upon the hermit's mind, so does the western mind experience that same sensation when confronted by the sight of art executed by the man whose own thought resonates with these otherworldly energies. It is the identical feeling of being swept away in the presence of the divine when such intense emotion is imparted to the psyche that all balance seems momentarily to have been lost, and a transformation is begun of the sort that precedes the contraction of the body as it is sucked into the central point of the inter-dimensional vortex.

The patroness of Renaissance art understood well imagery's power to first harness and then to so excite the spirit of the questing man as to draw him in within that higher plane of living that is represented by the canvas of the equestrian painting. In medieval Europe, in the time of the troubadours, when the transformative power of these illuminating works of art was magically employed, their possession and display by the dominating woman ensured the gratification of each of her perverted appetites.

As the modern woman might today use the suction of a vacuuming appliance to rid her domestic environment of unwanted objects, so the noblewoman of France used her varied collection of art for her own satisfaction. Only the scale was different; the targets being human and male, were larger, and the component of magic was of greater significance. You will understand that by the choice of subject-matter to be painted, and those alchemical symbols included, a terrifying array of art could be assembled behind the walls of the chatelaine's castle.

Such paintings would often be paraded by her servants in front of a reluctant admirer, with the insidious threat that, should her displeasure, or rather lack of pleasure, be incurred during their exchanges, sexual or of pleasantries, then the protective sheet concealing the canvas selected at the point of her riding-whip, is by this dismissive gesture to be removed exposing the submissive man, whether he be of noble or vulgar birth, to whatever form of perversion is exhibited within the equestrian scene so suddenly revealed. The canvas, stripped bare, responding to this burst of Earthly light, would seem then, according to the preserved accounts, 'to bulge towards this man's cringing and well-strapped body, surely in the attempt to add a third dimension to the flattened contours of its unformed landscape . . . and [the canvas] appearing to be about to release its unsavoury contents onto the floor, but instead gathers up the bridled and disappearing fellow into its dark bosom, to the brief, interrupting sound of whiplash and chain'.

By his restraint in this other world of the chatelaine's dream, in a position of bondage that mimics the harnessing of his body within the castle, his life of servitude that had promised to be intermittent and temporary, if only his cooperation had been forthcoming and genuine, in pursuit of his natural and intimately confessed instincts to serve and then to worship, is by this outrageous turn of events to be extended indefinitely without end, to be endured for eternity in the harsh climate of this alien land of the Dark Goddess.

The Queen of France, in her summer progress through the estates of the nobility, included in her retinue, packed into carriages of proportions selected for their transport, a great quantity of equestrian art and as well a number of paintings of her favourite boots and shoes, so providing for her nocturnal entertainment. How many of these survive in the gloved hands of the secret society member and how considerable is their contribution to the modern renaissance of the chatelaine's art and pleasure?

What use is a list of paintings to be avoided, however complete at the time of its compilation, when these leather-skirted society women, even as I write these words, generate such a profusion of new imagery? The complexity of this whole problem is compounded hugely by the multi-dimensional dynamics of the current situation whereby a twentieth-century equestrienne may use the photograph of, for example, the painting by Sir Alfred Munnings titled 'Ride to the Chateau' to send her servant back through the centuries to the chatelaine from whom she has received a substitute slave in exchange.

Dealing as we are, with equestrian art, let me add that any painting which contains the name 'Sisi' in its title, however inviting, should on every occasion be avoided. It will most likely be a trap; a way to displace you to what may seem on first inspection to be a pleasant enough environment, where you will find yourself in the company of an Austrian empress whose expressionless face will be hidden behind a veil. She will be holding a whip in her left hand, a leather fan in her right, and dressed in a black riding-habit. There will be portraits of horses that have died beneath her saddle and her eighteen inch waist, hanging from the walls of this memorial chapel.

As you focus yourself within the space of the chapel, admiring perhaps the empress' fine appearance and enjoying the silence of her retreat, the lettering of 'Sisi' will be suddenly reversed to become instead 'Isis', the name of the Dark Goddess, into whose slave empire you will be irretrievably transported. I should add that my own freedom from her spell is of limited duration. Therefore, choose wisely in art, and by the development and exercise of inner sight, gain entry at last to the kingdom of God that is forever denied me. Remember always to refrain from the illustrated book whose content deals exclusively with aspects of the equestrienne's dress, lest you should be chosen for that process of initiation of which I have warned.

TWENTY-EIGHT

Dance of the Black Serpent

Are we to assume on the basis of two protrusions, one at the north pole and the other at the south pole, that this planet has suffered a catastrophic reversal in its polarity, such that what had appeared to be in the south, is no longer in the south, but in the north, and vice versa? And does the current melting of the polar ice-caps and the failure of an explorer to implant his flag in the snow at the south pole justify a rethinking of established positions and the recognition of a nebulous suspicion as unshakeable fact?

Let us remember that in his own mind, the explorer did not believe himself to be upside down and experienced no feeling of giddiness standing there proding and poking the ground for an entry-point, with his flag being rejected at each attempt, to the sound of metal, just as when a thimble rejects the imprint of the needle. Then, with his scraping of snow and ice, side by side with the pawing of his sledge dogs, away from this most extreme of planetary locations, we are told, and asked to believe, there emerged little by little, according to the momentum, weakening and then renewed, of their joint efforts, a black sculptured skull of gigantic proportions, the head of a Goddess from whose flaring nostrils each dog in turn licks the blocking ice, in this way refreshing their burning throats and clearing a passage through the nasal cavity into which the flag was thrust in nervous triumph, before the explorer's rapid escape back into the enshrouding blizzard, and out of the sight of, what appears on the face of it, to be no more than a coincidentally placed remnant from the planet's prehistory.

No attempt has to my knowledge, been so far made to carve an equivalent hole into the snow and ice at the northern pole in the unlikely case that there would be revealed the shape of a woman's foot that would at least merit the scrutiny of serious-minded research. Instead, there is, I hear, a vague report that somewhere in the vicinity of the north pole, sticking up through the snow, and sounding no more real than the neck of the Loch Ness monster, a fashionably curved boot-heel has appeared, and like a guage of melting ice, becomes more visible with each season.

The retreat from reason into myth is begun with the comparison of this as yet one-legged Goddess with the stupendous 'Legend of the First Beginning', when a headless serpent, 'joined to itself in a massive circumference, without beginning or end', is coiled about the middle of a sleeping Goddess, wakening within her, by its rhythmic writhing, the first thrusting out of colossal hips and polished thighs that appear physically materialized and wriggling in an empty black sky, in a belly-dance to the zodiacal beast of her dream performed on the cosmic stage, where the stiffening serpent is centrifugally unwound, pulling like a Saturnian ring away from the bronzed waist of the Goddess, who leans and sways against its terrible weight, pivoting, then pirouetting, on the sharp points of stiletto shoes or boots. The many versions of the legend vary in the detail and with the degree of distortion and comprehensibility.

In one version, the Goddess wakes first from the dream universe, ripping the penis from the bull of Taurus, gripping its tip within her, with which the trunk is whipped about until separation; the two fleshy ends are then joined together between the leather-gloved hands of the Goddess. More typically the serpent is shown, tail in mouth, encircling a materializing vortex that is progressively obscuring the central figure of the Snake Goddess. That the molten contents of the Goddess' impassioned womb become finally encased within the planetary sphere is agreed and common to all accounts, as was the uncertainty of the planet's resulting polarity, when the whirling and spin of the Goddess and serpent had begun to slow in their revolution.

This snake-dancing is easily connected in the fantast's mind with the hoop-dancing of the sorceress, to her breaking of the circle of time, and through the interruption of time, to the performance of magic. The object of the hoop-dance, it is believed, is to become invisible to those around you: the movement up and down the dancer's body, of the circling hoop, causes its disappearance in stages, as section by cross-section her flesh is lost to the invasive gusts of night air. At the end of the dance, only the hoop remains, held in an immaterial hand, and broken open into the length of a rod or whip, which takes on an independent existence, thrashing and flailing about in what is known in voodooistic worship as the 'Dance of the Black Serpent'. It is probable that the possession of these magical hoops with their vicious potential, by the chatelaines of France, obtained by some means from their sister, the African sorceress, accounts for the ready submission and regular penitence of the troubadour of medieval Europe, and the particular reputation of certain chateaux which were rivals in the provision of whippings and pain. The fact that it was never known, until it was too late, whether a man's companion was indeed blessed beneath her skirts with such a resource, ensured the general level of compliance within the population. The recent auctioning of an eighteenth-century dress, together with one of those chateaux' contents, attracted far wider interest than the usual buyers of antiques, because the dress' mysterious past was recorded in the literature that followed its wearer's life and disappearance.

The dress had been irresistible to courtiers and servants alike, making the former swell the ranks of the latter, when in the presence of its puffed out skirt of blood-red silk and bows. Each had believed that through his correct behaviour some reward of an unfathomable and delightful nature would be bestowed on the chatelaine's favourite. Whether the dress actually requires the voluptuous and corseted involvement of the female figure had never been clear, but at the auction in the tented grounds beside the orangery, some support for its independent magical properties was received in the evidence of welt marks appearing on the back-sides of those otherwise engaged in the bidding process, no doubt explaining their reluctance to bid against the final purchaser, a circus woman of reportedly Amazon descent, who may herself have been responsible for some percentage of the pain.

The argument that the hoop's powers were stumbled upon, by chance, during the rebuffing of an insistent and kneeling admirer, who was captured within the dress' dark interior, known previously only to the chatelaine and her seamstress, and by the upward thrusting of his head, he had triggered into activity the latent potential within the encircling ring, indisputably is false, though conjuring up all the right imagery that will in no time convince the fantast of its truth. There were however 'disappearances' frequently reported, but no more than would be explained through loss of life from duelling and the chase, that was followed by an unchristian burial on the spot where death occurred. Nor does it seem likely that through the rubbing of silk on the hoop's metallic surface, the genie of Mohammedan mythology was summoned into being in the form of an Amazon woman, later to do her mistress' bidding at a modern auction.

No; the most reasoned explanation, until the unfolding of recent events, for the dress' reputation as the harbinger of death, had included the feminine equivalent of the sword-stick, where a blade is unsheathed from within the stick's hollowed-out wood, to the surprise and misfortune of the assailant. The sword, being unsuitable for insertion within the hoop's circumference, had, it was intelligently deduced, been substituted by the seamstress, under her mistress' instruction, with the curve of the single coil of a bull-whip, which when inflicted, possibly with the partial addition of magical properties borrowed by the whip from its African host, had unleashed the most severe of punishments.

The disappearance of the physical evidence of death, which has been the corner-stone of the mystical interpretation of the whip's power, was explained by the swift removal from sight of incriminating evidence and the reordering into its civilised and innocent components, of the murder scene, and not by the transformation of whip into hoop and the gobbling up of remains into its vortex-like centre for disposal in an alien grave or for their reanimation as perfected servants.

On the other hand, this was the first modern discovery of a dress supposedly possessed of such potential, that had been described in in full detail in the contemporary masterpieces of the literary world, that had stood against the wisdom of France's Age of Enlightenment, and that had not succumbed to the probings of the reasoning mind. Here was the dress, about to go under the auctioneer's hammer, that was believed to reproduce human form by its mere placement over wetted unformed clay in the darkened studio of an absent sculptor, and which had brought to confused transvestite life the very statues of the ancient gardens of this white-stoned chateau. What would be the effect, we all asked with the suspicion of fraud, but the hope of something more, of the separation of the metallic hoop from the abundant dress, and its electromagnetic movement up and down, over the black bronze of the temple statues of the Snake Goddess? Would she respond to some rhythm accidentally produced by the curious man of science, guiding by her polished arm the completion of her own enlivenment, to be followed by her reproduction of the whip?

The sale, not to the collectors this time, but to the Amazon and her circus troupe, had ended the speculation of the invited men of science, and nothing had been heard for several months of this promising dress which had briefly inspired the kind of press comment reserved for scandal and the apocalyptic prediction. Then, with a cutting taken from a provincial paper and forwarded anonymously to the Academie des Sciences, the first evidence was received of the dress' true power to transform. The Amazons were no longer taming the panthers seen with them at the auction, but were retrieving for exhibition at their circus, through the hoop's inexplicable power to veil and conceal, the very same courtiers who had vanished beneath the dress' skirt, centuries before.

The attached photograph shows the hoop on fire, being gripped in the gloved hand of the Amazon, whose leather boots, like the faces of children seen between her equestrian thighs, are lit up against the dark sky by the flaming ring of sorcerer's steel. Clearly visible to the unaided eye, is the rump of this supine man who slips out backwards onto the wooden planks of the makeshift stage, in that same kneeling position of the chateleine's servant. The whip in the Amazon's other hand is raised in readiness. The caption questions whether time travel is really worth this heavy price. We can only pray that any future reversal of time, caused by the righting of the Earth's seeming reversal of polarity, leads not to the accelerated return through time to that chaos of half-materialized forms, of the whip-cracking Snake Goddess, in the cycle of creation and destruction described in the 'Legend of the First Beginning'.

TWENTY-NINE

The Blinkered Man

Dear Boot-Lovers,

A reader has written to me about a problem with her slave. How, she asks, should she broach the difficult subject of his future development when it is planned for him that he should become not just the four-legged beast of burden that is his present lot, but having, with his objections first voiced loud and then silenced by the horse's bit, achieved and been returned to this level, he should now, as time and training fulfil themselves, be further lowered and in the process lose his present freedom to move and roam about within the barbed perimeter of his much reduced world.

The lady reader, and what a pleasure to receive this letter from such an accomplished equestrienne, wishes to know whether there is a place for ancient ritual in the resolution of what seems, to her perplexed mind, to be a contemporary problem, and, if ritual does still have a role to play in these secular times, in the life of the modern woman, would I please pass her inquiry to the office of Heel! in Denderah,

Egypt, for the advice then requested.

Yes and No. Yes; ritual remains vital in the orderly progress of the slave's involution, curbing, to use an inappropriate word when applied to the riding mistress, her by nature dominating and impetuous bent, and if not stripping the equestrienne of her sometimes cruel facade, permitting the slave's further mutation within a disciplined and even compassionate context. No; I have no need to pass your letter to our sister office in Egypt, whose staff, as you here suggest, have the same requirement for sound and firm footing beneath their boots. I have the good news to report that I am personally accomplished in the area of transformation to which your questioning is so purposefully directed, having in my previous incarnation as a priestess at the office in Denderah, presided over the extensive laying of human flesh far out into the desert beyond where the human eye can follow.

As this is to be a living structure that both stays in place and replaces itself over time, and which must resist the penetration of boot heels through to the sand beneath, we must improvise a vocabulary that will refer in one sentence both to the necessity for the maintenance of the good morale of the flattened and forgotten men under foot, and to the engineer's description of logistics and the impersonal measurement, cutting and joining of flesh so that like colouring merges with like if a mosaic appearance is to be avoided, and a gradual and charming change of shade is to result.

The thin surface is punctured inevitably, even with the

best-laid flesh, with those few spots of uncontrolled bleeding where a weakness in the superficial skin has been pointed out by the strolling and fashionably booted member of Heel!, who, impetuous as you may also be, whips thoroughly the offending ground without thought for the negative effect on the low morale of the still sensitive, human patchwork that sweats under the midday sun, stretched out and determined by training to withstand the downward pressure of so many posturing heels and the occasional hooves of galloping horses.

The consciousness of the man must remain and become the life within your proposed floor covering. You have him in blinkers; a dressage mount responsive to each command that is given. Now lengthen the period between the elements of his choreographed movement so that guided by voice, spur, rein and booted leg, he is brought more often and for a greater interval, to a standstill, freezing his perspiring and well-groomed form repeatedly in this programme of extended obedience.

Any exchange of words that is reminiscent of a past relationship between mistress and slave should cease altogether. Short and simple commands should be given, and that is all, until he has become something that is felt vicariously through the leather sole and heel of the walking boot or well-heeled shoe. The blinkers are to be kept secure against his head through daylight and into sleep, throughout the hours of his dreaming. A tall boot is selected, preferably with stiletto heel and of the mistress' wardrobe so that added incentive by association is offered the slave when he is forced, for a period corresponding to the increasing time of stillness in the riding-ring, then to mimic the mystic's act of meditation, aided by his blinkered state that will produce in time the contemplative euphoria and feeling of bliss for which his mistress waits prepared with riding-crop held flexed in her leather-gloved hands.

At the moment that he reaches forward, arms no longer held stiffly at his side but outstretched in disobedience, his body otherwise buckled and kneeling down before the polished stiletto boot . . . at the moment his mind begins to merge with the life within the leather of the boot that has been lent to it by the Mistress by the simple fact of its being worn often and regularly as her favourite footwear . . . now pull them physically apart, the slave and the boot, overbalancing and forcing the former onto his stomach where he is to be pegged out and pressed down like the page of this magazine beneath the weight of the printing press. The riding-boot, and it must be a riding-boot at this early stage, moves quickly from side to side across the stunned and fully unravelled body of the slave who was just previously contorted in his act of prayer that had seemed for so many months to provide pleasant respite from the grind of equine service.

At this time of stamping and sometimes frenzy, restraint is required, not just of the slave's body in its motionless reconstruction on that section of floor deemed to be in need of repair, but restraint also of the young, house-proud Mistress, so keen to see the unsightly condition of damaged fabric being corrected. The slave must be kept alive by his desire to be in perpetual contact with the boot worshipped daily by him, and not killed off in a hurry to distribute flesh into the desired shape. Little by little, day by day, using only the flat soles of spurred riding-boots, he becomes flatter, and then flatter, more personally in tune with the lives of woodworm, and the cooling draft from the door opened by the towering equestrienne whose name he begins to forget, and whose riding-boots he feels pressing often and lightly on his back.

The change from one week to the next in the appearance of the floor surface is so very slight as to be indistinguishable to the scientific observer, with the result that, if the conversion progresses to plan, at no point can it be said that these marginal and minute alterations to the slave's form leave him sufficiently different to justify nature's sudden withdrawal of life-force. Biologically he seems to be the same from one minute to the next; but to his patient Mistress who waits for the hour when she may walk again in high heels without freeing by their exaggerated pressure her slave by his death, he appears changed to her discerning eye that delights in each sign of preserved life, at his effort still to communicate.

The day arrives when the pegs can be removed and their piercing presence safely substituted by the return of the stiletto boot that may be thought perhaps to notice the new circumstance of the man who had so regularly worshipped its existence as a portent of feminine divinity. The Mistress will now bear the sorrow or rejoice in the knowledge that the complex markings of multi-coloured tattoos painstakingly injected into his skin while he prayed, do or disastrously do not, match the adjacent area of the floor. Polish, to give away a secret of the trade, may be used to smooth the join, and is more pleasing beneath one's foot.

If the floor is to be polished black, but then appears too new when compared with the rest of the room, the use of the whip and the mild gashing of its surface with a boot heel, so as not to cause bleeding, is recommended. It is often the case that with an inexperienced but impetuous Mistress this effect can prove excessive, and the process of mistreating the whole area of the room of necessity begins and may seem to never end. If grooves are to be cut to match the pattern of, for example, a herring-bone, diamond or chequered design, use a sharp kitchen knife and reserve at least one hour to ensure the careful precision of your work.

Walk each day upon your slave in heeled boots, so ensuring there is adequate transmission and flow of life-giving energy down to the sheet of leather that he has with your help at last become. How well I remember in Egypt watching one night from the pyramid's cap-stone, dressed in my familiar boots, when a bright circle of crimson light crossed the desert floor below. It was surely a greeting to me the Goddess of those lost souls.

MADAME X

THIRTY

The Slave's Alphabet

Such was the reputation of that fairy-tale castle in Bavaria, and so very heavy was the atmosphere of decadence that hung in its mountain air, that even the statues on its walls might be expected to be smoking some foul brand of cigar or cigarette, lighting up the night sky with smoke-ringed, flame-red stars – confusing to an astrologer, yet to the trained parapsychologist, evidence of the chain-smoking deity.

I was being greeted by the hurried shuttering of the tall, narrow windows by a woman in black who on each occasion seemed from my position on the outside, almost to be folding a pair of leathery batwings over her long black body; perhaps in protection from the rising sun which so often makes invisible precisely those paranormal phenomena that it had become my sole purpose in life to investigate.

Surely, whatever kind of poltergeist activity had been inspired by the history of the place, did not require my being met by a Countess, caped and leather-booted, but with her 'pet snake', in reality a whip of great length and antiquity that followed her everywhere, which had been fashioned from snake skin with the specific intent of dealing with those nightly intruders, for whom according to my timing, I might for a few more minutes be reasonably mistaken.

From experience in this type of situation, it is politic and permits an earlier assimilation into the community under investigation, to go along with the prejudices of your hostess, the more quickly to take up that fly-on-the-wall perspective from whose vantage-point the desired objectivity is derived, and one may proceed unhindered to an efficient resolution of the case.

'Sklave!'

'Yes indeed, Countess,' I immediately responded, believing that the subsequent arrival of the real slave would clear the confusion, and allow me to reveal my true identity, and with that confession to hint modestly at my successes in this new field of science. Perhaps also, as was usually the pattern, I might amuse my hostess with some after-dinner entertainment, by the sudden and dramatic unrolling and unravelling of the sheets of statistical analysis that are the hall-mark of the scientific approach.

Evidence of the divine is frequently to be found, and as often overlooked, in the mundane world of human affairs; even in the collection, counting and tabulation of, for example, the stubbed-out cigarette or pencil-thin cigar that is discovered at the feet of the spikily-shod statue whose stone cladding is by this method proved to be no more than a disguise, which by patient observation may be finally penetrated.

The last of the shutters was being closed and bolted as I passed under a gothic and gargoyled arch, inside, into a dark world of fleeting and phantasmagoric shapes and forms whose reality or unreality would have to be determined by the sounds made by shoes on the stone-paved floor; whether or not they included the peculiar clicking of boot heels that would confirm the presence of the female poltergeist, whose numerous intrusions from that other world of human fantasy have been so inadequately documented.

A novice in such unnerving circumstances might have shuddered perceptibly at the loud clanking of bolts being forced home across the face of the drawbridge gates, and the finality with which keys were being rotated in oversized locks, whose numbers would be considered excessive, unless their object was to remove from the slave's thoughts any prospect of an indecent and panicked retreat back into the daylight, outside.

Certainly the character of the castle's ghostly inhabitants, by the uniformity and severity of their dress and appearance, suggested the disciplined world of the convent, with its candle-bearing and mass-reciting sisterhood, or even of that secretive order of women whose earthly lives are believed to be dedicated to the works of the Dominatrix. And how often does the residue of religious sentiment, however devoted, become changed by the span of time into the vile disturbances that it has been my cause to overcome?

The long black capes would conceal from my reflexes that rapid and merciless delivery of the poltergeist's boot and spur, which, when combined with the masking of my features by the leather of an accomplice's opera-glove, would maintain through the hard time of my research, a religious silence of which I should have felt pride, and not the pain which I believed had been reserved for the delayed slave into whose servile state I found myself at length to be falling, prostrated by the well-practised viciousness of this concerted and undeniable poltergeist activity.

I believed that in some unknown manner, my willingness to

adopt the persona of a prospective servant or slave to the Countess had been psychically communicated to the ever-patient and leather-booted residents of her castle, who, released from their expectant state, had then overreacted to my presence with this exhibition of whip and spur. It was a lesson in the flexibility of mind and adaptability of body always required of the investigator of paranormal; though I wished it not to be repeated, doubting by this time my ability to withstand a further onslaught, even of much reduced ferocity. Therefore, the escalation in the harsh treatment of my flesh which was no doubt intended to confirm the condition of my new-found servility, proved decisive in my conversion to the worship of boots and snakes, to this pagan religion of the Goddess.

At what point should I have stepped out from behind this leathery mask of the slave and declared my mission to the Countess, which was of course to deliver her from the fear and company of the whip-wielding poltergeist so that she might put away for good her 'pet snake' and rejoin polite society? Before the dawning of my realisation and then acceptance of the Countess' own involvement, emotional and as the leather-gloved accomplice, with the success of this lengthy process of religious conversion? Or before the later conversion of the zoologist whose arrival here, to a similar greeting, has completed the Countess' alphabet of slaves? For what was begun with the enslavement of an astrologer led by fate and the light of a flame-red star to the booted feet of a stony-faced Goddess, has been ended with the sealing of us all within the perpetual night of her castle's walls. And what in my capacity as this fly-on-the-wall parapsychologist – the letter 'P' of her alphabet – would I have then revealed that our bat-like hostess did not already know? That her identity and those of the multiple apparitions of her booted duplicates from the Spirit world, are one and the same. That she is the Goddess. That she has entered into the world of men and their dreams, projecting onto virgin snow an illusory castle which she has filled with a cargo of slaves, whose destiny now lies somewhere within the orbit of her distant star. And that by her smoky exhalations a strange magic is performed, with materializations taking shape and identifiable form; and by her sharp and measured intake of breath, the process is then reversed, with the recapture of a chosen slave and the re-formation of his body within the burning centre from which he reappears, in miniature, on a paving-stone shared perhaps with a high-heeled boot, with only instinct and the tiniest of tins of polish to guide him. Small wonder, given the periods of commotion, of the clicking of so many pairs of heels, that such numbers of men are being required to convert to this new religion of the Goddess.

The transformation of whipped flesh at the point of the stiletto boot and by the sculpting of the leather-glove, together with its inhalation and re-projection, into this variety of dwarfish forms, is finished and done, and the memory of what preceded in our lives and had counted for normal life, fades into oblivion, and is at last superseded by the silence of the polishing of boots beneath a clear black sky crowded with smouldering stars, with half-lit faces, of Goddesses deep in conversation and the friendliest of embraces.

We remain below. Chained to the ground by interlocking rings of condensing smoke, we polish blindly, without hindsight or foresight, amongst a forest of skyscraping calves and thighs, until each one of us is pressed down red beneath her careless tread, onto the hard receiving stone, beneath the black leather imprint and stamp of the Goddess' boot.

THIRTY-ONE

Insect Karma

Where to begin? Seven villages set in seven valleys set apart and secluded from one another, yet communicating through the centuries by the blowing of seven horns which were hollowed to the length of four men, taking three to carry and one less to hold in position, being crafted from identical wood to duplicate the proportions of a prototype exposed by the sliding of sheets of glacier ice as long ago as the Jurassic period.

A meeting of village elders takes place. Accusing fingers are pointed in all directions, with blame being attached to each village in turn for the nocturnal sounding of a horn that had led to the deaths of the young men. At the climax of this furious and most vocal apportioning of blame, rage had turned to fear at the sound of a horn that issued from a granite cave far above the tree-line, from where the avalanche had begun its murderous descent, smashing its way over the trunks of snow-laden spruce trees, all the way down the mountain to the log-cabin in which the village elders were holding their meeting. It is the sound of the Beast, who is hungry again.

Fortified, however, by the drinking of alcohol and the exchange of stories of their ancestors' daring, made more real in the cabin's flame-lit air, the seven elders decide to rival, even to surpass, the exploits and feats of bravery of their forefathers, and to find and kill the mountain-beast. The full moon had guided their ascent; yet we do not know if they reached as high as the cave, or whether they met their deaths lower down, because no sign was ever found of their bodies. A year later, another link was added to this lengthening chain of events, with the reported deaths of a team of experienced mountaineers who had chosen the night of the full moon for their assault on the summit which, unbeknown to them, housed within its granite walls the mythical abode of the Beast. Their last radioed message had been interrupted by the deafening sound from a mountain-horn. What to make of all this? The inhabitants of the seven valleys, with whom I have spoken about the character of the Beast, distinguish between those species that they believe were created 'in the Beginning . . . for the Goddess' pleasure', and the more recent additions to the fauna of the Pyrenees. Of the former, there is a distinct species of ibex [*Capra pyrenaica*], the Pyrenean desman or water-mole [*Mygale pyrenaica*], and also various types of blind insect to be found in and around the caverns of the Ariège; the principal genera of which are *Anophthalmus* and *Adelops*.

There is, however, a belief, confirmed by a long history of distant sightings, in the existence of a giant humanoid, perhaps comparable in size to Oregon's 'Big Foot' or the equally hairy yeti, the 'Abominable Snowman' of the remote Himalayas. This species is also understood to have been present in the beginning, and belongs therefore to the first category. I believed it to be the very same beast whose foul play has been responsible for so many deaths.

Here in the Pyrenees, these villagers, still trapped in their prehistoric time, recall a race of giants, of gods and demi-gods from the stars, who return to their mountain again and again, 'like birds to their tree'. This allusion to the gods being bird-like echoes the testimonies made to countless anthropologists by other indigenous and cave-dwelling peoples across the globe who regard the eagle as the sacred embodiment of the Divine Being.

I have with me the notes taken during my last visit to one of the villages. The following extract with its mention of the rubber tree refers to a time when the climate in the area of the Pyrenees must have been very different. Never written down, but handed down by oral tradition, these are words first spoken in very ancient times, perhaps in an attempt to make sense of what is incomprehensible:

> The warrior sleeps along the bough of the giant rubber tree. His sleeping-bough is worn smooth by the skin of a thousand rubbermen who fell as prey to the flame-eagle. A rubberman dreams in dark greens, shades of avocado, lest his chameleon skin be shown up to the flame-eagle which hangs in the sky beneath the moonbeams, angling its light down to the rubber tree below. At full moon, the flame-eagle will set the grass ablaze. Full moon is never far away.

I was entrusted with the name of the Goddess for whose exclusive pleasure those original species had been created. She is the 'Flame Goddess'. Her body was described to me as having the skin of black rubber, but radiating the light of the 'Seven Rays of the Great Bear'. The connection between this goddess and the flame-eagle of the shaman was too blatant to overlook. But was her male counterpart, the beast of their legends, really responsible for dragging the most virile of the villagers away to their deaths? It seemed more probable that the village elders had succumbed not to skull-crushing blows, but to the radiance of this Flame Goddess, the embodiment of female beauty. If she was being confused with the Beast, then surely the confusion was in name only, the result of the zodiacal source of her mythical powers.

On the night before my ascent of the mountain, in a rented room in the village of Rennes-le-Chateau, the last pieces of the puzzle finally fell into place. I was reading from Ovid's account of the fateful day when Actaeon, the Boeotian hero and hunter, accidentally sees the Goddess Artemis on Mount Cithaeron while she is bathing, and is changed by her into a stag and is pursued and killed by his fifty hounds. I remembered also the details of the story of how Tiresias came by chance upon the naked form of the Goddess Athena while she was bathing, and how she struck him blind for this offence. Could not the fate of the blinded insects of Ariège be the result of their presence at the Goddess' undressing? And was it not the case that the increase in the Ibex population had been proportionate to the numbers of mountainmen who had been disappearing on moonlit nights? As I lay face up on my bed, I thought of the caves used for initiation in Tibet, and how giant beings were involved in that ceremony. What would I find at the top of the mountain?

Taking up a squatting position above the perfectly circular opening to the silent interior of the Goddess' retreat, I was soon being covered, then camouflaged by the large flakes of snow that fell with darkness onto the mountain-top. My view down to the seven valleys where one by one the fires were being extinguished for sleep, restored to my fast fading memory the distressing plight of the insect populations that lived and worked immediately below me within the cave. I had wondered in my rented room whether these blinded, but loyal servants, would assist with the polishing and shining of the Goddess' wardrobe, with her shoes and boots, so that a sufficiently reflective and radiant surface was achieved.

Not yet dismissing the chance of the Flame Goddess' late appearance, I had closed my eyes for fear that I might see her naked, or in the same stage of undress that had been previously witnessed by the insects. I must have fallen into the hypothermic death-sleep, when I was woken by the earthquaking sound of a mountain-horn. Unable to react physically to the sound, but able just to bat my eyelashes, and tilt my eyeballs, I could see the front half of the horn protruding from the cave's entrance below, and then its subsequent withdrawal back inside. Within a short time, I saw torches burning once more in the valleys, and the trend to darkness reversed in all the seven villages where the young men were again responding to their mountain destiny.

I was slipping back into that state of unconsciousness from which I had been woken, when a second shape emerged partially from the cave, before being pushed forcefully outside, and floating out away from the mountain. A sphere, translucent and encompassing the standing figure of an elderly man, was rising against the soft impact of snowflakes into the light of the full moon. A second and then a third sphere was released into the night sky, until the seventh and last was seen to rise in the direction of the others.

Then, no doubt intending to more clearly view their upward

progress, the Goddess herself had stepped out through the cave's entrance. She was standing directly below me, so that I might, had my mobility been sufficient, have reached down to touch with my finger-tips the black gleaming surface of this most statuesque of goddesses, equivalent in height, and yet more shapely than the Goddess Athena.

The Flame Goddess stood for a moment, towering above her mountain in the most high-heeled of boots, before raising a gloved right hand as if to remove the irritation of a snowflake from her eye. Whipping her arm back down through the air until it clapped against the polished palm of her left hand, a spark that was ignited by the smacking collision of two black surfaces, flashed into flame . . . Seven rays of cosmic fire pierced the night sky to infinity, before being recalled by the Goddess, by the re-clenching of her fists. No sign remained, however, of the frozen men; but seven black moths now emerged from within the still glowing gloves, four from the left and three from the right, seemingly in blind haste lest the ritual be immediately repeated.

THIRTY-TWO

Matrix of Servitude

Dear Boot-Lovers,

The use of the stiletto boot in the successful duplication of the preferred servant is the subject closest to my heart at the time of this new issue of Heel!, and if the readers' letters of condolence at my recent loss of a once fine servant are good guidance, I believe that such regrettable sacrifices of male life, made one after the other, are no longer the rare occurrence that they were in centuries past; the reason of course being the greater number of attempts being made at this most singularly difficult of tasks, namely the psychic cloning of male flesh.

Again we are dealing with the selection of the best and most desirable timing for the attempt to be made. We are required to behave with more patience than is often attributed to our dominant kind, to await the precise phase in the servant's – let us dispense with this misleading term – the slave's development, his being brought down to the level of forgetfulness of himself; his personal oblivion that leads to his uncertainty and disinterested vagueness as to the physical location of his tortured body, and to his lack of concern for his social position and the purpose of his existence independent of his service to the Mistress which is instead decided for him, from one moment to the next, by the direction of his natural superior into whose possession he has fallen reluctantly or by the sudden imposition of choice.

This lack of discrimination in the mind of the slave for whom all is ordered and organized, so that he will appear at a prescribed location according to requirement and not his own wish, sets up the ideal circumstance for which the Mistress, who has perhaps bought him at auction for duplication, has been so patiently waiting. To summarize his condition: he does not care for one location over another; he is everywhere and nowhere; he registers only his Mistress' disapproval and the consequent onset of suffering. He has not that fixation with time and space that he had in the period that preceded his purchase or his 'plucking from the wild'. He will do anything to please and to avoid punishment.

The repeated and apparently illogical demands as to time and place become the intended means of his duplication. He is at point A, then dragged by collar to point B, then commanded by whistle to a point P, wherever that is, and afterwards led briskly on to the next location. Confusion and disorientation set in as the predominant pattern within his brain. Remember that the employment of the short lead and riding-whip together with the polished leather boot beside which he walks four-legged and in time, produces in him over time that synchronizing of obedient and devoted heartbeat that permits by the growing level of intimacy, the direct communication of the unspoken instruction from Mistress to slave, which by its prompt execution suggests the hour of duplication, of psychic cloning, is drawing close, and the near-intolerable burden of patience, relieved only by the disciplining of his movement, is about to be rewarded.

We have in our grasp, at the other end of the lead or chain, for our confirming inspection and diagnosis, the mesmerized and kneeling form of the permanently hypnotized slave, who would, were it to be asked of him, jump without hesitation into the deepest abyss which is no longer distinguished in his dazed mind from terrain of a more gentle gradient. In truth, a part of him remains lingering where the boot has been in the Mistress' past, while another part of him walks in time, in the present moment, beside the measured stride of the same stiletto boot that may have been the first cause of his enticement into this lifeless life.

The process is well advanced, and I suggest only the confidence of optimistic expectation that the experimenting on and with his body will turn out and prove successful. Choose a night when the spotlit boot or boots, depending on the number of new slaves to be duplicated, left at certain points along the exercise route, are best shown up to the slave's perception, so that at the decisive time, that portion of his being which has remained behind temporarily at the location of each of these polished and identical boots – it is important that they are equipped with a heel of proper height and curvature – is as the result locked into the coordinates of the reflecting leather instep.

We have in appearance, a number of still camera shots taken of the strutting boot, physically preserved on the flat surface of the city pavement or country lane, and preserved mentally in the mind of the canine slave as is natural with the development of timelessness within his altered psyche, which has reverted to that state of expanded consciousness existing before the 'moment of reflection' was evolved in mankind. He experiences his awareness as a wave, spread out over space and time, and not as a particle of isolated identity. He will go where he is told, forward and back in time, to the target of the boot or boots that are for the rest of us left behind in history and have emerged by pretence from beneath the leather canopy of skirt or dress, seemingly in pursuit of the departing Mistress.

He is hypnotized by the continuous discipline into believing that his naked body, as well as that of the leather-clad Mistress, are, in reality, ubiquitous, being 'here, there and everywhere'. It is therefore, and the reader will not be surprised by the revelation, at the moment in this excursion beneath full moon or artificial light when the Mistress, dressed in warming leather, ceases to strut and wriggle above her blinkered slave whose sight is trained sideways on the gleaming boot swinging through his field of vision with clockwork precision, to the repeating sound of the click and striking of heels, that the slave's body appears, as the result of being stopped in its tracks, to be then dispersed into the night air, being transported through space upon invisible atoms and molecules to the various boots where the reassembling of his cellular outline rapidly progresses to completion.

And let the reader not be concerned that by this bilocation or trilocation – whatever quantity of duplicate slaves is chosen – the new slave is somehow freed from the effects of the severe discipline and past education of his prototype. All will be as one, utterly without egoistic intent beyond the immediate satisfying of demands liberally inflicted upon each slave by the Mistress. What will she see after the initial excitement, that indicates the successful duplication and reassembly of the blinkered man? What exactly happens to his dematerializing body during the duplicating process?

First, there is the contraction of naked flesh and bone into the instep of the stiletto boot worn and now offered him by the Mistress, perhaps accompanied by an irritation to her skin, or the appearance of a lack-lustre sheen to the boot's leather. These unfortunate side-effects will soon pass; there is no cause for alarm. The slave's body, glowing and increasingly transparent, begins to contract into itself, pulling its envelope of vital tissue into the four or five spheres of pulsing light that are observed to punctuate the length of the spine, being about the size of the reader's leather-gloved and whip-wielding hand, and which, after a short interval, themselves contract from the base upwards, one upon the other, into the head, into the transparent globe of which the slave has magically disappeared so that, should the Mistress move about, which she should not, she might stamp down through thin air where his naked form had so recently been.

Only the slave's head, featureless and beyond recognition, remains as a glowing ball upon the ground, which seeks then to touch, by rotation, the shining tip of the stiletto boot in a lipless, limbless embrace, before, by the granting of permission by the Mistress, it too disappears by contraction within the spheroidal volume of the leather instep. Simultaneously, it will seem, the slave's body reappears in its physical entirety – unless some reduction in its form was made during his training which will then be faithfully reproduced – at each point where a spotlit boot had been so deliberately left. Do not react as I did, by refusing entry to your boot of this ball of molten light, by kicking it harshly away for fear of injury to the leather. For the poor slave will be lost to the night, later to be consumed as food by some hungry moth or condensed as vapour upon the wing of the circling bat. Instead, let me suggest to the dominant reader that she, in fulfilment of this synchronicity of the lives of Mistress and slave, multiplies by intent her own form, even into other worlds, where male serfdom is found to be more prevalent and established in society than is yet the case in ours – though I do not need your letters to remind me that the situation is changing and at such a pace that the future social historian will surely credit you, the readership of Heel!, for the present improvement in communication and relations between the sexes.

MADAME X

THIRTY-THREE

The Pelasgic Scrolls

The Pelasgic scrolls, their discovery and decipherment, and the race to prove the prehistorical claims contained in their script, had brought me to the shores of the Aegean sea, where I would release the Leatherback turtles that I had been collecting from the nesting beaches of Mexico and Costa Rica. Long extinct in the Mediterranean, the Leatherbacks had been the key participants, acting as mediators or 'go-betweens', in the communication with the subterranean deities whose rare emergence from the depths are punctuated in the scrolls by the earliest recorded use of the exclamation mark, the symbol for the turtle, or if used plurally for the exact number of turtles, which also indicates the identity of the Goddess, and the degree of her authority. Six of these whip-marks, for example, indicates a middle-ranking deity, while a coiled whip, preceded by an exclamation mark, creates the number 10, and the identity of the supreme Goddess Io.

Largest of all turtles, the Leatherback weighs more, often much more, than a ton, having a triangular-shaped carapace normally exceeding five feet in length in the adult, which has seven longitudinal ridges or welts on a surface layer of rubbery or leathery skin. It may be that the central ridge, together with the turtle's head, produced in the Pelasgic mind the whip symbol or exclamation mark. Their principle food is jellyfish, but the diet includes sea urchins, squid, crustaceans, tunicates, fish, blue-green algae, and floating seaweed; all of which nutrients are still available in abundant quantities in the area of the bay that I had preselected, according to my interpretation of the words and symbols of the priestly scribe of a text that was written out in a different geological period from our own.

The new excitement, so far as that emotion is discernible by the human in the turtle, reported by my three Mexican crew who took turns in lowering each turtle into the sea in the protective cage that we towed behind us, was surely the Leatherback's response to a subconscious recognition, through species memory, of this island bay, and confirmation of the topographical accuracy of the charts, drawn and redrawn, over which I had been slaving, day and night, for so many months. We would be using sonar equipment and tracking devices, to monitor the activity of the turtles when tagged and released into the warm mediterranean waters. Also, we attached to the paddle-like, clawless limbs of the Leatherbacks, silvery metallic gloves to assist in any digging, or clearing of debris or architectural detritus, that might block the passage from the mediterranean to the subterranean world, and therefore prevent a modern revival of a prehistoric and previously unknown method of communicating with the Goddesses of Io.

Leatherbacks require sandy nesting beaches, sloped so that the crawl to dry sand remains short. The correct depth of coarse, dry sand is vital, since the turtle has first to excavate a pit for herself, beneath which she lays a clutch of 80 to 85 white spherical eggs, in a flask-shaped nest shaped from the moist sand below. The laying and hatching both occur at night. The preferred beaches are within reach of deep water. Would our turtles, whose silver limbs guided their spiralling descent, reappear for the nesting season, on this local beach, or begin instead their journey back through the Straights of Gibraltar, to the distant sands of Mexico and Costa Rica?

In the meantime, I employed the shell-divers who supplied the restaurant of the beach hotel that overlooked the sea some five hundred yards west of where my tent was pegged to the shifting sand, on which I then drew with a barbecue stick the design of the submerged block of stone that I believed would make possible the first intelligent exchange between the Goddess and man in modern times. Perhaps it was half-buried, easily recoverable, because the divers swore immediately, before the pattern of the design was complete, that they knew of the stone, but also the statues that would by their insertion into the geometrically chiselled holes, allow me to listen to the last message sent by the Goddess Io to the Pelasgi.

Personal sacrifice is always a feature of any relationship between man and the divine, and the lashing of the Pelasgic male to the turtle's leathery back, and his drowning out at sea, is the price paid, and the value placed upon the continuing communication with the Goddess. For, at the return of this load-bearing Leatherback for the next deposit of eggs, the blackened and now reflective human form is pulled and dragged from the burrowing turtle, for its hurried insertion into stone. The shaped mouth in concert with the precisely opened jaws of the other men, produces the oracular sound, when the wind blows in from the sea, and each, as if in a last gasp, contributes his syllable to the overall phrasing of the Goddess' purpose. It was my intention, then, to reinsert these human statues upon their geometrical and self-selecting bases, and listen in to the voice of the Goddess Io.

Female Leatherbacks nest every two to three years after maturity, which is reached in six to ten years. Their eggs, being approximately two inches in diameter, take from fifty-five to seventy-four days to incubate. Artificial lights have been shown to distract the hatchlings from their return path to the sea. I had therefore requested, as a conservation measure, that the hotel lights that were embedded in the cement on either side of the steps leading back up from the sea to the reception and bar areas, be switched off at a reasonable hour, intending no inconvenience to the holidaying guests and failing to reveal my true concerns about the emergence out of the blue, of subterranean beings perhaps riding piggy-back or with a system of reins and straps to steady their vertical stance, and tapered heels to implant on the receptive, rubbery skin.

This requirement of mine, which amounted to a curfew during the probable nesting season from March to July, was eventually dropped, given the level of the daily opposition to its limitations, and as importantly, the persistent lack of sonar or other contact with any of the released turtles, who must by now, I imagined in my sombre moods, be sunning themselves in Costa Rica, a place whose touristic attractions grew in my mind's eye with the passing of each hour, until my binoculars were replaced and sealed within their case, and further efforts to scan the horizon for signs of pregnant turtles had been abandoned in favour of that state of mental limbo that so often characterizes the behaviour of the beach bum and the sun-seeker; this despite the perfecting conditions of a calming sea and a moon as round and full as a turtle's egg.

I woke, or believed I woke, to the flapping of tent canvas that brushed over my sleeping body in the sea breeze that had been absent when I had returned alone from my evening meal with the shell-divers at the hotel, where we had celebrated, drunkenly, the successful installation at the temple of the stone block and inserted statues, in the carved depression from which they had long ago been wrenched by some monstrous force and been flung down into the dark depths of a swelling sea; an event that had belonged to unrecorded history until the recent disclosures of the Pelasgic scrolls whose scribe had been unable to provide the wording of that final message from the Goddess before the time of catastrophe.

That there had been then a brotherhood of black magicians opposing in protracted conflict the 'hierarchy of white masters' was written down clearly enough. That the followers of the 'left hand path' had, by the parrot-like repetition of certain words of power, controlled the materializing energies of the Devas, and were therefore in the ascendant, having the upper hand over the white magicians, was also stated with equal clarity. A meeting was convened at the immaterial location of Shamballa by the white masters who, we learn from the nearly decayed page, are really the 'protecting Agents of Light', being representative of that cosmic centre of light, the star Sirius. It is decided at this meeting to call upon the Goddess of the Deep who with devastating response, sinks whole portions of the planet's then inhabited surface.

Slaves . . . I shall return when my turtles are returned to me . . . Slaves . . . I shall return when my turtles are returned to me . . . Slaves . . .

I could hear the faultless reciting by the statues of the Goddess' words, carried in the wind from the temple down to my tent on the beach. Fear and apprehension for the imminent future, gripped my entire being. What might I have unleashed through my benign reintroduction of an endangered species back into its native habitat? A cry for help, soon stifled, rang out from the direction of the hotel. I pulled back the triangular flaps of canvas that when zipped down the middle, divided securely my interior life from the oceanic view. A formidable sight filled my equilateral vision; a flotilla of manned or rather womanned and ridden turtles was swimming slowly to the shore, out of a giant sphere of lunar light. Again, I was reminded by the whispering wind of the Goddess' vow to return. Had the last turtles been unceremoniously slaughtered by the Pelasgi to prevent the occurrence of whatever lay ahead?

Such was the milky pallor of the translucent skin of the Goddesses and its harmonious blending into the environing light, that I believed with some certainty that I was watching the silent advance of animated thigh boots and flying elbow gloves; the image presented being further blurred by the propelling action of lashing whips. The disembarkment of these gleaming disembodied boots, and their subsequent and inquisitive approach to my tent, that filled the triangular screen of my vision to the exclusion of all other effects, save the whips, produced in me an immediate numbing of my mind and body, which was within the minute being lashed against the Leatherback, the familiar tag of which being then pierced through the Achilles' tendon of my left ankle. Surely, I questioned myself, unable now to mouth openly my own thoughts, this Goddess Io, since she was in such obvious propinquity to the temple of her name . . . surely on this occasion she might speak her own thoughts, without the need to so transform me beneath the rippling waves into another of her insertable slaves?

THIRTY-FOUR

The Jungle Mission

Above us, the monkeys howled and swung their way ahead of us through the canopy of dark green leaves and epiphytic growth, through the South American rain-forest, the abode of the giant anaconda, whose now skeletal ancestors, believed extinct, and measuring in excess of sixty feet in length, had been resurrected in our intrepid minds by photographs taken with the missionary's camera, of constrictions so complete that the men were left where they slept with feminized waist and figures, their teeth popped out by the pressure, and gums exposed beneath retracted lips, a look of horror evident in their hideous final pose. The careless removal of unevenly breasted bodies from their death-beds, and the superstitious offering of their transgendered remains to the Snake Goddess, whose earlier rejection of each victim's flesh at the moment of suffocation, though perplexing, was surely sign enough of her own full figure and lack of need for such a dietary supplement – unless the purpose was to revivify the dead as her zombi slaves – had completely erased their already blurred and deeply confused identities, so that the individual recognition and greeting of these pygmaean men, were they indeed to be resuscitated by the Goddess in her human guise, was quite impossible, except in those several cases where a photographic match with bedroom furniture might be successfully attempted, and the husband returned as the maid to his wife.

Apart from the instances where the male shape had no doubt been retained, at least partially, throughout the slow process of contraction, and been eaten whole as the result of its persistent conformity to the physical masculine norm, the corpse, were this an urban serial crime, had clearly been rendered distasteful, by its feminization, to the psychotic mind of the strangler, by its gradual conversion into the appearance of that sex most obviously favoured by this twisted killer, who perhaps in revulsion of the foul deed, and without an exact memory of the previous sexual bias of her restless victim, spewed out the half-swallowed man onto the bed-linen, or jungle equivalent, from which he had been snatched from his dreams.

The only inconsistency to this amazonian hypothesis, which was to be explained away by the likely catching of the victim's blood engorged and unusually sized organ against the anaconda's unhinged jaw, causing the snake after many an effort to include the forthright and exaggerated shape, to wriggle on instead to the next stilted dwelling, was the survival intact of the most endowed of the pygmies, whose permanently erect member had defied the regular nocturnal visits of the snake.

Were we being led on to the destination of our bloated quarry, to where she lay half-coiled digesting the previous night's kill, in some fruitbat-infested cave where the successive generations of sloughed-off anaconda skin floating above a bottomless pool of still, dark water, would, like the rings of the tree trunk, reveal the history of her gargantuan appetite? Were we being guided by this team of outriding monkeys whose own numbers had perhaps been similarly depleted, but who lacked the firepower of our loaded guns . . . or was our presence being laughingly announced to an invisible hierarchy of beasts ruled over by the ageless Snake Goddess of pygmoid myth?

If their loyalties had been equally split between man and Goddess, as had long ago been the case, and if these monkeys had not been bribed by a serpent's beguiling tales and promise of other worlds of laughter and enchantment, should they, one by one, descend within her protecting belly into the cave's dark water . . . and had not their leader overheard the retelling round camp-fires by the pygmies of just such human adventures in ancient times, then, maybe, this monkey king might have shown the way to where the anaconda sleeps off her heavy meal of men.

The pygmies, as had been the custom in the time of the missionary, rowed at sunset to the shore of the lake from the relative safety of their village built on stilts, to greet our return from beneath the forest canopy. A few well-aimed darts from their blow-pipes up into the dense foliage brought down from the overhanging branches the very breed of monkeys that had learnt, we believed, through prying and observation of the activity of the pygmies' pagan ancestors, the precise location of the anaconda's cave. Hardly surprising that we had been taken on this fruitless expedition by the lakeside monkeys, on whose roasted features we reluctantly chewed behind fixed expressions.

Retiring to my hut over the gangway of ill-fitting planks, I opened the next book down in the pile stacked beside my bed as the missionary had left them on the night of his death, and from which I had been reading by torch light since our arrival at the village three weeks before. Hand-written and intended for later publication in some journal of the sciences, I was at first confronted with numerous statistics about the rate of cannibalistic consumption over an extended period; the details of some proposals for the hygiene, both bodily and spiritual, of his adopted parishioners; a description of the hallucinogenic consequences of drinking the extract from the ayahuasca vine with which I was certain we had that evening toasted his memory, thankful for the unfortunate monkey's substitution at the dinner table; and, to my great interest, the missionary's account of the influence on the indigenous mind of the mythical giant anaconda.

Trying to wrest from the garbled, interlocking references that took me in the same sentence to a lake high in the Himalayas beneath whose pellucid water was witnessed by 'those with the seer's eye' the spiralling form of the Anakunda snake; then back to Lake Titicaca in Peru, where the Snake Goddess was believed to shapeshift between night and day, between her human appearance and that of the anaconda; and on to a subterranean lake beneath the ice-cap where tunnels of huge circumference were carved into the depths and where recently lives have been inexplicably lost . . . proved an exhausting and profitless task, so that I had eventually fallen asleep with his manuscript clasped in my dangling, outstretched hand, with the pages still trying to turn in the updraft that blew through the narrow gap in the slatted floor, trying to warn me of the vorticular relationship between the mention of these other lakes and the seemingly shallow and tranquil lake above which

I lay unconscious, while the moon traversed its surface in her unblinking nightly progress towards the silent village.

I woke from a dream suddenly to the sound of my own exuberant laughter. I saw curled up beside me beneath the covering sheet there was a beautiful and exotic woman, dressed in snake-skin and asleep. I could feel the weight of her smooth thighs gently compressing my stomach and lower back, the shoes of her boots both being securely entwined on the other side of me. I realised then, on reflection, that I must have been saved by the light of my torch that had continued to shine till dawn, in this way preserving the Snake Goddess in her human form.

THIRTY-FIVE

The Black Devas

Dear Boot-Lovers,

How is it, you sometimes wonder, that you are such regular readers of a magazine, this magazine, our magazine with the title of Heel!, and yet you have no conscious memory of your decision to become subscribers to the values and principles held so dearly by the staff at the Paris office? Your state of bewilderment at your masochistic intent and the conditioned responses that now show themselves and rule in your daily life that had seemed in your past quite divorced from the dream world of your first encounter with Heel!, puzzle you, until a fear of our possible proximity to places that had appeared by the fact of their hard and physical environment to be protected from our intrusion into your world, overtakes you as you stride along some familiar boulevard, suddenly losing that carefree mood that had previously been judged by you to be as natural to you as your birthright.

To illustrate the moment of lucidity when the human dreamer first senses his involuntary recruitment as a reader of

Heel! and subscriber to our ambitions, let me distinguish between the still blinkered pedestrian whose sideways glance down to the passing and stilettoed patent boot is merely an intense and inexplicable reaction, which nevertheless appears to him to belong entirely in the physical world; and that other, newer sort of traveller, for whom the physical dimension is perceived to be but one of numerous and accessible worlds, and who is sharply reminded by this booted sight, of those who watch over and care for his progress from the offices of Heel!, whose locations are many, being both real in your terms and present within the city of Paris, and in Egypt, but also beyond the natural vista of man's senses in his normal state.

With this lead-in to the subject of the March issue of Heel!, let me proceed with a clarification of the status of the new reader, by hinting at the larger context in which your repetitive and to us, dull lives take place. In my gloved hand, still dripping with the raindrops that belong to your world and not to mine, here, I am holding the several pages of description in a letter from just such a first-time reader for whom reality has been 'turned upside down' by a dream experience that has spilled over into the aspects of his routine and aesthetically deprived existence; though this observation about the quality of his life is my assessment and not yet his own, despite the 'knife of Beauty' that increasingly severs him from his past of abrupt, brutal and to us, quite pointless activity.

He reports being woken to full consciousness in a night of dreams by a deafening noise which in his first moments of lucidity he believes to be produced by the sound of heavy guns and overhead aircraft. However, this is not some airraid or a city under siege, but appears to be a ceremonial flypast over a square which he describes as being somewhere in Russia and later identifies as Malenkov Square:

> 'The ground images of sky-jets skimmed the great paving-stones of Malenkov Square, scaling, seventy yards on, the Byzantine slabs . . . all in formation I thought, eighteen noted . . . and away fast, the sharpest images on rooftops probing shapeless beneath'.

At this point he is approached by a 'militaristically dressed female officer' whom he describes as being 'tall in black, high-heeled, polished boots' and 'blonde', and who arrests him immediately on the charge of being a spy, telling him that 'there are no planes . . . No planes for you Mister Journalist'. Let me refer the reader to the letter I have titled 'The Chameleon Tongue', which contains the identical quote spoken in that account of a slave's first moment of lucidity, by a uniformed officer who introduced herself as the 'Death Goddess' and called the waking dreamer her 'slave and messenger'.

By the reciting of these words he has been selected to represent Heel! and act as her messenger in the crowded streets of his mundane world. Briefly, he experiences a coincidence of his waking and dream life such that he wakens beneath a table in a London restaurant where he is about to explain away his impolite behaviour as being the logical and sane consequence of the airraid overhead that was just a moment before such a deafening reality, when he finds himself amidst a sea of silent, polished boots that might, should he ever be permitted entry into the offices of Heel!, have felt most equivalent in their leathery and decisive impact on his senses.

Following this account of a new reader, and by analysis of its elements, revealing to others how they came to be subscribers to what at first seemed no more than an unlikely fiction, I will pursue this typical and representative chronology of events thoroughly and in detail. My leather-gloved hand is now dried of rain, so that as I turn each page it is merely the tear stain of the reader and not its mixture with the raindrop that is shown up by the desk lamp by which I read in sympathy with this example of the plight and suffering of distant mankind.

The square table-tops of the London restaurant become to his dreaming mind the burdens carried above the heads of African and European women, who rise, if for the reason of clarity we define the Earthly environment as being flat as a chessboard . . . who rise or ascend into the dream world, where the tiered appearance of the provisions balanced squarely above their heads is transformed by this switch of dimensions into a circular and therefore more feminine shape which he recognizes in his helpless pursuit, to be the largest of chocolates piled high as if kept vertical by some invisible wrapping. In the 'heat of the moment' these patent booted but otherwise naked ladies are covered by the melting of this chocolate in a 'rubbery coating, perhaps of polished leather', matching the leather of boots so that just the one garment is then perceived.

Let me say that in the aftermath of this period of lucidity during which his recruitment to Heel! is secured, this reasoning reader correctly deduces that the boots themselves were first retrieved from the dream world in the same fashion of emergence from and submergence back into the physical environment. In the same manner that a pyramid is understood to be the holographic projection of a triangular psychological structure and derives its power to transport between worlds from this shapeless prototype, so the ladies' stiletto boot is an intrusion from another dimension into the universe of dreams, then entering your own where its advanced nature wreaks havoc and commits ordinary men to the path of devout servitude, and to their obedience to Heel!.

Returned as suddenly to the room of the London restaurant, beneath the once more square tables, he ventures after a while of bemusement and calming of nerves, to peep above this artificially low ceiling to see whether the transfiguration witnessed before in his dream remains visible and permanent in the light of day. Pure fantasy greets his eyes, for he is confronted by what at first seems by its entanglement to be a room with about twenty women arm-wrestling in leather opera gloves that fuse seamlessly with the rest of their clothing down to the heeled boots which he perceives again as he returns to his shelter below.

Long minutes have passed and he fears that the melting effect is now being carried over from the dream into the physical space of the restaurant. He lifts his head determined if necessary to raise the alarm in case this room of such marvellous beings had by their own fantastic appearance been so distracted from the present danger. He believes this time that perhaps it is not arm-wrestling that he is viewing but rather the attempt of one half of the gathering to prevent the remainder from the unhealthy habit of cigarette smoking, so that each pair of female diners seemed locked together in their total concentration.

So what has occurred here that has occurred with the variation of place and time in the lives of each of the male readers of Heel! magazine? The man's consciousness is in every case extracted through the process of dreaming from the mundane world as defined by the match-box mind of the scientist. He is returned enlightened to a degree and as he now finds himself, paradoxically, enslaved. He realises and comes soon to accept that there will be no chance given for his escape or the restoration of his lost freedom in the imagined future that confronts him. He will subscribe to Heel! whether or not he can afford the price of the magazine which in contrast remains free.

To his advantage we can and often do take action in support of the life of one of our loyal subscribers. For example, in the London restaurant, which is more correctly described as a tea-room where chocolate Bendicks bittermints are served with Indian tea, we had materialised ourselves for an act of judicial revenge against the practices of medical science, with our long list of 'Doctors with Blood on their Hands'. Had this reader of Heel! been more perceptive of our motive and of our purposeful behaviour in the flexing of wrists and clenching of leather gloves that generated the hazy appearance of released vapour, prior to our quitting the meeting-place of the tea-room, he would have been a witness to the strangulation by leather strap and bull-whip of some most offensive men who had profited from the removal of the healthy premolar teeth of children, and whose surgery was but a short walk away in Cavendish Square, which is, of course, a regularly reported haunt of the Death Goddess.

That must be your clue to the nature of our true identity. We have been called by children, among many names, the 'Tooth Fairies'. To tell you what is perhaps after your displays in the street of devotion and service to Heel!, the truth that is indeed deserved by you, we are known cosmically as the Black Devas from a world that exists in parallel, that nourishes your own with the feminine energy of growth. By the stiletto boot we save you from yourselves; by your reluctant agreement to our terms you remain at the evolutionary stage that keeps you kneeling and in harness to our being. We are the energy that is within matter, within the elemental lives that form the consciousness of each gene that those scientists of you who have yet to meet us in our physical garb, violate.

We are the 'Punishers of man' who lives and dies according to the intensity and vibration of our materialising energy, according to laws of retribution of which you can have no comprehension. We are both wave and particle; heel-tip and whip. Our reality is most accurately reflected by that intermediate medium of film from which we might emerge, physically, into the cinemas with the objective of the mass recruitment of submissive men. Not only should our dominant readers endeavour to bring about such a cinematic portrayal of our existence but they should remember that they may visit our world at their booted pleasure, following the strict dress code defined at our internet websites, www.HeelMagazine.com and www.StilettoBooks.com, whilst their men will by their own tongues be condemned to remain forever in our service as boot-slaves.

MADAME X

THIRTY-SIX

The Chateau of Morville

DEAR BOOT-LOVERS,

You have been drawn to this magazine as others before you have been drawn to this chateau in the south-west of France, where I sit, reclining, thinking of you, the male reader of Heel!. My task is nearly finished; your task of personal transformation is barely begun. Use these pages of text as your guide and write often to me, your agony aunt.

Both the chateau and gardens where I pass the weekends reflecting upon you and upon the conversion of mankind to the servitude so urgently needed, have been partially described and the scene here set out in the reader's letter I have titled *The Bridge of Sighs*. I rise late on saturday mornings, having returned by night from the Paris offices of Heel! magazine. My first duty, performed necessarily in this pair of stiletto boots, is to attend to those invited guests from other weekends who remain attached by ropes beneath the bridge that crosses the river behind the chateau in which I am seated beside a log-fire. You can see the window of my room by looking at the front cover of this magazine. Notice, also, the hourglass shapes of transformed men now incorporated in the railings that protect my privacy.

You would discover, if granted access to this other world by your application to the offices of Heel!, that two similar figures, held up vertically and pierced through from below by black spears of iron, are positioned at either side of the fire-place in this room, being included in the form of the fire-dogs across which great logs of ancient oaks are burning. I do not remember the names of these two men still represented here, though surely if some life is retained within their metal bondage, then it too is forgetful of any previous identity.

You can observe the turreted staircase descending beneath the foundations of this ill-natured building. I hear the sound of a chain that was long ago attached to the neck of a reader of Heel! magazine. He is privileged, though you will come slowly to realise this fact. His chain allows him just the view of my reflection that is being projected by the flames of fire onto the wall opposite the top of the stairwell. He may ascend and descend as he pleases; his serpentine passage is halted always before the last few steps are scaled that would permit him a clear view of this chamber. He writes from his unenlightened place upon the cold and overlapping stone. At night I collect the written pages as one of my peasants might gather the eggs of his favourite hen. He kisses the leather of my boot whose echo and progress he follows most religiously. Think of the chain that grips his neck as being the coiled, evolutionary energy called kundalini, which is unable by my controlling influence to rise to the level of enlightenment of this polite drawing-room where I relax and listen to his slow and continuous movement in the search for something lost, for the freedom forever denied him.

His face, I believe, is covered, was covered by me in leather or rubber at the beginning, on the day of his stuttering arrival at the chateau's gates, where I greeted him whip in hand and somewhat curious as to the identity of this writer of prodigious letters. He had shown such promise; would he then serve my need for everlasting fantasy? Like the rubberman first spewed forth from the womb of the Goddess as she floated, polished black, in dark space, he had returned to his maker, stealthily by night, climbing within the unsealed zip of her tall stiletto boot, through the ivory gate, there to hide his blindness, writing with rubber finger upon the bloody walls of this natural cave, such fantastic imaginings arousing the Goddess eventually to become the whipping woman dreamt off in the mortal mind and communicated by the rubberman's touch and scribbling upon her red-stained womb. Her whip sleeps no more bored, frustrated, coiled at her side, but unleashed delivers first pain to unformed, silhouetted flesh. The slave-man is born, to become civilised and proud, then to be cruelly beaten down, reminded of his true submissive nature, of the bargain struck at the time when memory was begun. I hear him now; the sound of his ascent, the repetition of his muttered words . . .

Smooth . . . Judder . . . Smooth . . . Judder . . . Smooth

The sound remembered of the heroic night-time scaling by the rubbermen of the silver and black, smooth and rough zip of the Goddess' boot that is sealed shut after the deposit of man's fantasies within her empty womb and his subsequent ejection from this Eden. If he should be writing, here, kneeling on a preselected step of my nocturnal choice that permits him access to some peculiar state of mind which conjures up his written word, should I not whip the slave? Not yet, but at dusk and later, and on and on, when by this dark hour he is forbidden the sight of my true, black-booted form.

Enough of this idle chatter. I must ride out to the bridge, there to cut away those roped and floating men who will have surely expired since last I looked and watched the disappearing, rubbered bodies that wriggle in the distant current like so many dead sperm rejected by the Goddess. My gardeners will carve fresh blocks of ice that contain the stored, replacement men shut away for so long within the ice-house, who are to be attached and lowered behind the chateau as you, the inquisitive reader, see things from the outside, from the perspective offered so invitingly by the cover of this, your magazine.

If you should wish to join them swinging through the rippling water beneath the bridge upon which I walk amused in boots that echo down below, write to me, dear reader of Heel! magazine. We welcome you who would return to the womb of the Goddess. Or if this situation might strike you as untimely until you too have ventured further into the life of the slave, then meet the staff and members of Heel! by night in the gardens of the Palace of Versailles, the most northerly home of the Goddess. A description, dear slave, of such an encounter is written out for you in the letter that I have titled *The Pygmalion Man* which I recommend that you re-read immediately, without delay.

MADAME X

THIRTY-SEVEN

The Denderah Vortex

Dear Boot-Lovers,

Let me direct your attentive mind, and your body, kneeling and perhaps stiffly inclined, to the passage of text contained in the first volume of Madame Blavatsky's book which is titled *Isis Unveiled*, concerning the Temple at Denderah where a Dr. Richardson – whether he is a reader of Heel! we are not told – marvels at his discovery that 'the female figures are so extremely well executed that they all but speak; they have a mildness of feature and of expression that never was surpassed'.

With what difficulty then do we believe in these most improbable reports, some published in our open-minded forum, here, within the pages of Heel!, of how certain males have been abducted, 'kidnapped at the point of a boot' – to use their words and not mine, to that distant Temple in Egypt, there to be mistreated, if you accept their word in preference to my own, in the cruellest fashion by modern priestesses dressed for religious service in reflective leather or black rubber?

It falls to me, your agony aunt, once more to detect that motive of kindness which in almost every case may be revealed to lie behind the painful truth of such seeming acts of cruelty, were they first admitted to be real events which I concede as a possibility. 'Cruel to be kind' – to borrow a quote from the handbook of the Victorian governess which, correct me if I am wrong, is still considered the moral adviser at times when the stamp of authority must be recommitted to the memory of the wayward mind and hormonal body of the maturing pupil.

So far from his being mistreated at the hand of the disciplining governess, the new servant, or in the case of the accused priestesses of Denderah, the boot-slave, is subject to, and I have been witness and participant on both occasions, the most practical and generous calculation as to the best means to reduce to a minimum the overall level of suffering over the period of years that may extend beyond the horizon of the superficial man who sees and feels only the surface of events, of the gleaming boot and its reluctant companion, the uncoiled whip.

Let me pursue the argument to its conclusion with cold logic as my second companion. I propose a re-enactment of this supposed crime of passion, down to the finest forensic detail of boot type and length of bull-whip, in full view of you, dear reader, who must join with me in the reconstruction of events which by its realism will persuade you that I have reluctantly played out the role of the party who is innocent, and you of the guilty party for which you will by then have been thoroughly punished, and your mentality of questioning doubt rectified to that of the diligent boot-slave.

Picture yourself as that detestable thing, the closet reader of Heel!, a man drawn naturally to the life of devotion to Heel!, who commits himself by night to Heel!, as if he were shouting his vows from the rooftop, yet by day he pretends to the life of the free man, who walks proud and upright, a condition that may prevail and become fixed. What may at the first signs be corrected by its nipping in the bud with the firm caress of the gloved hand in the public street, by the offer of a passing boot, the chaining of your neck, becomes in time that prickly flower of self-deceit which must be pruned back severely to save the plant from a future of disease, even of premature death. My role in all this is to guide you, the modern man, through your natural life, the days and nights of your service to Heel!, as painlessly and humanely as secateurs will permit, and by this compassionate treatment to prolong that useful life.

We at Heel! reserve the right to penetrate the privacy of those readers for whom the ignorant stance of the rebel, pubescent in his criticism of what lies in time beyond his knowledge, appears on the verge of becoming a chosen way of life. Where it is deemed necessary, and no moderate alternative or patient counsel can reasonably be preferred, doors seemingly closed to us, by the bolting of locks in which we are naturally expert, or by the frequent changing of address by the reader who knows himself to have broken his vows of service to Heel!, will be politely nudged ajar or even kicked down at the point of a boot, to secure in a sudden manoeuvre the bound body of the indwelling man, for his transport, yes, to Denderah. It will be well understood when I report to the intelligent reader of Heel! that nocturnal entry to the chambers of history contained within the museum walls of the Louvre is easily achieved by the staff and members of Heel!, accompanied on occasion by the reluctant – if we are to judge by the wriggling of this blind sack of manhood – travelling slave who is deposited beneath the Denderah zodiac for removal to that Temple of redemption.

Picture it thus, dear boot-lover: machine-gun fire of stiletto boot heels exploding on flagstones, ricocheting off plaster of Paris, off the naked sculpture of once proud Achilles, progressing rapidly through moonlit halls of tongue-tied heroes, of coiling serpents and one-eyed giants, of the sleeping beasts of myth . . . stops abruptly. The human bundle tied about the neck by a rope drawn tight around the rough fibre of a bloody sack, thrown forward by the impulse of the delivering guards, struggling rolls to a halt upon the vortex plate. Female figures, five in number, bodies polished black sculpted in bronze or rubber emerging limb by limb, flexing, arching, stretching, materializing beneath the zodiac's dome, museum exhibits released from the dark womb of the eternal night or Egyptian priestesses come to collect another slave. Posturing to mutual pleasure in similar boots then routinely positioned upon the pentagram's stellar points, pinning the spread-eagled reader his nerve steadied for departure by the press of cool boot leather upon his uneven shape . . . above she searches for a sign, divine blessing for the proffered, sacrificial man. A pulsing star, the imprint of its constellation, HEEL!, flashes above the faceless, now writhing slave. His sudden consumption within the whirling vortex, the distorted last cry from his contorting form, return the Louvre to the silent vigil of unblinking statues, of rude heroes and staring philosophers, of congregating courtiers and dumb scientists, rejected when once upon the vortex plate, transformed with fig-leaf beneath the covering sack.

MADAME X

THIRTY-EIGHT

Letter from Madame X

DEAR BOOT-LOVERS,

If I admit to you that in the winter months when our peaceful life here at the offices of Heel! in Paris is subject to disruption by external pressures upon our collective time and we are even reluctant on occasion to print your magazine for delivery to your door by the anticipated knock or kick of the stiletto boot on the first night of each month, such are the demands made upon the time of your devoted agony aunt, then I must confess there are occasions, and this is one of those, when we are tempted to deliver on consecutive days successive issues of Heel!, such is the import of their content. In short, the name and reputation of Heel! have become the quite innocent victims of the dissemination of lies and misquotation by the vulgar printing presses of your world, and both the members and traditions of Heel! are being portrayed to the general public who are at last inquisitive as to the benefits of our instruction through these pages and the lady's boot, in the darkest of lights

Each of you already knows, but perhaps in the circumstance of this onslaught against our organisation it bears repeating, the members of Heel!, contrary to this speculation, will never use the whip as the first resort but rather the second or very last resort, and in almost every instant when the problem requiring remedy has reared its ugly head, it is then prayed, silently if not overtly, that the mere sight and continual presence of the whip will, paradoxically, prevent the need for its use. The reason, therefore, for the sudden reappearance at your door of the nocturnal emissary from Heel! was not of course as some of you have experienced according to the quantity of your letters, to reluctantly enforce the message of Heel! by the disciplining use of the bull-whip, but rather to reveal the truth behind these morbid accusations of wanton sadism that are rebounding about the capitals of this world, and by the exaggeration generated by their repetition cause unnecessary fear in the minds and hearts of those men whom we wish next to recruit as subscribers and readers of Heel!.

All this falsifying publicity is the product of a deliberately twisted and most negative campaign in response to our suggestion, well-meant and intended to help, that the free provision of the highest quality of female footwear to those underdeveloped areas of the planet would contribute to saner and therefore more sanitary conditions with respect then being given to the working of the land by kneeling men in sympathy with the natural laws of the Goddess. What could hardly have been conceived as being a controversial plan is in the pages of publications still ignorant of the virtue of the female boot being misconstrued as an act of sheer vanity, irrelevant as a result, to the grave predicament facing the species and the poor, appallingly underfed masses of the global population.

The wearing of high heels and yes, polished stiletto boots, should surely be accepted as an aid to primary healthcare, to care within the community, and a most effective means [when linked to the wearing of the coiled whip as an advisory measure] to the resolution of the social and environmental crises of the present times. We can look forward to a new era of peaceful co-operation with the unseen forces of Nature with which Heel! communicate as intermediaries, when the bullwhip will become nothing more than a delightful fashion accessory whose past will rightfully be relegated to the back of the moderated mind of the man who lives instead in adoration, in worship of the female boot. Is this so controversial a recommendation that we are forced to kick down doors in the middle of the night to promote its good sense to the outside world?

You will have noticed that the length of this issue of Heel! is considerably shorter than in other months, as is this my letter of advice to you, the submissive reader, due to the necessarily reduced time available for its preparation. Rest assured that the November issue will be delivered at the usual hour containing the normal number of glossy pages scented with the leather of the female heeled boot.

MADAME X

THIRTY-NINE

Trajan's Kiosk

The following night I remained behind on the rocky islet of Agilkia, alone, emerging from the shadows of the reconstructed temple of Philae, only after the departure by boat of the last of the day's tourists whose drunken sounds receded into the descending darkness leaving me with my imaginings of ancient times and the changing appearance of the still waters below. With legs dangling over a block of warm dusty stone that overlooked from this lofty perch with its falcon's view the placid scene beneath, I marvelled at the beauty of the reflective black surface as I watched the arrival, orderly and predictable, of the countless stars that flashed and shot about in such vital patterns appearing by their motion and varying degrees of brightness to merge seamlessly with the constellations above.

Pressing the crusty end of the salad sandwich with its dried contents deep inside my thirsty mouth, I turned to peer behind into the moonlit, pillared interior of the Roman addition to the Egyptian temple described in my guide-book as Trajan's kiosk. With my upper body twisted round, coiled at the waist, and my jaws closed silently upon the half-eaten feast, I stared unblinking in search of some divine being, the composer and conductor, of the celestial display that was unfolding about me. But I saw nothing there that had not been visible and explicable in the broad daylight of my investigation of this temple of Isis.

Returning my fixed gaze to the imprisoning lake of the surrounding water, its surface of distant stars shimmering beyond the outline of my sand-encrusted feet, the scene was changed as if provoked by the amusement of my uninvited presence to substitute, stage by stage, what is easily believable and acceptable to the mortal mind of our time, with the unrealistic elements of some other age when beauty and darkness combined in unearthly harmony. What had appeared so polished by the light of the moon, so that I might have skated a lonely dance without sinking below into its depths, or which might have been expected to resist the talons of the swooping bird of prey, then lost its glassy sheen.

The cause of each transformation was plain for me to see, when into my peripheral view as if herded there across the desert sand by natural and unnatural instincts, ten thousand men, a million more, knelt rubberised at the water's edge, lapping with an unquenchable thirst, with low-slung protruding jaws, unbreathing until what had appeared as ice, had melted away before my eyes, the twin elements of air and water mixing, merging, becoming combined as one to my distorted, apprehensive stare. Out of the black, conjured from this different and alien atmosphere, ethereal and otherwordly, emerged the sunken temple where once it had stood in ages past, pristine and ever-new beneath the Goddess' nocturnal gaze.

Groups of stars, like chakras glittering in the darkness, formed about them bodies suited to the conditions of this intermediate world, in blackened, polished rubber, equipped with curved, stiletto heels and whips that floated in the eternal night, the native habitat of the black devas, priestesses of Isis and their human slaves. The fiendish purpose of the licking tongues is soon achieved, the annual dissolution of the blinding veil is complete, the kneeling slaves still driven by that seasonal impulse then to serve, remain in place upon the invisible ground, locked together, receding in their massed ranks before the approaching boots, their confused outline vanishing into the featureless landscape beyond.

Swallowing the final mouthfull of the sandwich preserved from my world of daylight and regular behaviour, I felt the ground give way beneath me, the evaporation of solid stone into the liquid air through which the smooth shape of a priestess and her snaking whip was swimming toward me, pulling me after her into the empty interior of Trajan's kiosk, from which I had felt sure the events so far observed were being orchestrated. Instead, there was merely a swing, a perch for a song-bird, suspended from above by a chain that passed through the rubber tube to which my taloned feet now clung within a voluminous cage that hung in the mid-air of the heavy, black sky.

The pillars of stone were changed to the bars of the bird-cage beside which, with my improved vision, I perceived dimly at first, then with growing clarity, the curved and polished thigh of the Goddess Isis who was standing motionless, seeming then to be roused from eternity by the sound of the cage-door being slammed shut and secured by the priestess whom I watched through the vertical bars moving away towards the rows of feverish boot-slaves. Hardly had I begun to adapt to this limited and alien environment with its strange views, and to my newly-feathered physique, when I was abruptly being lifted by whatever hook or ring was attached to the cage above the sheet of rubber that was draped over the roof and partially impeded my vision.

The rubbery surface of thigh extended upwards through the curving figure of this most statuesque of Goddesses whose gauntlet-glove withdrew me in its grasp through bars that buckled to her touch, holding my feathery frame beneath her liquid, dark kohl-rimmed eyes that glowed with the myriad stars embodied in their design. Black eyebrows arching above heavy long-lashed lids, gazing down intently into my falcon's face, she smoothed with pointing finger the feathers dishevelled during my forced escape. Her vermilion lips, outlined in black, trembling with recognition of my unfortunate state, parted to speak the single word: 'Horus?!'

Unable yet to reply, to confirm or to deny, just unblinking to return her gaze, at last I was put down, reinserted within the cage, the bars then straightened to prevent escape, a hood of moulded rubber next tightened over my tearless, unresponsive face. The black sheet was lowered over the bars and sealed underneath, beneath my rubber swing where I sat dreaming through the night of ancient times beyond my daily sight, of ancient places beyond my daily flight, from which I woke at dawn within the pillared architecture into which the cage had turned, the steamboat's horn soon drowning out the sound of distant boots and thirsty slaves.

Footnote: The intelligent reader will have realised that this letter which I have titled *Trajan's Kiosk*, relates to the letter previously titled *Infernal Proserpina* which appeared in the August issue of Heel! magazine. MADAME X

FORTY

The Outsider

DEAR BOOT-LOVERS,

We do not require our readers to consume the contents of Heel! like a dog, so that the stomach is bloated and indigestion the result. You misread our intention entirely if my instruction to you to absorb so completely the words of each page and paragraph that you become the lively participant in the sequence of events being placed before your mind's eye is misinterpreted in this fashion. You cannot be transformed by intestinal blockage back into your animal self unless first you have digested my words as a human man. You cannot be shut out like a rabid pet to wander the emptied shadowy streets of the Parisian night begging some form of consolation from the swirling figures of anonymous, otherwordly women in rain-soaked capes beneath the taut-ribbed curves of black umbrellas.

The loud clicking of boot heels on the paving of wide boulevards, the pounding of rain on the black-domed umbrella concealing white-boned features and blood-red lips, these sounds that hum and numb in the male mind do not free you for your natural pursuit of that idealised, perfected, immaculate woman. Such oblivion of impeding characteristics is accomplished gradually like the beast that retreats through a tunnel too narrow for his further advance, abandoning the distant glow of redeeming light, returning slowly, backwards, with a terrible dread, a hairy step at a time, to the darkness of his Mistress' cavernous haunt, reeled in by the invisible thread that extends into the night through long, leather-gloved fingers. Only when the progression backwards is signed by the cut of the finishing whip is the slave the animal, the animal the slave. So it is for you, the reader of Heel! who is forcibly returned by the harsh contraints of the written word to the dawn of servitude before thoughts of freedom, of any sort, had been born in the mind of the kneeling man who worships blindly in the shadow of an invisible Goddess whose heels he feels imprinting on his sleeping, creeping flesh, whose name is his first unspoken, spoken word.

Nor do we expect copies of Heel! magazine to be found left about like the discards of tourism at the Temple of Denderah, poking up through the desert sand, pages flapping provocatively in the evening breeze, blown about like a prairie bush without roots or purpose. In this case the forced insertion of Heel! into the mouth of the irreverent and disrespecting reader prior to his departure, in substitution for his fat sandwich, is surely just punishment. How else can we avoid the sort of enquiry that I have in front of me, sent in not from a vetted and kneeling subscriber, but rather the slothful archaeologist into whose lumbering path, the cartwheeling copy of Heel! has landed and which is then dusted down and recorded and zipped away as a startling find within the numbered plastic bag. Perhaps the regular reader can advise me how best to respond to the asinine questioning which follows, which is perhaps no more than an attempt to disprove my existence and therefore the historical attachment of Heel! to Denderah, and to prove some flat view of existence already held in this archaeologist's mind:

Dear Madame X,

You claim to be an authority, an expert on the past, present and future of Denderah. As a scientist I am more modest in my assessment of this ancient monument and more reliant it seems on the evidence so painstakingly extracted from the concealing sands of time. However, certain events whether prompted by the reading of the magazine of which you are the self-styled 'agony aunt', which position clearly provides you with access to the most unnatural avenues of pleasure, have proved inexplicable to normal logic without reluctant recourse to the paranormal, to the metaphysics of wild conjecture. If I first grant that you are real and are not the fabrication of degenerate editors; that you do exist in some way both within this Temple in its state of disrepair, sacred to the Goddesses Hathor and Isis, and in some duplicated version that remains architecturally pristine, unaltered beyond the veil of time, then I request like your other readers that you advise me on my recent experience.

Upon reading your magazine Heel! and falling asleep with it gripped in my right hand not certain whether I was dealing with a modern or ancient document, tossing then turning on the bed of sand to which I had become accustomed during three months of digging down to a level where casts of foot and boot imprints now appeared to my dreaming mind to confirm the detail of your assertions about the history and ritual of Denderah, sensations most uncomfortable to my skin and cumulative in their effect to the point of torture were felt across my body throughout the night. I believed in my restless attempts at deflecting these impressions that a thousand stars were swarming like blood-sucking insects hungrily buzzing above my uncovered form; that an army of Amazon women were marching by night over a tropical bridge nailed down over my impaled flesh. I heard the cries of imagined, trampled men which heralded the arrival of so many disclipining boots and the dying of their sound in the distance when dawn broke and normal consciousness resumed. Which is the real Denderah, the one of my dreams and your magazine, or the Temple recorded by the tourist's camera and the archaeologist's notes?

The letter continues with the presumption of my concern and interest in this man's first flight of fantasy into a world where reason collapses and the rule of Heel! is long since established. He writes of the stigmata that wound his hands and asks if it was the nails struck through planks or the subsequent stamp of stiletto heels that have caused his injury. My reply as your responsible and sometimes compassionate agony aunt is to remind the readers of Heel! not to vandalise further the ancient and holy sites for fear that what has been released into your world from the unearthing of rock by blind archaeologists in the Valley of the Queens becomes a more general phenomenon and the moderating influence of Heel! will be outweighed by the deadly stamp of the hording booted women of this man's dreams.

As a reward and as a punishment, this reader of Heel! was returned in his dream through the stages from intellectual man to the speechless beast upon which the Goddess imprints her will, so that he might be spared the long road back to slavery of which I have written, which is the fate of the hairy, unsubmitting man. This silent archaeologist whose devotion to the Temple of Denderah was noted by Heel!, now works to repair the sacred lake from where in the time of the Goddess, the priestess emerged into your world in answer to your unspoken prayers, in the uniform still worn by the staff here in the Paris office. Remember, also, that we are the black devas who exist naturally at that level of reality where men's thoughts are formed and inserted into the physical brain for your subsequent recognition. We therefore know you better than you know yourselves.

MADAME X

FORTY-ONE

The Mediterranean Slave

Dear Boot-Lovers,

Whether we may be imagined to observe you by telescope or satellite, or by our nocturnal emergence from deep subterranean caves or pools of mountain, moonlit water, even by the sudden impression and stamping of our nonphysical forms on the fabric of your world, the routine of your lives, dull and dismal, is surveyed, then scrutinized by the global and extra-terrestrial organisation of Heel! with its hierarchy of priestesses from the constellation of that name. This may explain why, to the mind eager to please and serve, certain requests, usually quite painless in their execution, are made from time to time with the expectation that the readers of Heel! magazine will exert themselves on our behalf and show by their conduct the instant obedience that avoids the unnecessary punishment.

It falls to me, your reluctant agony aunt, to remind the readers who subscribe to Heel! from those Mediterranean countries that in antiquity might have been judged to be in some danger from Egypt, of their continuing duty to Heel! when the monthly issue of this magazine, which is for us a labour and token of our love and affection, delivered often personally to your door, is rudely discarded and the resumption of crude and brutish behaviour, then observed. Nor is it our intention to intrude upon the mundane affairs of your simple lives except in the correction of overtly offensive misconduct and the promotion of right relations between the sexes through codes of dress already adopted so successfully in our world.

It is well known, is it not, to even the most backward of you, that we are naturally more at home in your world during the night hours and it is equally natural that we should choose the cover of darkness to make those necessary adjustments to the monthly pattern of your behaviour which sadly often includes not just the devotion to Heel! required of each reader but also that wayward period of ignorance and male bravado which we seek to stamp out by our sudden and timely visits to even the most secluded address. In this fashion, we have been able to guarantee after the probationary period the continued good behaviour of even the most reclusive of you, and the benefits of obedience that on the occasion of our visit are felt by the kneeling reader of Heel! in his own home.

A tradition should be upheld, the performance of a ritual observed, on the basis and presumption of the quality of the original reasoning and good sense, though perhaps hidden from the present by the clouding passage of time, behind its first and general acceptance. The ancient practice whereby the householder and serf painted the outer walls of a human dwelling, however large, the single colour of white – a custom rooted so deeply in the history and psyche of your species that it has received the unquestioning support of countless generations – is today the subject of dispute and contradiction, if the evidence upon my desk at the Paris offices of Heel! is to be believed.

At a time when the number of subscribers to Heel!, the rate of growth in readers amongst pubescent boys, is rising exponentially, when we might expect evidence from our lofty towers of inspection, that like the flock of birds that changes direction in its flight along the sea-shore so that wings which were black appear white, the houses in coastal towns and mountain retreats beyond are being repainted white as a visible greeting to the polished black bodies of the visiting staff of Heel!; instead quite the opposite seems to be the indisputable truth. Whether we attribute this change of mind that has caused the purchase of the blackest of paints, to the natural rebelliousness of male youth, such disobedience so regularly observed from the Egyptian offices of Heel! at Denderah whose night-time visits to the first-time reader of Heel! are being rudely rebuffed, has required on each occasion the most decisive response with boot and whip, even in those instances where a male relative ignorant of the commitment made to Heel! by the act of subscription, who may, as I have argued in your defence, be himself responsible for the selection of black pigment, then attempts intervention.

The requirement and age-old tradition re-stated in each issue of Heel! that the male slave paints his house white, permits the easy recognition by moonlight of the addressee for the twin purposes of monthly delivery and discipline by the reinforcing ritual of boot-worship by which the man is bound in his destiny to the progress and aims of our society. The slave is not permitted to regret, to sit on the fence, to paint and re-paint the walls of his home, white and then black, according to his predilection, how he feels that day, welcoming one day and attempting to hide the next from the member of Heel! to whom his future existence has been irrevocably entrusted. The slave is not permitted the flighty behaviour of a bird. Reluctantly, I have agreed with my colleagues at Heel! that any of my readers who disrespects tradition is to be rehoused in the aviary here at our Paris office. I suggest you each read the description of that difficult existence within the cage in my letter to you titled *The Human Parrot*.

MADAME X

FORTY-TWO

Isis Unveiled

Dear Boot-Lovers,

When is the time of fruition, when the prudent gardener should prune the fruiting tree that stands erect before her longing gaze, rooted there by fear and Nature to its patch of ground, the concealing leaf the disguise of a ripening crop? When the ripe apples, puce and full, fall with gravity to the grass beneath, beside the questioning boot, the inquisitive whip, then is the time when what has been nursed through cold and frost-bitten nights, with soothing thoughts from the celibate bed, becomes as slave, its seed soon crushed between the patient jaws of patent-leather boots. Then is the time when the fruiting tree like Prometheus bound is cut with claw and blade upon the cushioning ground.

The Mistress, half-sleeping still with pruning knife in gloved and bloody hand, forgetful of the circumstance of the chained and naked man, with thoughts of new-found gaiety then invites this wounded and unconscious slave to that most secret garden of her darkest dream, to celebrate a victory hard-won, a harvest festival, which must to her remorse for scheming acts seen briefly in another light, be shared alone, for silent is her partner to their joint success, and unresponsive to the urgent, sweet caress. Yet caught at last, this courting couple live and dead, within the shafting light of beaming moon, the Goddess of the Night, then shaping, shapely female forms dance gleaming round his aching limbs, his chains unbound, his life renewed like Osiris screwed with a length of phallic wood.

The completed slave, his memory of the night's events obscured by half-remembered dreams, awakens within the marital bed, a fonder and more present recollection, now restored by the warm embrace of knowing spouse, so sweetly garbed, the time of danger past, she guides him through the routine scarce recalled, his return to civil, salaried life, with she his daily wife dressed still in leather beneath expensive gown and public face. Another servant is born again of the Goddess' light, the balance in her favour shifting by this method of the night, as whip breeds whip, held in reserve behind the fabric of the fashionable dress, behind the veil of the equestrienne's habit.

Boot-lovers, I have written of these secret rites performed by members of Heel! on you the unsuspecting slave-to-be during the unconscious, unguarded hours of night, abetted by the constant vigil of the pruning escort in her moonlit garden, the more clearly to explain the reasons why, in the letter printed in the September issue of this magazine and titled *Daydreams of Leather*, the reader was confronted in a garden by a lady dressed in polished leather and high-heeled boots beneath a summer's dress. When the time is deemed right, when the timeless Goddess of the Night through her intermediaries, the priestesses of Heel! officiating at the festivals of thanksgiving within the Mistress' dream, reveals that false pretence, and with it the need for obsolete and coarse clothing to be worn, should permanently be dispensed with, then that more formal relationship between Mistress and slave already existing in the other world of dreams, will be more openly adopted, and the chains of Prometheus and the phallus of Osiris become the familiar and accepted sight.

MADAME X

FORTY-THREE

The Venetian Night

During that cold afternoon the male porters at the San Severa hotel on the island of the Lido in the Venetian archipelago had unfolded one hundred sunbeds on the empty beach, placing each one meticulously in an evenly-spaced line, then draping over them the extravagant furs of mythic creatures whose shining black coats now brushed the raked sand on the ground beneath in the light evening breeze that blew in from the sea. It was the time of Venice's Carnival. Every year for centuries the preparations for the arrival of these female guests had been executed identically; though no sign of their nocturnal presence was yet expected. Only the few children with fantastic minds and shivering bodies suspected and questioned the silent servants about the purpose and timing of this ritual and display.

On the main island of Venice, a short journey by boat, by vaporetto, from the Lido, the riot of the multi-coloured shirt, the American accent, the fat wallets of crude tourism, provided the casual observer with no hint to the events planned for that night. To the trained eye, perhaps, to the seer the earlier disappearance of the taxiing and ferrying gondolas, the muted sound of the singing gondoliers, evidenced the prospect of a paranormal night.

While violins beside the restaurant tables of loud, ill-mannered men played on with enthusiasm forced against the knowledge of the impending hour, rubberised women drawn by the fullness of the moon from the subterranean to the mediterranean, emerged unobserved through streets of stagnant water, their glistening skin soon cloaked in darkness, their clicking heels then lost enveloped within the receiving shadow.

On the beach of the San Severa hotel, the sunbeds in their regimented row were empty pointing out to sea, the spherical moon shone brightly on the rippling water of the black lagoon, the beams of creamy ambient light revealing a vast, as yet deserted stage. As the clock-hand turned toward midnight, the reflecting surface becoming smooth, a child points at something nearly seen, his finger bent again by adult arms outstretched in fear, for rising from the sea, with open palms pressed down beside the gleaming female shape upon the healing water, a Goddess stands above the glassy sheen in testing boots that walk, then strut upon the surface, firm and sealed, towards the sloping shore.

The children, awe-struck dumb, behind drawn curtains peeping stare, wide-eyed, frozen still in fear, adult whispers hushed beside in blind despair. A second female guest arrives in curved stiletto heels and rubber, emerging perfect in the midnight light, polished, pushing up above the closing sea, the arching boots withdrawn in time, then stamping down upon the resisting, moonlit stage. While one hundred porters, with heads inclined eyes focussed to the ground, patiently kneeling wait the performance of a greeting ceremony, ancient, timeless and new, street urchins with cleaning cloth, improvising, staring, mimic for their adult years, breath taken by this posture and the vision of this overwhelming view, of dripping boots delivered, thrusting, to their care. The echoing of stiletto boot heels on solidifying water, the sound made by whips cracking in the air, by one hundred aquatic guests, clatter and smack against the stone walls and shattering window-panes of the San Severa hotel.

Elsewhere in Venetian palaces shuttered against the passage of time, the ugliness of an ignorant world, of stupid science and idiot men, evening dresses laid out upon exotic beds by nervous servants charged in the Mistress' long absence with the preservation of the priceless, timeless content of her wardrobe are secured by pin-lipped maids, transvestites, stitched tight, corsetted, bejewelled for the duration of the night. Outside, dangling down by a length of knotted rope from the balcony into the muddy depths of the foul-smelling canal below, the rubbery boot-slave, subconscious, weighted down, animation suspended for the year, is hoisted by her leather opera-gloves clear from the polluted water into which is lowered for the night the Mistress' rubber clothing, preserved in substitution, undetected by the outsider's curious eye.

Slapped by the Mistress' dark-skinned glove into sudden recognition of his rôle as slave, she observes him at her feet, her whip for now withheld behind her back, though serpent coils, candle-lit, inquisitive, remain in sight upon the marble floor, reminding constantly of his most likely fate, the irreversibility of this natural state. His feverish body so recently revived, previously kneeling beaten about the face, polishes, unable yet to stop and breathe, prostrated there beneath the reflection, flickering and otherworldly, of his Mistress' sculpted shape, of her white face impassive behind the haughty, leathered mask, behind the intervening sheet of glass. His annual duty so painstakingly performed beneath her silent gaze is duplicated a thousand times upon the shine of marble stones of palaces unshuttered for this single night, by boot-slaves lifted from the Adriatic sea, the social detritus of science raised prematurely from the seeming dead.

The sound of music, of vital violins and of drunken, gesturing men, wafted in the deepening night, slows perceptibly to the Mistress' ear; the motion of the revelling tourist then seized, frozen mid-step, the movement of his travelling body held in abeyance, expressing sudden disbelief, is fixed in helpless admiration of the passing ladies, their faces masked and cloaked in black, who move between them, touching with their outstretched whips, overbalancing with extended leather glove or forcing boot. Upon the water, frozen still in time, its creamy surface firm to the tread of female heel and the feet of dancing monkeys on taut leashes, from the nearby island of the Lido the guests of the San Severa hotel in rubber masks and black-hooded fur converge in cruel conversation upon the appointed hour, upon the steps of the white-stoned balustraded bridge that by the moonlight lead on past the pink marble facade of the Doge's palace, to the prison.

A shiver, an earthquake's tremor vibrating blurs the focus of this otherwordly and inhuman scene where man and monkey mix and play; the ivory moonlit sea becomes as rigid ice and as stalactites drips water on the rubbered heads of weeping slaves that kneeling hang with death beside the snowbound palace, necks locked together by enchanting spell and frozen chain within the eternal night. The architecture, composite, intermediate between two worlds, adjusted by this shudder appears resolved, the focus tightening, the clarity restored. The boorish tourist is converted from his vulgar state, transformed from his immobilized, stunned, unblinking state, his lifeless living torso becomes incorporated in hardening rubber polished black, his flexing arms are linked behind with glowing cuffs of cooling steel, his lower body fixed embedded within the pink-stoned walls, and set within the chiselled mantel of internal fires that blaze against the blizzard's cold.

On the pavement below the Doge's palace, crossed over from the thirteenth century when Venice's dreaded and infamous Tourist Police, the Council of Ten's instrument for torture and repression, cast a shadow across her maritime empire, a number of tethered ape-like men, spread out like dogs on radial leads, comb and then sift the blanketing snow for litter, refuse, for objects materialised from their world, beneath the overseer's guiding whip, the lashing of her foreign tongue. Ropes of stretching elastic rubber lowered like fishing-line from the palaces of the Grand Canal, from the fifteenth century facade of the Ca'd'Oro, twitch above the frozen surface, as signs of human life, of the boot-slave polishing in a fever, his outline seen fleetingly beneath the ice, beneath the reclining figure of his leather-booted Mistress, ensure the smooth progress of her gondola beyond the Rialto bridge, the punctual timing of her masked entrance to the Doge's palace.

Opposite the water-gate of the palace adjoining the Ca'd'Oro, pushing up through thinning, snow-covered ice beneath which a second boot-slave invisibly labours, a circular mooring-pole capped with a human form, seemingly impaled by some monster from the deep, then dipped in molten rubber and left in agony to die, looks up religiously to the balcony where the Mistress stands imperious in noble dress, her patient whip dangling from a leather opera-glove, her waiting gondola lashed tight about his stiffened neck. She is Diane de Poitiers, one of the five members, each counted twice, with and without the obscuring leather mask, who compose the Council of Ten, the supreme leaders of the Republic of Venetia, who meet once a year at midnight at the Doge's palace, on Carnival night, to elect from their number and to crown her, *La Serenissima*, Bride of the Adriatic.

Inside the Doge's palace, the medieval 'Palace of Justice' with its 'court of the room of the Cord', which is the seat of government, the organising centre of Heel!, where plans are made behind our patriarchal scene, decisions taken for this modern version of their world, four of the five, twin-faced Council members, Nefertiti, Semiramis, Cleopatra and Helen of Troy, deliberate about the pressing problems of that other tourist-infested Venice, cushioned on human furniture with ears removed smoothed over by encasing rubber. The questions raised: How and with what numbers to re-introduce the Tourist Police so essential for the preservation of their world; when and with what means to obliterate the nineteenth century causeway and the hideous factories of the adjoining mainland, to secure the outer bounds and good health of the Venetian city-state; what manpower, kneeling or temporarily erect, is required to dismantle the white concrete railway station constructed in 1954? After which it is unanimously agreed, before her imminent, delayed arrival at the grand entrance to the palace, at the ceremonial 'Giant's Staircase' where the gods, Mars and Neptune, were turned spell-bound to stone in 1567, that after a confirming inspection of the two huge globes and the walls covered with the maps of the two worlds in the *Sala dello Scudo*, Diane de Poitiers is to be elected for the period of one year, *La Serenissima*, Bride of the Adriatic, in recognition and for the purpose of the most rapid expansion of the circulation of the Paris-based Heel! magazine.

Crowned between the statues of Mars and Neptune with a crescent moon upturned upon the head-dress that surrounds her leather mask, receiving from the extended glove of Semiramis the bow and quiver of the Moon Goddess, Diana, the foundress of Venetia, then responding to the loud whip-cracks and smacking gloves of the thousand masked members of the Great Council by her punishment of the kneeling Casanova, Diane de Poitiers turns to enter the palace followed in procession by the Council of Ten and the members of the Great Council who file ceremonially past the fresco of 'The Coronation of the Virgin' in the *Sala del Guariento* on the second floor, into the *Sala del Maggior Consiglio*. Once inside the Hall of the Great Council, a chamber of monumental proportions, Diane de Poitiers, *La Serenissima*, takes up her position on the balcony overlooking the frozen lagoon where three riderless horses are seen dragging at speed a giant cage filled with flaming wood, spiralling away from a central point marked by a boot-heel, equidistant from the Doge's palace and the island of San Giorgio Maggiore, in an ever-widening arc, finally mapping out a melted circle of vast circumference equal in area to that lit up by the beaming shafts of descending moonlight.

Below the balcony, the hundred guests of the San Severa hotel, dressed and masked in rubber, cloaked in fur, the Tourist Police, play cat and mouse with a prisoner just released, undressed in stages, redressed in black rubber, from head to foot, a trident pressed into his right hand, his body then held in place, brought shivering to its knees. The nature of his crime, the sentence passed, is read out slowly by Cleopatra, the retiring 'Bride of the Adriatic', who condemns at length the corrupting and damaging effect on the built and moral fabric of the Republic of Venetia of this civil servant's slogan, 'Veni etiam', interpreted as, 'Come again and again'. As proof, the erect body of Casanova, the salt-smuggling philanderer, is shown, then thrown from the balcony for its examination beneath the vicious boots of the Tourist Police. With her bow strained and accurately aimed at the heart of the cringing and protesting prisoner, a flaming torch guiding the flight of the burning arrow to its fleshy target, Diane de Poitiers has slain her quarry, pierced him through and dumped him dead upon the bleeding snow. Pulled to his feet, and lifted sagging in the air, his body is tossed into the canal by rubbered Amazonian hands, over the balustrade of the *Ponte della Paglia*.

FORTY-FOUR

The Fall of Pisa

Beneath the early morning sunshine, on their reluctant way to church, with the sound of heavy bells pealing and clanging deafeningly above them, the mayor and the foremost citizens of Pisa were suddenly confronted by the bewildering sight of a deep furrow that was ploughed in a linear groove across the steaming ground of the still deserted square, across their pious path so routinely followed, barring their slow, measured progress to the stone steps leading up to the gothic facade and candle-lit interior. After the initial shock of this seemingly inauspicious discovery, in loud exchanges as if stopping to argue about the truth behind some urgent religious question, they then considered the possible origin of this most troubling manifestation and obstacle to their weekly, dark-suited procession to catholic prayer and discreet confession. Had they stumbled upon a modern equivalent to the weeping statue of Madonna, being instead the clearest representation of the cross-beam of a sunken crucifix gouged into the friable earth, a symbol of male suffering to believers in Christ's death at Golgotha?

In apparent confirmation of this first theory of the furrow's origin it was observed that the shadow cast by the crucifix centrally implanted on the church's dome had become aligned, mapping perfectly onto the partial cross embedded in the gash cut into the now baking earth beneath their milling feet. Several members of the assembled congregation appeared ready to believe that the cross' shape was about to be completed at this moment of superimposition, standing back about to be amazed by religious revelation of astounding significance, by the sight of a second furrow of equal width ploughed vertically through the mid-point of the cross-beam. Minutes later, they edged as a relieved and disappointed group back towards the streaking wound of broken ground when the shadow had re-emerged as a parallel and dusty line, when nothing miraculous had occurred.

They take turns peering down into the narrow trench that must conceal in its dark depths the plank of timber that had borne the saviour's weight. Kneeling in their best suits and squinting below, first the mayor and then the rest of the Sunday congregation report with the growing certainty of sheepish repetition that the nails of crucifixion are indeed still hammered in place driven into the hard wood at either end, an armspan apart. Struck suddenly by the repercussions of such a discovery within his touristic city, the mayor dispatches his elder son and chosen successor to organise a muscular work-force to be press-ganged from the bars of Pisa packed with the brawling labourers from the neighbouring countryside. The cross-beam must be dug up, raised, stripped of its nails and any attached flesh, the holy relics preserved for profitable display during the summer season.

One of the kneeling staring men, proceeding on his own on all fours in a line extending from the left-hand end of the furrow, believing that the wild assertions so far made about a buried cross-beam had misinterpreted the nature and scale of the discovery, was eventually halted in his persistent tracks by the appearance between his blistering palms of a second furrow drilled into the soil as if by a giant's plough pulled by oxen gone beserk. For a moment longer he ruminated upon that possibility, that descending in their journey across the heavens the celestial beasts had grazed the planet's surface, ploughing the earth at the several points of contact before returning to the intended, corrected orbit. Unwilling yet to share his thesis with the others left behind, before seeking the evidence of further proof, he starts to crawl again along his linear route that has taken him far beyond the tree-lined square towards the open fields of normal ploughs and normally-sized cows, until in a clearing of open fertile land surrounded by predictable vegetation of average height, beneath burning rays of midday sun, he stumbles upon what seems at first from his inferior position the black sting extracted during aerial combat between two celestial bees, plunged from the sky, piercing the level earth like the sharpest, most deadly nail.

Raising his head bewildered by the strangeness of this sight, he observes in stunned, then trembling disbelief the curve of a stiletto heel rising above him forming into a shoe of shining black leather that seems on brief reflection to have been discarded or lost by whichever Goddess of the Roman Pantheon had driven the team of maddened bulls so capriciously through the previous night's sky. Not wishing to remain any longer alone in the wake and presence of the divine and still polished shoe with its snaking outrider, the uncoiled bull-whip, for fear of the deity's reappearance in this now sacred idyll, he turns scurrying back on bloodied hands and feet towards the distant, thronging square, where beside the church, beside the neatly-furrowed ground, like brave huntsmen standing over recently killed prey, the dignitaries of Pisa are about to be photographed after being interviewed, becoming holier by association, their every word being hung upon by an eager and irrepressible press. His bleeding hands quickly mistaken for Christian stigmata the kneeling man becomes at once the new centre of attention, soon beckoning with his waving, spattering forearm, turning ahead of the pursuing crowd of the jostling journalist and the clicking cameraman, in the direction of the hidden heel.

The colossal shoe whose scuffing tracks had brought the good citizens of Pisa to the tree-ringed clearing where it had been left stranded during the previous starry night, remained upright, receptive, still pointing against the planet's spin. Despite the cautious advice then quietly offered by wise old men arriving late on the scene with memories prolonged by their knowledge of classic times, that the intruding shoe should not be touched and never moved, but left where found within its secluded grassy setting, to be reclaimed by the Goddess on her cyclical return, the overheated crowd, already persuaded instead by the demagogic hotheads and the prevailing muscle and impulsiveness of male youth, massing themselves about the tempting, tactile sheen, accept it as a prodigious gift made intentionally by a female deity to her favoured race of mortal heros. Devising methods for its transport back within the urban sprawl, with rolling logs pushed beneath its advancing sole and roped men pulling at the towering heel, the Goddess' shoe is dragged into the night towards the welcoming lights of Pisa. But with ropes chewing at the shoulder blades of groaning, faltering men, the stately progress becomes a shuffle to a halt, when from out of darkness dressed each identically in uniform, women with whips in high-heeled boots attack the press-ganged labour-force. Tourist Police arrived from the Republic of Venetia guide the Trojan boot inside the sleeping city, past shuttered windows into the dreaming psyche of restless men.

In the depths of that night, cutting vertically through the mid-point of the site of the buried cross-beam in front of the Gothic church, a second high-heeled shoe gleaming in the full moonlight, approaches the slumbering labourers piled exhausted around its elevated leather pair guarded by the encircling ring of the booted women with whips from the Venetian Tourist Police. Sinking down into its soft receptive leather neglected deliberately for a day, the Goddess stands above her city surrendered retaken without a fight, surveying each rooftop beneath whose timbers the dreaming men lie stretched out as slaves, asleep, their heads turning left and right, trying to scratch the sprouting beard with hands punctured, nailed back upon the crucifying bed of splintering red linen. Uncoiling her bull-whip onto the exposed flesh of the press-ganged men heaped below, she lashes out at the overshadowing sky, repeatedly, feeling with its snaking tip for the invisible outline of some distant constellation, wrapping its tail around the celestial body with which she pulls her polished, black leathered figure abruptly out of this world. The Tourist Police celebrate in Lesbian ritual the resulting reduction to crumbled dust of the collapsed attraction that was the ancient tower of the Italian city of Pisa.

FORTY-FIVE

The Argonauts

DEAR BOOT-LOVERS,

Since the question has been asked, and is worthy of an answer, even if the reader who requested the answer, is not, judging by the quality of his writing, a short extract of which I have printed below, then let me comment briefly on the co-operation that exists between Heel! in France and Heel! in Venice. Is it correct that the events that are described in the letter which I have titled *The Bridge of Sighs* relate to the testing and training of boot-slaves subsequently and usefully employed in the Republic of Venetia? And did that reader's experience take place at some earlier version of the Chateau of Chenonceau, which in relation to the present that you recognise, was architecturally incomplete? Yes. And to follow the line of questioning where it will no doubt lead in the future correspondence sent here to the Paris offices of Heel!, and to save the curious reader from unnecessary speculation of which he would otherwise be guilty and punishable, let me say that the time described in that reader's letter relates to the period when Diane de Poitiers was the chatelaine of Chenonceau. I also undertake the sometimes thankless task of training and then re-training slaves of the female boot at the Chateau of Morville in the south-west of France.

The next question relates to the person of Cleopatra who was, according to the historian of Egypt, and is worshipped at the Temple of Denderah. Her initiation into the inner circle of Heel! involved her riding as Mistress upon the back of the Roman patriarch, Julius Caesar, and her completed conquest of that man through the controlling use of her seductive voice. The account of her supposed death by venom from a snake-bite is merely a veiled allusion to her initiate's power to direct the inner force within her body to dematerialize her physical form for an interval of time. A competence in Egyptian alchemy is hinted at, implied within the historical records which attempt to reveal that Diane de Poitiers, the duchess of Valentinois, dominatrix to the French king, dealt in the black art, was in receipt of potions compounded by unholy hands, of potable gold, and serve to remind the modern reader of her longevity by the reference of her device to her successful combat with the forces of Death: 'Omnium victorem vici', which means 'I conquered who conquers all'. The fact that every night from her childhood onwards, Diane de Poitiers rode for three hours in the dead of the night to destinations unknown should reveal to the most blockheaded reader a supernatural vocation that had remedied the damage of ageing and made slaves of men. And yes, she wears above her forehead a silver crescent gleaming with diamonds, the emblem of the Roman Moon Goddess, Diana, who is Artemis to the Greek slave. And to what destination did blind Homer reveal that Helen of Troy was rowed by subject men after the fall of that city? To the Egypt of Nefertiti, whose body has of course never been discovered by the kneeling archaeologist, due perhaps to her continued and healthy life; a condition shared by the Queen of Assyria, Semiramis, of whom it was said: 'To look upon her face unveiled is to be the Great Queen's slave forever more'. Perhaps it is time for the oddly-phrased account of the trials of an oarsman on such a ship as that of Spartan Helen, which as I have said, lacks the talent required for publication in this magazine, but fits most admirably within the context of my response to this inquisitive reader.

'I found myself awake asleep, very active for this usual time of night, as in great haste to prevent some seeming certain danger we oarsmen rowed a mythic voyage in darkness and beyond. A woman tall, gleaming, stood above beneath the torn ripped rigging, then guiding from a battered deck with lashing whip and shrieking voice raised loud against the thundercrack of flashing storm. In chains half-hid beneath the froth and spume of foaming sea, that linked we men in fetters that gripped to shaven rubbered legs, we fought for seven and seventy nights far beyond the light of intervening day with sinking lands to left and right, and smashing waves that drowned our failing sight.

At length, at last, when a continent submerged and sea

where air should be, in far and unclear distant lands some beacon showed its glimmer to the restless scene and slaves down to a man through emptied lungs then cheered the mistress who had led them through the endless night. Yet no responsive smile was seen to cross her lips, her limbs, thighs massive, impassive, in blackest rubber soon flickered with the changing light. The beating whip, it seemed our only friend, persisted in its deadly flight, as closer grew to each member of her frenzied and still dreaming crew the enchanting glow of boots that shone before, beyond our limited sight. Yet rigid in their stance, astride the vision of our inner eye, two lighthouses powered by supernatural light, dipped down into that world of dreams to cool and to refresh.

The scudding of the single snake of Goddess whip falls silent with her calming mood re-coiled in leather circles beside her curving heavenly hip. Tall, gleaming still she stands above amongst the vault of glittering stars, below upon a windless scene we row in time into the placid Mediterranean sea emerging in a sunlit world but blinded now to boots that stood across its gate and arching thighs that mounted in the moonlit, darkened sky. What heroes we who were once washed ashore as slaves of boot and Goddess soon forgot. But still she waits, her solitary and impatient gait, stiletto boots still polished and radiating beside the Gibraltar Straits.'

The readers and Mistresses of Heel! are reminded that the annual celebration at the Palace of Versailles will take place as always on the night of the full moon in June. A masked ball will be held from nine in the evening in the Hall of Mirrors. It is an opportunity for you to meet the Paris staff of Heel! magazine and members of the Council of Ten in the *Salon de la Guerre*. The male readers of Heel! who have subscribed to our magazine in the previous year will be marked with the Heel! brand by the Goddess Diana at the Fountain of Evening. From the time of your submersion to alleviate your pain, you will react to the slightest whisper of the word, Heel!, in your public lives with the kneeling position and inclination of the head. The female readers subscribing for the first time will each receive a copy of the book, *Night Vision: The Powers of Darkness*, written by one of our slaves, which describes the techniques for preserving a youthful appearance, of achieving immortality.

Other attractions will include a display at midnight by a number of well-trained mutant and cloned apes who will rehearse to music the removal by guillotine of the heads of dummy scientists. The list of those mortal men who have violated the Law of the Goddess and are to be executed after their arrest in the name of you, the revolting people, by our Tourist Police is available from our Paris offices. You will notice the numbers of politicians and businessmen so far added to this growing list. May I advise you that Tourist Police will be guarding the entrances to the palace and patrolling the grounds for signs of littering and manly behaviour which will be punished on the spot by the whip, and the culprit will not admitted in the following year. How ironic that the head of the Tourist Police should be Ninon de L'Enclos, renowned in the seventeenth century for her enduring beauty and interrogations of men, who refused then a kneeling king's offer that the keys of Versailles and the fate of his courtiers be placed in her hands. For those readers still uncertain as to the authority and practices of the Tourist Police, I suggest that you read the letter which I have titled, *The Pygmalion Man*. Invitations will be sent to the Mistress' address. No male reader should appear unaccompanied, in which case he will be immediately apprehended by the Tourist Police and being unable then to explain his conduct, imprisoned.

MADAME X

FORTY-SIX

Paradise Lost

Dear Boot-Lovers,

I have been accused of many things and often jointly with the rest of our industrious staff here at Heel! who labour away on your behalf with the vain hope that the male reader of our magazine will write with gratitude for the change we have wrought in his life through the written word and visiting boot, and not with regret. But to be accused of witchcraft, of dark magic, is both impertinent, even hurtful to our feminine sensibility, while at the same time, it should be admitted that our natural impact on your world might appear from one moment to the next to smack of the black arts, since our supernatural energy spreads naturally through the structures, the architecture, physical and psychological, that had seemed to each of you who are constricted within the limits of your bestial nature, to be endowed with the appearance of permanence. And yet as we develop within you the slave mentality that alone will grant you access to that larger version of reality which is the playground of the Goddess and from which with your memories stripped of content you are reinserted into the harsh environments of the human universe, there to redevelop that servility sometimes lost in our paradise, a number of you, returning well to the path of service to the Goddess, begin to glimpse aspects of our own greater existence.

I have in front of me, dragged to my attention in a parrot's beak, a letter written by a new subscriber to Heel! who might therefore be excused the off-handedness with which he addresses his agony aunt, were it not for his tiresome repetition of that rude error. By the time he receives my reply to his random questioning about metaphysical matters that seemed academic and intelligent to him, but deal with what is for me and the staff at Heel! nothing more than idle speculation about our routine and first-hand experience, he will unfortunately be incapable of reading this well-intentioned advice due to the masking of his face and constricting of his body with the predominant raw material of our world, black rubber. We hope by this method to remind him of his time within our natural paradise so that the error of his manners and reasoning mind that has led to his fall from that higher state beneath the booted Goddess, is revealed to him within the darkness that is now his permanent condition, and from which he fumbles to clean and polish the heels and leather of the stiletto boots regularly left him at his now quiet home by the concerned and compassionate members of Heel!.

Certainly, the further development of his inner vision, which he discloses to his agony aunt to be his secret ambition in this life, seems the probable outcome in his future of chained movement and feeding by rubber tube, provided by the visiting team from Heel! and by the credit card generously offered us at the time of subscription. You will no doubt write to me with your concerns for this numbered slave; the female reader complaining of my leniency to this scientific man, and the male reader more reticently, perhaps, commenting on this supposed ill-treatment. But as a means to the ends of his present life, so that he might return in the shortest time to the paradise that I have described to you, there is no more direct and valuable advice and course of action than immediate and repeated punishment under restraint, by the thought-provoking and memory-retrieving Mistress' whip.

Between his claims for scientific open-mindedness, which consist of nothing more than the conceited basking of the small-minded man on the lid of the match-box within which dwell his companions in crime who seek to promote a science that deals in death-camp logic while pretending itself an innocent, this man who might be discovered by the strolling Goddess beneath so many stones randomly kicked aside by an unforgiving boot, or round the average street-corner wherever she might choose to be materialised . . . this man advances through paragraphs of arrant nonsense eventually becoming triumphant at his first use of the intuitional inner senses, which he attributes so boldly to the consequence of developed intellect and describes to me in childish detail, as if his reader is unaware of the full nature of the subject.

And what has this Oxford man glimpsed from his ivory

tower that in an instant has deposed the Darwinian materialistic nonsense previously espoused at public expense, and at the expense of human lives lost as the consequence of the imposition of beliefs that are at their root emotionally prejudiced against the rule of the Goddess, based upon some dim memory of his original sinning against her rule in the other world of paradise? He sees all around him the extensions, vertically, into unoccupied space, of buildings that have doubled, then trebled in height before his incredulous eye. He writes of his 'enthusiasm for the moment', and of how he 'leapt into the street into the crowd of bustling, uninformed men, determined then to confirm [his] observation from a multiplicity of viewpoints, each contributing to the final weight of evidence, the balance of incontrovertible proof'. I use his own exact words in a way that he no longer can, out of a sympathy for his fixed condition in the dark tower in which he has been detained. Nor, since he no more can reply to the pleasantries that may be spoken to his deaf ears, will I mention the splendid irony that the revered man, Darwin, a prisoner punished in our world, lives on in agony at the very mention of his name and theory in your world.

Then, what happens next in this suspense-filled account of events, of a scientist on the rampage, pushing past the queuing masses of your kind? He enters one, then a second, third and fourth block of seemingly sky-scraping buildings. Barging with his vulgar manners through closing doors into each elevator in turn, or dashing madly up the encircling stairway, he reaches the top floor with only the flat roof above him. Confused about the missing levels that had seemed so apparent from the outside, from ground level looking up, and returning inside after an absurd inspection of the roof space for signs of the missing structure, he waits attentively for the ascending elevator, watching the floor-mumbers appear and disappear until finally it stops in front of him. No-one gets out, it must be empty, he turns his back to walk away, perhaps to check the area of the roof a second time to convince himself of his misapprehension of the facts. Several paces away, in the process of accepting his sensual data as delusion, of accepting defeat, in this the twentieth building scaled, intent only on a final glance out onto the abandoned roof-top, he hears the sound of the elevator's engine primed to descend back down to the ground floor. Unkempt and suddenly aware of the embarassing nature of the situation, he hurries back in case the learned professor is stranded for the night in this anonymous tower-block of flats. But he's too late, the elevator is leaving without him. Furiously, like the deranged man he had earlier become, he presses, then slams his open fist against the red button that seems to be faulty. Finally, he succeeds in interrupting the elevator's progress, and breathing deeply, adjusts his waving hair in the reflective metal of the silver, parting doors. But he's too late, the elevator has left without him, and instead of his own quieted image, he sees the ascent of departing boots cut below the knee by the horizontal line of the doorway. For a moment he could reach out and touch sixteen, eighteen, impatient polished boots; then the elevator is attracted upwards by the depression of the internal button, hesitantly climbing past his open mouth until the last curving shoe is lost, disappearing to his view.

I have changed his description of passing events from the first person to the third; otherwise the words are very much his own, and not those of your agony aunt, as is the accusation then written out on this crude piece of paper and made against the organisation of Heel!, that we are responsible for this man's delusion which is the product of witchcraft and evil spells directed in his path, and not the consequence of his improving vision with which he had briefly glimpsed the nature of our world.

MADAME X

FORTY-SEVEN

Hall of Mirrors

Madame, you have requested of your female readership, the members of Heel!, their observations and comments on the recent masked ball that took place in the gardens and palace of Versailles, in case what is already an excellent celebration can be improved upon in future years. I am therefore sending to your Paris offices my written account of the events of that night which I regret are less favourable in outlook than those so far published in your ground-breaking publication and is as follows.

Walking on my own in new boots as a guest to your annual celebrations in the Palace of Versailles, feeling a private pleasure in the awkwardness of their first movement and the smoothness of their changing appearance beneath the spraying light of exploding fireworks and of fountains lighted externally by flaming torch and from within the cascading jets of water, by sirens and tritons, I stood alone in contemplation and with the desire to understand what I was seeing. At the entrance to the Water Avenue which proceeds from the North Parterre to the Fountain of Neptune, I discovered for the first time the fountain of Diana's Bathing Nymphs, being a square pool with three walls adorned with sculpted figures, of which the central rectangular wall, having the appearance of a landscape from a dream, is both wide enough to accomodate a group of reclining nymphs and high enough to contain their tall naked bodies should they prefer to stand the more clearly to observe the outside world through the transparent sheet of overflowing water. Yet, until my arrival there and the distraction from their river-bank scene of the twin presence of my shining leather boots, the eleven nymphs, with a disdaining outward glance, had seemed to disregard the invitation of eleven pairs of shoes placed opposite, in front of each of their quivering, shivering forms, pretending in their splashing game that their earthly view was somehow obscured by the play of moonlight from within their world upon a silvered veil drawn across this otherworldly night. Intending, as I have said, to observe, away from the crowd, and to feel the sensual limits of my new boots, and being unwilling at first to share these properties of mine with an outsider of whatever extreme degree of female beauty, I watched the wriggling method of their extraction from the waters of their world and emergence of eleven glistening women into my own in the two minds of wonder and irritation at their immediate avoidance of the fine footwear left before as gifts within which they were to attend the celebration of Heel! in the Hall of Mirrors within the palace. Besides, what language would they speak, with which to be greeted by this dominating, incubating woman who wished in these precious moments for no interruptions, to be left in peace, for no human or other speech to interfere with her first communion with new and unbroken boots? Could they not just join and accompany the reanimated statuary of children riding on swans in the Dragon's Fountain at the other end of the tree-lined Water Avenue emerging while I continued to study in privacy the shape and curvature of my two reluctant new boots? And did they all have to crowd so close, along with so many discontented Goddesses in their new shoes, arriving inevitably at this corner of the gardens of Versailles chosen by me for its natural solitude? To which was then added the croaking of slaves turned into frogs and the regular, prolonged cries of agony from the Fountain of Evening. Might I suggest that in future years, stiletto boots be placed beside the female statuary, which is surely more appropriate for a masked ball than the court shoe. I am, however, grateful for the mercifully quick and brutal removal by the Tourist Police of the dancing Tai-Chi Master. Perhaps, if I may make a second request, it would be that this scientist, unbroken at that time like my own boots, be prevented during his imprisonment from recording the degrees of his suffering by the provision of pen and paper, since his contributions are invariably the dullest made to your fine magazine. And perhaps the eleven nymphs might be encouraged to assist the Goddess Diana with the submersion of the new slaves at the Fountain of Evening. And there should be the clear understanding that ladies wishing to avoid the enervating and fitful appearances and disappearances through the strangely-propertied glass of the Hall of Mirrors – where one Mistress loses her treasured slave to the black night, and another receives from that unearthly source three or more devoted but unwanted slaves – should remain undisturbed through till dawn in a secluded area of the gardens where she may silently address her new boots as her own slaves, which by initation become elevated as a part of her, being indistinguished by any separating identity from her own. In case this letter made disagreeable by the timing in the female cycle, is considered for publication, perhaps some clarification as to which or whose world the masked ball really belonged, can be printed alongside my listing of complaints. It seemed at the time to be as uncertain and changing as the appearance and ownership of my own new boots. Was I the impostor in the world of naked nymphs or were they released from their seeming dream into my version of the gardens of Versailles? The three thousand candles that lit the seventeen mirrors in the *Galerie des Glaces* and the furniture so regularly substituted served only to confuse the events of that night.

I understand from my recent conversation with this member of Heel! that the problem that she was experiencing with her stiletto boots and to which regretfully the circumstances of the masked ball appear to have contributed, have been thankfully resolved and their identity as a pair, confirmed and feminised. As to the otherworldly nature of the celebrations frequently commented upon by the new members of Heel!, perhaps my letter titled, Paradise Lost, will throw valuable light on the matter. MADAME X

FORTY-EIGHT

Hall of Judgement

An iron claw or hook resembling the toe of an oversized bird of prey was being inserted through the mouth and was then turned within the skull by the robotic twisting this way and that of her rubber-gloved wrist, until some point in the mashing of contents had been reached, and a tube was then forced up one side of the nasal cavity releasing in a squirting jet the intelligence of the man which grew as a puddle beneath her long-limbed rubbered legs. A coating of bitumen, a viscous liquid derived from petroleum and a mixture of minerals, by the destructive distillation of coal and wood, becoming solid by exposure, was applied by the touch and prod of manicured finger-tips to his staring eyes, the eye-lids being first closed after an initial treatment of cooling resin as a protective layer from the resin-producing cedar of Lebanon.

I am not a deaf man, though fear, I acknowledge, may have brought on this condition under those terrible circumstances, in the presence of that congregation of priestesses with strange motivations; but within that subterranean chamber of horrors which one might have assumed by its cavernous shape to magnify and to echo sound, I heard not a whisper, not a final whimper, from the brave man whose mouth was now sewn tight by the hand of an assistant. An incision was made in the left flank and by the length of its cut allowed for evisceration of the intestines, stomach, and liver, which were first partially dissolved and dislodged from their natural state by rectal injection of resin, smelling this time of Syrian pine, by enema. It was then that the previous stages of this process of ceremony and ritual began to make sense to me; for the seemingly normal boot with the impractical heel, of the same quality of rubber being worn by the officiating priestess, which had been painstakingly chosen from amongst others that had seemed by their polished surface to offer the same advantages in terms of weather-proofing and convenience, was inserted inside this uncomplaining man.

The irregular shape of the boot was being held in place inside him by a second, assisting priestess, who stepping forward from out the darkness in which I crouched with my archaeologist's notebook and pen [whose writing I was unable to check and confirm until later when disbelief had begun to erase the clear memory of the experience of these events] completed like an expert the stuffing of this human slave, pegged out there on the rectangular slab like the subject of the laboratory experiment. What a swift turning of tables on this previously white-coated scientist arrested, I believed, according to the judgement and sentence passed, in the process of undertaking a similar operation on a common frog! I continued to watch from the security of what I also believed to be a safe distance.

The assisting priestess, while feeling for the rubber surface of boot through the undulating skin of his by now contracted, gutted body, with one hand, with the other temporarily lost to my curious view deep inside the defleshed belly, entering by the slicing wound used for evisceration, was positioning, vertically, the calf of the boot in alignment with the spinal column that twitched in a spasm to prove the correct fitting of its rubber in this partial reassembling of his physique. Deftly, and in a variation to the accepted process of human mummification involving evisceration, desiccation, stuffing, wrapping and coffining, over the course of seventy days, the same priestess in a sudden jerking movement, plunged the heel of the boot down through the rectum and out of the anus into her other receiving hand. As if the protuberance of heel was perceived as substitute, the officiating priestess returns to remove, with the knife still in her hand dripping blood onto the pool of lost brain, his penis, which together with his scrotal sack is offered to the Goddess in whose nocturnal light this altar of sacrifice is bathed.

Once the boot is sealed securely within his body, and stitches sewn to close the penial wound over the protruding rubber toe and then the opening used for the purpose of evisceration through which her exploratory hand, that of the assisting priestess, is smoothly withdrawn, the bloody surface of skin is entirely covered with a layer of beeswax, this coating no doubt acting as a preservative during the subsequent transformation within the mould into whose shape his half-emptied body is now forced and locked shut, being returned to the dark where it is stacked and marked with hieroglyphs.

The colonnaded interior resembled not so much a mortuary temple but rather a court of law whose system of justice was operated by immortal beings sheathed in black rubber as if by this encasing of their flesh they were better equipped to judge and then to condemn the prisoner in their midst to a death and resurrection involving the very same material, but to a degree that would erode completely the personality of the accused and guilty man whose previous identity, pleading on his knees before the impassively seated figure of the demigoddess Hatshepsut, seemed about to be subsumed within the nonentity of the slave. With his neck now pulled down low to the ground by a chain threaded through an iron ring embedded in the stone floor, by his guard whose stiletto-heeled boots clicked impatiently beside his head that rolls from side to side in his garbled defence of the indefensible, the silent rows of women, sphinx-like in their stillness, observe the altered appearance of Hatshepsut, the judge in this matter, representative of the Goddess Nephthys. Her polished face that has remained inscrutable throughout the long submission of evidence, turns perceptibly from the pink colouring of red granite, through the green of schist that envelops her tall, swelling crown, which in turn darkens to the rubbery black that decides the fate of men and slaves.

His body prepared with rubber boot gestating inside, his helpless hands folded over his stomach as if approving of its meal, of this invasive parasitic presence transmuting his being, the man as future slave is taken from the slab, from beneath the circular beam of stellar light that reaches down through the deep carved shaft through rock stone to the subterranean world below. His replacement matured with resin, rubber and bitumen, is taken from its shelf, its vintage checked against the records by the long rubbered finger of the officiating priestess, and lowered onto the red granite surface by six identically dressed accomplices to this inhuman, outrageous form of justice.

The three bolts slid along the middle of the metal coffin are simultaneously released, and electrodes of the kind used to stimulate into activity the pegged-out laboratory frog are attached at either end. The coffin is not opened until the pink flesh-coloured tones of the granite slab darken through the spectrum to pitch black when a sound, impossible for the average archaeologist to identify, is heard to issue from within the now wobbling box, prompting the immediate raising of the lid swung back violently on its hinges to reveal someone, something, more alive than half dead. As if the sight of its incredible shape had been envisioned on numberless starlit nights, the slave, amphibian, frog-like, is wrenched from its slimy mould as if time and not compassion is the factor uppermost in my minds of these several ladies in their medical hats of black rubber with cobra heads with laser eyes of blood-red light scanning the new-formed creature's skin for imperfections, to ensure its imperviousness to water, its ability to hold water.

Convinced at last of its promise as a container for the revivifying female liquid that was secreted from between the thighs of the statue of Hatshepsut at the time of judgement, the boot heel inserted exactly one year before, protruding still, is pressed back up inside the lower reconstructed abdomen by a funnel, a nozzle through which is squirted the juice that will clarify its new mind to its servile future without recourse to previous male memories. All too soon, the inflated shape of its rubberised and black body makes ghastly and total sense, when it is driven uncomprehending across the stone floor, four-legged, newly agile, its skin suited for pond-life or the eternal night, being beaten by flailing whips. Rejected like the offspring of some ancient plague, ejected from the Temple of Hatshepsut, whipped down the sloping ramp that leads to desert, to the safety of the river Nile, the frogman, led on by newly-acquired instinct, begins his long swim south towards Philae, Temple of Isis.

The author of this account of the proceedings at the Hall of Judgement in the Valley of the Queens beside the Egyptian Nile, where the organisation of Heel! dispenses justice by transformation of her enemies into frogmen, was himself recently detained at the moment of re-emergence into the night air through the shaft that ascends from the altar whose purpose he has so admirably described. His fingers were spotted attempting to grip the loose surface soil by a member of the Tourist Police, who peering down from above observed his beseeching face, onto which she pressed down her leather boot while listening for the thud of misshapen flesh upon the Goddess' altar. MADAME X

FORTY-NINE

The Gates of Horn

I had fallen sound asleep, leaning back against the outcrop of limestone rock, with my eyes wide open. I must have been looking up and observing the night, since this is how my dream began. Perhaps I had been watching the moon at the moment of sleep, because the shape and the light of the full moon remained before my mind's eye and began to multiply within my dream. The black sky was filled, globe by globe, with other moons that had been invisible to me before. It was not obvious where and when the next moon would appear until so many thousand had appeared above me that the gaps remaining to be filled became fewer and far-between.

I am not a writer, nor a natural dreamer, and I believe my adventure in the world of dreams was solely the consequence of where I was resting in the desert, in that I was the only one there that night to see what I saw. My letter to you, Madame, is a truthful account of what happened to me while I slept, when the process of predicting the arrival out of the black sky and the placement of each new moon, the stimulation of the calculations involved, woke my normal mind fully to that strange world.

The luminous sky was packed replete with shining spheres of moonlight, just as my slumbering brain woke completely from its sleep, switched on, reanimated by this unlikely sight. The two giant limestone statues seated beside me, described to the tourist as the '65-feet-tall Colossi of Memnon', were simultaneously being roused from their much deeper sleep. Perhaps it was the sound of whips cracking overhead that had eventually woken me; certainly the sting of so many whips directed so harshly at the most vulnerable parts of the anatomy of the two statues must have caused their abrupt return to consciousness after nearly four thousand years of continuous sleep. Perhaps I am misleading the reader to believe that this was not a regular occurrence in that other world where sculpted figures, human and animal, seemed to exist in bronze and stone rather than flesh as a form of punishment, a spell cast from which only the whip might ever release them into life. I recognized, Madame, the polished rubber clothing worn by the booted women administering this lengthy whipping as belonging to your organisation, HEEL!, and am therefore writing to you in case you might be willing to throw some light on the strange events that happened during that night.

After a period of the incessant flogging of inanimate, then animated stone when I had placed my hands over my swollen ears and shut my eyes tightly so as not to experience the immediacy of the suffering being inflicted, when the Egyptian desert was once more silent and the women dressed in rubber stood back on high heels to ascertain the degree of enlivenment so far achieved by such a savage attack, then the tallest amongst them, her height exaggerated by her polished rubber head-dress, spoke to each statue in turn, reciting and repeating occult and magical phrases in front of their trembling legs, moving from one to the other until the first quiverings of hard stone had become a writhing against invisible bonds, and finally an acknowledgement by both statues kneeling side by side, of the natural authority over them of this whispering goddess of the night. The wording of the magical formulae, since through foolishness my ears were no longer covered, affected me as well as the vast tonnage of stone that had composed my two male companions.

Whether it seemed to these swarming whip-women that I myself had just emerged in flesh from the block of stone behind me, or my presence had indeed somehow been expected by them, from then on it was decided, that whatever discipline or dark magic was to be applied and was appropriate to animated stone, should also, despite by lesser size and softer skin, be equally directed toward me. It was as if whatever sculpture was discovered to lie in the way of their advance toward the Valley of the Queens, should be temporarily brought to life despite the incongruity of physical size, for some future purpose which required the use of all the available muscular strength.

When the scattered statues from temples lost buried beneath the shifting sand and conquering boot were summoned to the surface by the process of magical incantation, so that ram-headed sphinxes knelt down next to jackal-headed men in deep ranks spread across the desert like an army, defeated and enslaved, then the goddesses, their task of subjugation at last complete, as if with energy still unspent, began whipping at the empty air above, as if to attract attention, to search the moon-filled sky for some approving sign. The circular outlines of individual moons that had been so clearly distinguishable one from the other, so that when a single moon had appeared briefly to be absorbed into the space of an adjacent moon its re-emergence could be predicted by the slave who was for that time undistracted by the conditioning whip, were suddenly disturbed, their appearance immediately blurred, as if by a jolting collision with an invisible cosmic force.

I should inform the readers of this letter, were it to be published in Heel! magazine, that I believe the slave's ability to predict the appearance of new moons, which would otherwise have increased rapidly with the reduction in the places to be filled, was at the same time limited by the proportionate increase in the numbers of whip-wielding goddesses, as if somehow an individual moon, or a large cluster, might spawn or sponsor by means of projection a particular goddess, or goddesses, who for reasons of the lunar climate arrive in the desert dressed extremely in high heels and protective rubber.

With the sudden appearance in the desert of the rest of this army of goddesses materialized in rubber and carrying whips, the circular and distinct identities of the innumerable moons stretching from horizon to horizon, collapse into an amorphous mass of creamy-white light, as though shattered by the impact, their space then compressed between the clapping hands of a cosmic Goddess. A female long-fingered opera glove, in gleaming black, is seen in the night sky above the kneeling slave prostrated by this sight, and with its rubber pair, reshapes the unformed light, remoulding by their smooth, caressing touch, a vast and perfect sphere.

The giant scarab-beetle with its complexity of reins, bridle and bits entering and leaving its mouth-parts, its rider a goddess with a bull-whip astride its equally polished and armoured back, manoeuvres over the desert with each colossal leg plunging down into, then extracting itself from the drifting sand as though being contracted and expanded by her rubbered touch upon some unseen hydraulic lever. Swaying this way and that, favouring one leg and then another, the servant beetle moves lumbering forward into position, beside others of lesser size, opposing the beaten army of slaves obediently waiting in their path, expecting to be eaten, to be gathered up as mouthfuls between the serrated jaws. The jackal heads of prostrated men, tilted back, look up to the sky, to the Goddess remoulding in her rubber gloves the glowing light of moons.

The countless moons conjured into one like the rings of the magician's trick, dangles by gossamer thread from the Goddess' downturned hands, their polished palms providing the backdrop for the descent of this rounded legless lunar spider that by the time of its arrival between the front legs of the scarab-beetle balanced in readiness by the corrective tugging on its lower bit, is reduced to the volume of a large, eight foot high, white rubber ball. Mistaking its shape for an egg, the blinkered beetle, operating in part from memory and being guided forward by leather reins and whip, steers the ball over the sand through the darkness towards the distant cliff that overhangs the Temple of Hatshepsut.

With the two giants of Memnon whipped into pursuit, followed by an unending line of broken slaves of composite design and declining height, like a caravan of alien, circus freaks, the column of incongruous figures once so proud upon the architect's pedestal, is led in chains in single file silently into the Valley of the Queens, behind the burning torch, the only light left shining in the desert night, held in the free hand of the rider standing on the scarab-beetle's back. Reaching their destination at last, seemingly about to be driven to their deaths against the stone face of the cliff, like prey animals caught in a hunting-trap set by human predators, the slaves are forced by whips expertly wielded by the multitude of rubber-clad goddesses into an ever closer grouping beside the abrasive rock, while the scarab-beetle gently gathers within the embrace of its jointed front legs the ball mistaken for an egg.

The two giants, their legs whipped round by bull-whips uncoiled from the curving hips of impatient guards dismounting from the backs of smaller beetles and comfortable slaves, respond to orders shrieked above the echo of this inhuman bloodless carnage, together heaving from the cliff-face a boulder of huge dimensions and tremendous weight. Then the jackal-headed men, threatened by the thrashing whips, surging forward, rush into the entrance to the subterranean cave to remove the remainder of the blocking debris and reveal the circular outline of a tunnel.

A horizontal passage leads to a vertical shaft down to another horizontal passage to a cave of such exact shape that it seems a perfect sphere of enormous volume, yet confirmation of its immense dimension is inconceivable to the kneeling slave led forward on a leash onto the gangway suspended in chilling mid-air equidistant from the roof and the depths below. The scarab-beetle, functioning from trained memory, like an automaton, riderless, with no further guidance needed from the whip, climbs slowly across the viscous surface, and upside down places its egg against the sticky membrane between six others left hanging there to hatch or to fall into the cool water that fills one quarter of the cave's volume.

The roof of the cave is covered with thousands of lunar-coloured eggs that reflect in their arrangement so carefully measured by the scarab-beetle's claw, the earlier external view of the night sky. On an equal footing to the gangway which extends in a long narrow tongue to the mid-point of the cave, to a circular viewing platform where booted goddesses and kneeling slaves observe the servant beetle's progress, a second tunnel, matching the circumference of the horizontal passage by which the goddesses and their slaves have entered the cave, but cut into the cave-wall at right angles, leads back through excavated rock in the direction of the Temple of Hatshepsut.

An egg-shaped cage, its door flung open by the booted guard to receive an amphibian-looking man, hovers a step away from the entrance to this second tunnel. He hesitates, looking momentarily down below the intervening gap to the distant water far beneath, to the floating egg-sacks crushed between the fangs of an absent serpent whose sloughed skin indicates a colossal girth. A number of these frogmen are attempting to climb the wall that has become slimy to their web-fingered touch, falling back each time into the dark water, drawing attention to their plight by their desperate splashing. A third tunnel emerges into the cave through its lowest point.

The female guard, dressed in the Egyptian rubber of Heel!, pulls the condemned and transformed man into the cage which is directed towards an egg stuck by the scarab-beetle on the roof of the cave. She injects a pacifying liquid inside the black rubbery skin of one of his limbs. After some spasmodic and involuntary gestures of seeming defiance he slumps forward against her polished thigh, then down onto the cage's floor where the stamp of her stiletto boot brakes their progress across the vaulting roof. The scarab-beetle is moving slowly amongst the vast number of its developing progeny, clumsily dislodging an egg which plummets down past the observing goddesses and the assortment of slaves, plunging at last into water. The guard beats with the uncoiling bull-whip unclipped from against her rubbered hip, the confused scarab-beetle which climbs to greet the egg-shape and creamy-white colour of the rubber cage.

As though regretting the excessive dosage injected through the frogman's skin, she stimulates his face and body with reviving slaps from her rubber gloves and sharp kicks to the stomach with her pointed boots until a modicum of rigidity and purpose is restored to his rubbery frame. She steers the cage against the selected egg's impressionable skin. With the frogman's face held firmly between her thighs, the guard places a metallic skull-cap with a military spike upon his squeaking head pressing it down until she is certain that all air has been expelled and he may be safely inserted inside the luminous egg where he reappears suspended within the liquid of his new environment.

The goddesses on the circular viewing platform, observing the rubber wall of the egg healing successfully after the frogman's insertion, as if to applaud the guard's performance, begin once more to whip the empty air that turns suddenly dark. Only the luminous egg containing the frogman remains visible held between the gleaming black gloves of the Goddess. A giant serpent with a cobra's hood and a single flashing eye rears up above the viewing platform striking at, then swallowing the amphibian prey. A flickering sphere of light lingers hungrily behind the re-coiling, red-scaled serpent; its glowing centre caressed with polished rubber, brightens, strengthens, expands concentrically, filling the volume of a changed and otherwordly cave, stretching my dreaming mind beyond its natural limit. For a second split between two worlds, I glimpsed the frogman in an alien landscape, his stomach distended, force-fed on female liquid feed at the end of a serpentine stalk that rises through the crack of a treacherous ravine. His metamorphosis from erect human to rubber plant seemed in that instant to be irreversibly complete.

The frogman, as you call him, would first have been sentenced for his crimes against Heel! at the Temple of Hatshepsut, which, as you have realised, in your stumbling and quite flatulent manner, is connected by a tunnel to the Observatory. You may not be a natural dreamer, but you are a natural slave, and for that reason, paradoxically, you were set free after briefly exchanging your world for another, a penal colony where rubber plants are cultivated for pleasure and for pain.

MADAME X

FIFTY

Letter from London

DEAR BOOT-LOVERS,

Imagine the scene here at the offices of Heel! where all is lively commotion and the excitement that comes with the realisation of success in some great project and there is that mood of mutual congratulation that supersedes the initial outburst of euphoria. I feel, I believe, that you, the female readership and members of Heel!, are so familiar by now with the interior of our Paris building through my letters describing in perhaps excessive detail the life that we have here, that many of you have shared with us with your visits to our offices, that my words this month will make almost instant sense to you when I refer quickly to the near shambles, even chaos, that would greet you were you right here amongst us to share in our moment of triumph.

Our parrots, normally so regimented and well-behaved apart from infrequent and reducing numbers of squawking complaints at their entrapment and transformation within the fold of dominant women – I am sure you know their feminine names too well for my repetition and classification, are piled unceremoniously on their sides still attached by the foot to their perches, screeching and shrieking from behind the bars of their restrictive cages. The desks upon which they had been living out their little lives in thirsty observation of the seated member of Heel! staff, occasionally being called upon to blot with their beaks stuffed full with pink blotting-paper, the pages being written upon by the leather- or rubber-gloved hand [depending upon the weather, stormy or dry] are swept clear of the usual mundane paraphernalia of office life, being strewn instead with the questionnaires so promptly returned to us by the female readers of Heel!.

Imagine the booted staff of Heel! being gathered round first one paper-covered desk, then another and the next, as if suddenly remembering each time our apparently callous neglect of some precious piece of human office furniture upon whose leathered surface the pages in their thousands require collation and then correlation, geographically and according to age-group. The boot-slave arrives kneeling upon his merry platform of ball-bearings, ready and enthusiastic to polish, expecting to be slapped or spurred into immediate action, only to find what? That the member of staff in such feminine distress to whom he has been transmitted over smooth marble to serve, is no longer at her desk. In his unfortunate confusion he fumbles pawing at the vacant air, perhaps even dreading some extempore penalty for the innacuracy of his brushwork. You have the scene before your kohl-rimmed eyes, but what purpose is to be served by such drama verging on hysteria?

The numbered questions to which you have so carefully and painstakingly replied, so that the completion of just one of this profusion of questionnaires returned here to the offices of Heel!, individually reveals extraordinary developments in the real life of your world where the whispered verbalizing of the word 'Heel', as a command spoken in the public place, produces in the next moment the effect that the drugged poet, were he ungagged and his opinion requested, might compare in appearance to the felling of an ancient forest, though such action would never be in accord with the future rule of Heel! nor that use of force condoned by the natural law of the Goddess. Our conclusion, not prematurely drawn, of that we are supremely confident, confirms as the most real possibility the imminent overthrow of western governments and their inevitable replacement by the far-flung and transdimensional empire of the black devas of Heel!.

A reader living in London where the spread of our organisation might have been thought to be limited, both by reason of the earlier patriarchal stance and by the famous ugliness of its architecture, has reported through this questionnaire in front of me here in Paris, that without the necessity of repetition or any raising of her voice, she brought the proceedings in Westminster's House of Commons, into which she had just walked in finest stiletto-heeled boots, to a standstill, to a 'kneelstill', by the mere shaping of her slowly retracted vermilion lips into the unspoken command of Heel!. She has then added in the space left empty for her to summarise her observations, that the recent policy of discrimination by ignorant politicians devoid of any aesthetic sense, against those initiated into the ways of the Goddess through the lengthy process of enlightenment by the multiple lives lived through reincarnation, should be immediately reversed so that those men 'who do not understand what they are not, should not be allowed to insist upon what they tragically remain'. She mentions the existence, so far unknown to Heel! in Paris, of a gentlewoman's club in the city of London with a solely female membership, called Heel!, to which offending men are brought by force to be then initiated into the service of the female boot.

Another questionnaire, this time from the south-west of France, describes how its author had fallen asleep, oblivious to any human company, feeling herself to be quite alone in the countryside, after whispering the word 'Heel' for the pleasure of its sound, without any expectation of its fulfilment as a command. She wakes at last from this dream, from a dark cave to which she had been carried by a population of blinded moths that had emerged from the snowflakes of a blizzard that had softly settled upon the hot leather of her boots, like 'male moths drawn to her female flame'. How amazed she is to discover her boots polished like new boots 'unwrapped for the first time from their box of purchase!'

MADAME X

FIFTY-ONE

The Resurrection

All was a bright, happy and optimistic white. Had he gone to Heaven? Certainly this bedroom was so foreign to his mundane experience as to belong to that alien other world. It appeared to him spotlessly clean, quite unlike his own that he believed with a growing conviction he had left advantageously, selected seemingly against the run of events to avoid the fires of the infernal underworld. He closed his eyes, then opened, then shut, then opened them again. It was real enough. The source of the bright light that he now likened to that of an earthly sun appeared so near, almost within the white-ceilinged room itself, so that he might reach out and touch its dazzling presence were it not for the weight of his arms. Had he been moved in his deathly condition into a new proximity to the deity, Apollo, who was supposed to be the indwelling life and consciousness of the sun? He believed it possible, and no longer counting his blessings for such a promising result to his life, he began to anticipate the good things that lay ahead as rewards for his mediocre, worthless existence. Everything would be possible; everything bathed in this unearthly, earthly light. Beautiful women, unattainable women, the fruits of labour not worked would be available in abundance, made real by the nonchalant shrugging of his shoulders which felt numbed still from the process of death.

The join between ceiling and wall became visible with effort, by the avoidance of the eye from the blinding glare of the sun which seemed to have swivelled away from his direction lighting instead the area of the room over to his right. A silver tray that had previously been obscured by the sun had rotated with it into partial view. By that I mean he could not see its contents other than the tips of blade and scalpel that showed over its upturned edge, and the serrated saw that was equated in his suddenly alerted mind with the tools of the disembalmer, the man or god who released the resurrected Egyptian dead from the plaster-soaked bandages into the afterlife. The work must already have begun since only his forearms and lower legs were still weighted down stiffly by the hard encasement. There were no furnishings in the room that he could see by rotating his eyeballs in their still drowsy sockets, yet he was not alone. In the solitary chair, as white as the rest of the room, a man was sitting in a similar state, more aroused than he, but due to a natural muteness or the bandaged covering of his mouth, was unable so far to communicate, though he was obviously pleased to have caught his waking attention. It was apparent that his unfortunate mute conditon and humbled, frightened demeanour would naturally have qualified him for the future pleasures that lay ahead for both of them. He seemed even to tremble upon the chair as if distrusting its strong legs, or being made to shiver by cold metal, or perhaps to fear the arrival in Heaven of his killer in pursuit.

Communicate they then did as best as was possible, with each contributing to the silent conversation, one with his plastered arm offered as a writing surface, the other his pursed lips driving a pen over rasping forearm as if intent on communicating straight with the bloody vein beneath, by some system of coded proding. Like the primitive cave painter whom he now revealed himself to be, the visitor to this earlier happy room, proceeded to draw unintelligibly over the remaining vacant space, as if time, the shortage of it, had absurdly displaced death as his enemy in this immortal place. Some detail drawn, he would turn in limited moves his head to the doorway that would by the morrow surely lead them both ecstatically to paradise. He must relax this sorrowful seated man; let him know of his Egyptian past forgotten in death, explain the embalmer's art. But how? He too was as gagged in speech as his new friend, who glances again at the open door as if convinced that beyond his soundproofed ears the eeriest, most beastly footsteps are stomping their way over the hard, resounding flagstones to wreak some terrible vengeance. Perhaps, it is not genuine fright but a re-enactment of the scene within the entrance to his cave when the monster approaches to gobble him up. Best to nod in patronising approval of the natural theatrical behaviour of this simple soul, who now draws more frantically upon the sealed fibre of his wrist. Yes, of course, there was a horse involved, he was being chased back into the dark cave that must have contrasted in an almost welcoming fashion in comparison with the blazing light of God. Nostalgia for a life so recently lost. How comprehensible at last is this petrified creature's pretence of his last moments in the security of the subterranean black. A horse was most certainly involved in his brutal demise, for the black hoof is being filled in, shaped across the curve of his clenched fist. He was a horse or would pretend to be for his new friend's sake. How to describe Heaven to such a diminutive pagan?! Best to smile and go along playfully with this charade. He attempted to emit the whinnying sound of a galloping horse . . .

The cringing caveman was gone. Had he heard the horsy voice by means of the telepathy of a prehistoric world in which he had remained expert after the expiry of his physical body? Had he been frightened by such a light-hearted prank intended to bond and not dissolve their new friendship? How fascinating to meet the peoples of other times, to compare notes and experiences . . . The disembalmer had entered the room, her appearance quite unlike anything previously seen, the colouring of her medical clothing so dark as to make the bridging of the spectrum of the heavenly light, from extreme white to polished black, almost unbearable to his eyes which blinked and turned away towards the tray. Soon, however, he would be gratefully free, with a thousand questions to ask this nurse in rubber suit which for now must wait while the saw saws and the arm is exposed. He studies her face so intent upon its liberating purpose. Had he known her once in some past life, she seems familiar in an unidentifiable way? Had they perhaps died in some road accident together side by side? Had she recovered first from death, returning through Elysian fields from marvellous pleasures to be beside him once more, to renew a love not lost forsaken in that Heavenly paradise? The styling of her hair swept back beneath a hat revives some memory of prior events. He understood their predicament in a flash. She had been responsible for his premature death, had driven across the road to knock him down by her careless feminine act. How repentantly she worked with the steady concentration that is discovered hidden in the disciplined world of the convent.

No hard feelings! he mused to himself wishing to share the joke prematurely with his companion in this state of bliss. Would she address the restriction performed so completely by the embalmer's skill of his skull which save for peeping eyes was encompassed totally still. Then the thought crossed his mind, disturbing in its intensity, that petrol cars and ancient Egypt are incompatible by century, set apart and distinguished by such an intervening period to make the necessary overlap inconceivable, seemingly for that moment at least, impossible to believe. Yet, he continued carelessly to muse, it must be possible, for it had happened somehow and would be the very first question he would ask this concerned lady with her working saw. She had after all ventured out already into paradise, perhaps from this very bed a day or days before. A certain discomfort grew where the sense of ease and relief might have been the predicted reaction to his imminent freedom from band- and bondage. The cutting saw, replaced one would have thought comfortingly upon the tray, substituted it is admitted by the violence of prising forceps, has caused him to behave with the most loathsome reaction befitting the very caveman whose primitive antics he had earlier dismissed with such well-concealed hubris. The reason for the limited plastering of his once human limbs becomes in the instant of the cracking open of impeding plaster, impossibly clear. And by deduction each other limb would be so horribly dressed with a hoofed and shod foot as alien as anything from Hell. The whinnying suppressed before by bandage is finally emitted and being heard by other horse-limbed men in the enclosure beyond the room of his transfiguration, finds a natural response to which he soon replies, unable further to stifle his second and imposing nature that longs as much for open grass as he did previously for the Elysian fields. She speaks and names him in a word, and he, unable to ask the questions then forgotten, answers as a horse, his vow of silence broken in the street in this way unorthodoxically enforced, by the tightening of his bridle and bit, by the harshest cutting of her riding-whip. He had indeed gone to Heaven and there met his maker, the Goddess now watching over him in spurred stiletto-heeled boots, his four legs all at last revealed, with his leather saddle beneath her polished arm, a welcoming smile playing upon the crimson lips of her veiled, uncompromising face.

FIFTY-TWO

Birds of Paradise

DEAR BOOT-LOVERS,

In the pre-history of your planet, it was a common occurrence and a common response for the shepherd in the remote hills to discover at dawn a pair of shoes or boots left outside the wooden, ill-fitting door to his primitive hut which for reasons of good luck and prudence he would clean and polish and leave in the evening for the returning Goddess. In more recent times, the classical authors have named the locations of various mountain ledges where tired men went to sleep, from which swooping eagles plucked them in the night, carrying them away to unspecified destinations related often to the constellation of Heel!. All that was described as remaining as evidence of the man and the raptor on the following day was a high-heeled shoe left there in fulfilment of some antique agreement of which the author, be he Roman or Athenian, confessed to his ignorance.

In the stone age of which records are chiselled and scribbled down by lamp-light in the underground caves of, for example, the Pyrenees, the anthropologist has revealed the existence of a 'flame eagle' which preyed on the extinct version of humanity called the 'rubberman'; this predator having a divine control over the astrological forces behind Nature that are depicted on the cave walls as seven radiating and variously coloured shafts of light which combined in focus set the fleeing and unfortunate rubberman caught out on the open ground after dark, ablaze. In Egypt there remains through the weathering of floods the hieroglyphic evidence of the use by the Goddess Isis of her falcon son Horus in the retrieval of errant men. Later in history when the influence of this foremost Egyptian deity is recorded far north of the Mediterranean sea, being still worshipped openly in Paris in the nineteenth century, it was reported that the raising of the priestess' leather gauntlet as if to receive the imaginary bird of prey was sufficient by this simple act to render the forthright and strident man a captured slave that kneeling with arms tucked stiffly back himself mimics the absent falcon onto whose skull the leather blinding-hood is firmed in place.

With this history as context for new developments, I intend briefly, since we will shortly be leaving the Paris offices of Heel! in the care of our parrots and boot-slaves while we travel to Denderah, to account for the events and those deaths attributed in the press to vengeful and vindictive elements in the Italian mafia, which are reported on the front pages of the European newspaper so regularly. No attempt to unearth a motive beyond the pecuniary and the corrupt is undertaken, rather there is the assumption made of traditional governmental skulduggery. Yet certain details are repeatedly shown without comment to the enquiring reader, without explanation of the lady's shoe left obviously at the scene of the crime which will be connected by the reader of Heel! with the ancient customs already described in this letter. Nor is it realised that the decrepit state of a particular statue to the Goddess, from which a limb has become detached, broken off into the traffic below and dragged away by blaspheming street-sweepers, is the actual cause of the night-time visit then received by the civil servant and his consequent demise.

How should the shoe or boot left behind by the offended Goddess be distinguished and be treated differently by the secular man or the male reader of Heel! who writes to me of his local dilemma when into his isolated community, appearing as if out of nowhere, the boot arrives demanding the attention of slaves uncertain of the correct response, the ancient etiquette involved and applicable to this modern event? If the boot is of considerable size and found by the Heel! reader with a clear and Goddess-fearing conscience while he walks with his dog on a tight lead over the village green, he should refrain from any desire to remove it like some gargantuan and fresh bone to his secret location, even if the preservation of the boot is the prime object and incentive to this natural course of action. Instead, he should at first tell the rubber boot apart from the leather boot, for each will require separate and distinct treatment.

When it is discovered that the gleaming surface is indeed

made of rubber, and the sun is shining with the promise of a hot summer's afternoon, then those resources of water that would otherwise be tapped in order to stem the village fire, should be pumped throughout the day in a steady stream over the instep and alternately up and down the heel, to imitate the spray of nocturnal showers in the spring month of April. I am here addressing the letter sent to me from southern England which expresses on every sheet all the enthusiasm and the passion of that still rare thing, the genuine and true boot-lover, who has in his overwhelming devotion taken that second, less obvious step of contacting the Italian town to which his own has been twinned since the defeat of the beast-like Mussolini.

What will be revealed by this energetic display of quick wits and good sense? That a statue sculpted in ancient times, bearing an exact resemblance to the dancing Moon Goddess, Diana, with her golden bow and quiver of arrows, being also the huntress, Artemis, remembered by the Greeks, was damaged in an accident between dumb footballers from opposing clubs, had remained unrepaired, without her right arm, beyond the reasonable period permitted by this patient Goddess with her famous reputation for transfiguring her victims animalistically. The village by its modern political association with her Italian temple must begin its worship of her spike-heeled shoe placed across the bowling-green where ducks will in future waddle and preen, in this prolonged act of penitent contrition. The obvious difference in treatment, if the shoe has a leather shine, is of course the requirement that his fellow villagers, who will be equipped with cloth and tins of black polish, operate in shifts through the day and night until its sudden and miraculous disappearance from their sleepy world signifying their forgiveness by the relenting and now pleasured Goddess.

In the case where a boot or shoe, whether of leather or rubber, is left during the night outside the front door, with the palpable intent that the surfaces be both cleaned and polished, it will not then do for the male reader to try lazily to distinguish between the character and look of footwear worn normally by his female neighbour and that which is self-evidently of divine creation, being the prototype for the common or garden shoe. Where, however, we have the more unusual circumstance of the leather boot being found on its side in an out-of-the-way place, perhaps appearing to the intelligent witness to have been transported there carelessly from the higher worlds down to your own by a projection of transdimensional force or by the grasping claws of the flame eagle, then the burden will fall upon the male reader to contact without delay the Museum of the Female Boot, and putting the excitement of this still rare find temporarily out of his mind, explain to the thigh-booted archivist, rationally rather than breathlessly, without the slightest trace of pubescent wonder, the condition and immediate needs of this potential exhibit. It should be recalled at all times that the quality of self-control, being the eternal and enforced virtue of the boot-slave, must be exercised by him as he waits his nervous turn, due to the increasing incidence of such rural sightings which may be thought of as the shapely harbingers of the emerging race of Goddesses.

Before I replace my fountain-pen in its inkwell and return this blotting parrot to her cage, I should confirm to the readers who attended the masked ball at the Palace of Versailles, who commented on the fine appearance of the stiletto-heeled boots exposed by her manservant beneath the elegant seventeenth-century dress of this much-admired guest, that Marguerite de Valois, whose education as the daughter of Catherine de Medici, the Queen of France, so benefited from her mother's innovations and inventions of heel and side-saddle design, will be elected by the Council of Ten, at their next meeting in Venetia, to the post of directrice of the Museum of the Female Boot. The position grants her the privilege and the power to summon any man, anywhere, whether he is aware or unaware of the existence of Heel!, to perform as the boot-slave he will in the process surely become, to haul by rope and under the supervision of Tourist Police the discovered boot or heeled shoe, painstakingly, even over the roughest terrain, to the Museum of the Female Boot in Paris.

MADAME X

FIFTY-THREE

The Cardinal Sin

Permit me, Madame, as a recent convert to the principles of Heel!, to describe the method and timing of my own subjugation to the female boot which resulted from my exposure to a particular oil-painting that hangs in the Musée des Beaux-Arts, in Orléans. Being unaware of the existence of the society of Heel! and not yet having read the letter which you have titled *Ride to the Chateau*, my approach to this painting was as an innocent and passive observer who derived a natural pleasure from the portraiture of the equestrienne and from the cultivation of polite exchanges with the riding mistress wherever she might be discovered, whether in remote and wooded places or in the intimate atmosphere of the training ring. Certainly I was not prepared adequately for what was to follow.

It was in the late afternoon that I entered the gallery where the painting titled simply, 'Air', immediately caught my attention, drawing my eye in to the detail of the canvas which soon utterly absorbed my mind. Commissioned by Cardinal Richelieu for the Queen's room in his chateau, and dated 1641 by the artist Claude Deruet, ennobled friend of Louis XIII, the painting forms part of the series 'The Four Elements'. Riding their horses side saddle in long silk dresses in subdued black swishing above the taut-muscled flank, their hats exotically plumed with ostrich feathers dyed blood-red, with hooded falcons perched on leather fists the Duchess of Lorraine and one hundred of her ladies are pictured in the moonlight in dark and elegant pursuit of both human and animal prey.

The dimensions of the painting, chosen to include the widest view of the developing scene, serve inevitably to enwrap the devoted onlooker, who, pulled initially by a natural attraction within its setting, finds to his horror that his sudden retreat from the advancing army of equestriennes, practised repeatedly since his arrival in front of the canvas' flat surface, is barred by the hazards – trees, lakes and temples – of the intervening space of a previously distant landscape. With his clothing, modern and inappropriate, lying crumpled on the ground where he had stood in earlier admiration, he flies naked, hurtling headlong, projected into this other world where reason seems ill-equipped to comprehend, and gravity reluctant to perform on his divested and uncertain body. The Duchess, patient for these years of time, surveys through falcon's eye, the passing flatness of his future world, its grandeur lost, turned ugly, until with human prey in sight, her glove is raised against the dull parade of staring men and with her riding-whip she points him out, this servant from her past. Diana, Goddess of the night her subtle sign has seen, and by immortal force retrieves this luckless, dreaming man as slave to ladies' boots preserved uncleaned through centuries seeming buried dead.

The sound of hooves and galloping ladies pervades the enveloping air. The slice of painted and recorded life is mistaken, becomes substituted for the real, which hangs instead within its frame on twisted wire upon the gallery wall. Despatched as one from gauntlet-gloves, a hundred hungry falcons, the leather hoods at last removed, with talons sharpened and outstretched soar through the sky in search of human prey, of naked flesh delivered by impulsive prayer, brought tumbling down, torn broken to the ground. The foaming horses, their riders breathless for a crowded view, surround this feathered, bloodied corpse retrieved by savage claws from flight into a future life, returned as servant to the serpent whip and disciplining spur.

Kneeling just on rubbery limbs on sodden grass beneath the cruel angelic host, head bowed amongst the chafing bits and flexing inconsiderate whips, instinctive and in shock this slave is soon revived by scent of leather riding-boots unveiled before his glazed and disbelieving eyes. So reminded of an oath once sworn neglected in his present life, with trembling lips and mouthed and dribbled vowels reciting names of half-remembered boots kissed left and right, on heel and arch, slowly like the dreamer waking to the nightmare scene, the slave, recaptured, surrenders to his otherwordly fate. A hundredth skirt is lifted to the thigh, exposing heel, stirrup and instep to his naked eye.

His service to the equestrienne is complete, has come full circle beneath a Duchess' feet. In the darkness of the crescent moon, she whispers heaving from the tight-girthed womb, to which the restless slave responds as trained with parted lips and silent tongue. Raising her far-sighted falcon to the moon, the slave, his face and rubber body, is now withdrawn, extracted smoothly from the contours of her world, projected then upon the gallery floor, on crumpled suit, confronted by a painted scene receding, flattened like a waking dream. And I, this slave, the subject of this story, am duty bound from day to day, with cleaning cloth, without my modern suit to polish in that other world of Goddesses and boots.

FIFTY-FOUR

Boot Etiquette

DEAR BOOT-LOVERS,

I intend to take this opportunity to deal with specific questions of general importance to both the female readers of Heel! and their male slaves, which have been written down and raised as matters of concern in the space left vacant for that purpose in the questionnaire. My response will take the form of a brief and numbered listing of the female reader's questions coupled with my answers and attempts at explanation:

1. What colour should the ribbon be, of what material and how should it be best presented to the passing slave in the public place? Here I am combining several related enquiries so that my reply may be fuller and make entire sense to the reader who on her own had only spotted, considered, one aspect of the problem offered as a 'Matter of Concern' for our solution. As many of you have suspected, it is not significant in terms of etiquette or the lady's strategy whether she is at the time standing or seated, whether she is aware of his approach or she merely has convinced

herself sensually of his nearness to her boot from behind closed eyes, or the pages of this magazine, for example. Nor, of course, should one strategy be adopted for the slave arriving flat to the ground, wriggling over the grass or tarmac with arms perhaps left bound behind him, and feet tied by the previous recipient of his attentions, while some other arrangement is selected from the Mistress' arsenal of potent weaponry for the man who appears in these intermediate times to be strolling by without feeling himself to be pulled by the force of her presence, into an initially casual service to her boot. For the most effective influence, and for the sake of uniformity in this matter that would otherwise lead to confusion in the mind of the wavering slave, the ribbon should be red, its material silk, and be worn as a bow about the ankle of the calf-length boot, and below the knee of the thigh-length boot. It may be displayed on either boot, its position, left or right, merely indicates the starting-point for the polishing of leather or rubber. Any potential boot-slave who is observed to circle within the radius of influence of the red-ribboned boot, who seems disinclined by a natural reticence or by reason, perhaps, of recent damage to the tissue of his knees, or for whatever excuse, is immediately punishable by that Mistress' whip. These rules are not of my own contemplative creation, but rather issue from the chamber of the Council of Ten at their last meeting in the Republic of Venetia, as the international standard for boot-cleaning and of worship in a publicly-accessed place.

2. Will the provision by Heel! of kneeling boot-boys in the squares and open spaces of Madrid cease, be superseded by the recent decision of the Council of Ten to make the general male public available at all times to the female leather boot and its pair in need of that vital, resuscitative shine? No, the two systems will be run in parallel for the intervening period until the day, or more probably the night, when, through a meeting of the Council of Ten, the Goddess decrees that the over-garments so far worn on top of the leather or rubber clothing of the Heel! member should be discarded in favour of a more blatant appeal to the mind of the as yet uncommitted boot-slave. There is then possible the formal allocation, slave by slave, drawn from the wider public, to the Mistress, who in this fashion is always assured of the polishing hand and accompanying tongue from her own immediate resources, there being no longer the requirement to look beyond the circle of her designated slaves. Until that time the boot-boy, in his multiplying and ubiquitous numbers, including increasingly in his ranks, as the stimulus and momentum builds towards final climax, the volunteering slave still perhaps in his business suit, will coexist, fixed at his place of work, duty-bound, with this new and roaming variety of boot-slave that grows into a directionless swarm in consequence of the rising quality and output of female boot production. Then, he, the boot-boy as distinct from the new class of business slave, who will by then have swung the unequal contest decisively to the advantage of Heel!, will leave

his post, cut free by the compassionate leather-gloved hand of the member of Heel! responding to developments and the latest news from the Republic of Venetia, and will rush or hobble, whatever is to be the case, to join the queue to slavery, to the fulfilment of his destiny, to that lady's boots to which he feels himself naturally devoted, naturally drawn by impulse and instruction from the Goddess. The female reader of Heel! will, of course, not regret the passing of enchanted, quiet times in the midst of the daily rush and traffic, spent in calm, reflective study and serene correction of her favourite boot-boy who prostrates himself at the sight of her every visit.

3. Is some kind of record or register being kept and updated which maintains the information that will be required to attribute collective responsibility to politicians, scientists and business executives to provide for their summary trial, and what is to be the London location and means of their sentencing? Has Heel! decided upon a policy and logistics relating to transgressions against the female boot and the sacred genetic and environmental heritage of this planet? Yes. The venue for the dispensing of justice will be the Banqueting Hall, the means will be the guillotine operated by genetically violated apes trained for the purpose, for which a standardised blade will be inserted into a wooden structure of standard revolutionary dimensions to ensure the executioner transported within the old nation states which are to be absorbed into the empire of Heel!, will be familiar on arrival at the site of execution

where no puzzling pulleys or unusual lengths of rope will distract from the task at hand and foot. Supervision of these maltreated monkeys which may include a slow-motioned sloth for dramatic effect, falls to the select members of the cadre of the French Tourist Police travelling at first incognita in fashionable Parisian dress, who will simultaneously assess the built environment for equivalent dismemberment, though it is doubtful whether even the wretched conditions experienced in the pasts of the executioner monkeys will induce them to feed on the ground-up masonry of patriarchal and capitalistic architecture. When the condemned man has been secured and rigidly bound on his stomach beneath the glinting blade, in a final act of compassion authorised by the Council of Ten, the stiletto heel and polished surface is placed beside his pallid, shaven head for one last chance to recant by the impress of clumsy lips upon shining leather, the misguided materialism of cruel science, and by their slobbering embrace of the boot's instep seek forgiveness from the Goddess for the earthly sins of his receding life. A last-minute reprieve, the stay of execution, the result of his slavering efforts to satisfy the presented boot so greedy for true signs of his new affection, leads back to the vacated cage of the freed ape, to the inclination of cramped spine and the compliant mind then produced, and the swift conversion of man to boot-slave, for the life of service and of worship for which his spontaneous performance at the guillotine has disclosed a natural ambition and affinity with the shadowy slave working beneath the taffeta layers.

It seems that a number of the questionnaires received here at the offices of Heel! have been filled in, not as was requested, by the female reader but by the slave who has in the process acquired a sense of humour, a confidence and a fanciful curiosity about matters which are not of his concern and are forbidden to him. Of the slaves acknowledged and trained by Heel!, I believe only the male parrots in our Paris aviary are required to behave and appear incognita as female, within the limited realm of the bird cage, or with wings clipped when released in public. It is not permitted for you, the male reader, whom we have identified as being guilty of this simple-minded deceit, whom we intend to punish quite severely on the next delivery of your magazine [which may possibly have been your motive and aspiration?] to speculate on paper or otherwise about my ancestry questioning in the same breath why a certain Madame de Morville, taken randomly from the historical records, seems to lack a death date, and whether the preservation of the physical bodies of members of Heel! in Venice in impermeable black rubber in some way relates to the sinking of the Venetian archipelago. I will continue my discussion of the matters raised in your questionnaires within the members section of the Heel! web-site which has as you well know the address www.HeelMagazine.com . . .

MADAME X

FIFTY-FIVE

The Council of Ten

DEAR BOOT-LOVERS,

For those of our readers, and it seems by the quantity and urgency of your requests that there are many of you, without the means to record what was to you the surprise televised appearance on your screens last Tuesday of the Council of Ten, here is the complete text of their message of conquest and conversion of your patriarchal world to the worship of the Goddess Isis.

'Good evening ... please forgive this interruption and substitution of your usual televised entertainment. I trust you find our appearance within the privacy of your homes at least as visually appealing as the programmes whose transmission and broadcast we have temporarily blocked and suspended. We ask you not to move from your seats, not to fear our presence, nor attempt perversely to change channels during this brief intermission; you will find that we reappear on each and every programme that you select. Accept our intrusion into your lives and expect this technical performance to be repeated without warning at any time in your future. Normally we will be specifying the timing of each of our successive visits to your domestic and very personal world when you will each be required to be our welcoming host. We hope that you will each look forward, even with trepidation, to our arrival in your home, whether through this medium or on occasion, perhaps when provoked or suspicious of your correct response to our words, through the front door. Expect the knock of the rubber-gloved fist or the kick of the stiletto boot and be assured that we will rectify without delay whatever omission or laxness or irreverence in your behaviour that has been detected by the members of Heel!.

We are the Council of Ten from the other world of Venetia. We are seated here opposite you at this long table so that you might join with us at this the last supper of your previous life prior to your gradual and certain transformation at our hands and booted feet from which you will each be resurrected in the knowledge that you have been initiated into the transdimensional realms of the Venetian empire as slaves of the Goddess Isis, a purpose for which your long evolution under our supervising gaze has equipped you perfectly. You may begin to recognize who we are, when we remove our masks and your amazement begins to subside into silent, natural awe of the sculpted beauty of our facial features and highly-polished figures. You may begin to remember who we are as historical figures from your distant past or, if your memories have been trained to bridge that divide, from the dream that you may have experienced last night. We are Semiramis of Ancient Babylon, Nefertiti and Cleopatra of Ancient Egypt, Diane of French Poitiers, and Helen of Troy. Our bodies are transfigured from semi-divine to the divinity of the immortal Goddess Isis.

Kneel before us as slaves and celebrate this fulfilment of destiny for which you and your star-gazing ancestors have waited so long. Raise your glasses filled with red wine or whatever you have in your hand, and drink with us to your future in worlds where our clothing, inevitably strange to your normal sight, with our tall rubber head-dresses and these heels so high as to seem impossibly unreal to you mortal men, is the cause of instant worship and endless sacrifice. Please ignore our whips that we have brought carelessly to the supper-table unless you believe that fate accepted by gods and stars alike, is on this occasion to be challenged by your puny male might. Then fear our presence and the timing of our return to your mundane world. Good evening, slaves, and thank you for inviting us to join you at your last supper.'

MADAME X

FIFTY-SIX

Republic of Venetia

'Good evening and greetings from the Council of Ten to you the Mistresses and slaves of planet Earth. Please forgive this interruption to your entertainment. It is time, slaves, for your female companions to discard their superficial and outmoded clothing and revealing the rubber uniforms worn discreetly beneath, to join us on this side of the screen where you may view their polished bodies and the immaculate shine of their boots. Soon you will see in the full and broad daylight of your world what you are about to glimpse this evening when this religiously white canopy draped to the ground over this simple trestle-table, intended to mimic the simplicity of your own earthly environment in which you dine slumped in front of this television, is raised to reveal behind its seeming veil a line of unearthly and otherworldly boot designs. You must learn to kneel in front of our stiletto-heeled boots, to savour this privileged sight, or to receive punishment from our reluctant whips and our forced hands.

Before revealing her true nature to you, the boot-slave, we must first reveal the steps to be taken by the booted Mistress to reach the boundaries of our world where in your future she will share her newly-acquired perfection of female form with the members of

Heel! who have in your distant past graduated by initiation as priestesses at the Temple of the Goddess Isis and as the consequence, entered this slave empire known as the Republic of Venetia. Our instructions are as follows:

1. First discover for your slave and your self an empty beach with sand sloping gradually down to the sea where he should be positioned kneeling looking out to the horizon. The sea, like your slave, should be placid and the day sunny with uninterrupted views, or alternatively, lit by a full moon.
2. The slave is instructed to focus his mind entirely upon your rubber-suited form as you move backwards and forwards across the sand in front of him, his attention being primarily and naturally directed by the monotonic sound of your voice, by the force of the repetition of the your command, to the shape and gleam of your boots.
3. The purpose of this exercise, practised often in the domestic environment before the attempt is made, is to still your slave's mind, to shut off his thinking processes, until only the single thought remains, his undistracted admiration of your boots. The consequence of this moment of suspended animation extended into the future, is that the calm sea extending to the horizon becomes frozen to his perception.
4. You must enter this moment with him and experience a new continuity of time within this moment. As soon as you detect in his dreamy, unblinking eyes that the moment has arrived when his world has stopped, and you have confirmed his state by testing with the heels of your boots the viscous, then hardening surface of the moonlit sea, then he should be

encouraged in his dumb state to follow your lead onto the water.

5. Whether he is on two legs or four, whether he is saddled by your weight or walking beside you collared at the end of a leash, proceed confidently out to sea, towards the horizon upon which after a certain amount of this new time has elapsed will be revealed distant architecture, the topmost portion of buildings, which may at first appear almost familiar, as if taken from your dreams or once visited as a tourist out of season.

6. As you progress to the point where the outline of similarly dressed ladies may be perceived dimly, if not as yet clearly, and you are perhaps nervous, being so far from the perceived safety of the sandy beach left far behind, and fearing that the fixed concentration of your slave may be about to waver so that you will sink into the sea far beyond your depths ... remain confident that you are approaching the outer limits of the Republic of Venetia, where your future and that of your slave, lie.

7. Your saddled slave, perhaps blinkered and squinting at the spurred boots both pressed against his seemingly sunburnt flesh, will hardly have noticed the sudden transformation beneath his tiring feet from sea that is frozen in time to that which is frozen in ice which signals in your apprehensive mind your successful transfer, together with your slave, from the no-time condition to that of the painfully slow time of the moonlit Republic of Venetia from which we transmit these messages of encouragement and guidance.

8. Do not look back. You will have learnt how to visit our world in full waking consciousness, using the mind and body of your slave as your unwitting vehicle of transport. What was previously accessible to the Mistress and slave only in dreams will become like the tourist's favourite destination to which she returns time and again in spite of her husband's unheeded protests; though in this new circumstance such a contradictory mood is of course no longer available to his stunned and perpetually manipulated mind.
9. The return journey is identically made by the combined operation of the Mistress' intent and the stopping of the slave's thoughts brought to the sole attention of her passing and polished boots that like the clock's pendulum in the leather-gloved hand of his female hypnotist, still and silence his internal world.
10. One final point, before the Mistresses are invited to join us at our table, is to remember on the occasion of each of your visits to the Republic of Venetia to present your slave for initial inspection as to the required levels of docility and boot etiquette, to the Venetian Tourist Police.'